THE INVESTIGATION

"Geoffrey's upset with your investigation, Quintin."

"He has nothing to worry about...if he's innocent."

Felice gave him an impatient look. "Please don't play policeman, Quintin. What did you say to Geoffrey that upset him so?"

"I just asked him a few questions, but he's holding something back. Some key piece of information. I can't put my finger on it, but there's something."

"Quintin, in all honesty, I think Geoffrey's innocent."

Felice reached for her cigarettes. Quintin watched her elegant fingers moving expertly, without the slightest tremor. There was a hell of a lot more to Felice Fallanti than her interest in his body. She cared about Geoffrey, and probably about Daphne and Leslie as well. He wondered what she was really up to and if going to bed with him was a part of it...

MADE IN BEVERLY HILLS

RONN KAISER

AVON
PUBLISHERS OF BARD, CAMELOT, DISCUS AND FLARE BOOKS

Authors' Note

Ronn Kaiser and Janice Sutcliffe-Kaiser wrote this book together. But for the flip of a coin, the byline might be different.

AVON BOOKS
A division of
The Hearst Corporation
1790 Broadway
New York, New York 10019

Copyright © 1986 by Belles-Lettres, Inc.
Published by arrangement with the author
Library of Congress Catalog Card Number: 86-90914
ISBN: 0-380-75225-5

First Avon Printing: December 1986

AVON TRADEMARK REG. U.S. PAT. OFF. AND IN OTHER COUNTRIES, MARCA REGISTRADA, HECHO EN U.S.A.

Printed in the U.S.A.

K–R   10   9   8   7   6   5   4   3   2   1

One friend in a lifetime is much; two are many; three are hardly possible.

Henry Adams

For
Larry Weiss, Mary Keown, and Roberta Holden

MADE IN
BEVERLY HILLS®

BEL AIR

May 4, 1985

4:25 P.M.

The Maserati Quattroporte rolled to a stop between the two rows of royal palms that lined the drive. Its color was metallic taupe, the same hue as Felice Fallanti's eyes. As she expected, a parking attendant stepped out from his concealed station in the shrubbery and swaggered toward her car. Felice set the hand brake, but her eyes were locked on the figure approaching her.

He was young, as they all were. He could have been handsome, but she really didn't look at the face—except for a general impression of sun-bleached hair and tanned skin—rather, she focused her attention on his crotch. The boy's strut told her he knew what he had. Felice wondered if he was the one Helene had balled in her pool house while Jed was doing laps.

Breaking her gaze, Felice reached over and took her newest Judith Leiber purse from the seat beside her. Glancing in the rearview mirror at the elegantly mature face that continued to please her—though her fortieth birthday was already a memory—she turned her head to get out and for an instant she froze. On the other side of

1

the glass was one of the most impressive bulges she had ever seen.

Her first thought was that he must have been reading girlie magazines in his shaded retreat. Evaluating him for a moment, Felice decided this was indeed the object of Helene's celebrated liaison—celebrated because of her audacity in screwing the kid under her husband's nose. "The challenge of it is what made it interesting," Felice remembered her saying in her characteristically supercilious way. *The bitch!*

The young man pulled open the door of the Maserati, revealing more of himself. He offered her his hand, but Felice ignored it. She was aware of how he had positioned himself to look up her skirt as she climbed out of the car. He seemed eager enough; maybe the bulge was for real.

Felice relented and gave him her hand, and as he lifted her out of the car his biceps flexed under the pink shirt emblazoned with the Hotel Bel-Air insignia. Felice let her breasts brush his chest, then ran her hand across his thigh. She glanced up through her lashes. "Is this for sale?" she asked huskily.

The boy was momentarily shocked. "Well . . ."

Felice's smile revealed traces of amusement, though her startled admirer didn't notice. "Not now," she whispered. "Maybe on the way out we can talk. I've got an appointment." Every weekend Venice, Santa Monica, and Malibu were teeming with an army of faces just like his, and any of them were hers for the asking.

Felice quickly made her way toward the entrance to the hotel, feeling his eyes on her ass, curious whether its promise made him harder. She had to laugh at herself, for being outrageous was her style and being able to laugh about it was her salvation.

Geoffrey was probably already there, she thought—dear, sweet, limp Geoffrey. They had agreed to meet for a drink and talk about the shock of the day before. He had said four, but that meant he'd be there at four-fifteen. It was now four-thirty, so Felice was right on time.

Geoffrey was in the bar when she entered. At a glance

she could see that the bartender was not as impressed with him as Geoffrey would have liked. The smooth image, the pale lavender Armani suit, the monogrammed shirt and Bally loafers were wasted on the man who seemed more interested in his tip.

Adolfo, like the fun-loving Italian that he was, always considered Geoffrey's attentions a badge of honor. "It is a compliment to be desired—whether by a man or a woman," he had told her in bed one night, after a party at which Geoffrey had come on to him very strong. They laughed about it, and Felice even felt jealous—which was rare for her. They had made love fiercely that night, as passionately as they ever had.

Every time Felice saw Geoffrey after that, she wondered whether Adolfo's zeal that night had been a result of Geoffrey having insinuated himself into her husband's fantasies. It didn't matter, of course—given the result, she would have gladly let the decorator parade through their bedroom nude all the time—now it was academic. That was all before Helene. *The bitch.*

Geoffrey rose from the bar stool when he saw Felice approaching. The brief smile on his lips transformed into a pucker as he planted a kiss on her mouth.

"Felice, you look gorgeous, as always."

There was a tiredness about his eyes that she noticed immediately. "It's good to see you, Geoffrey." And it was true. He was the only faggot among her acquaintances with whom she ever got past girl-talk. "Lord knows it's been months, though." She patted his cheek and looked at the puffy flesh of his face, sensing something was amiss.

Geoffrey hadn't been himself for a long time. On the surface there was the same familiar panache, the outrageous bravado, but underneath something had changed. He was suffering as only gay men can suffer. *Poor, dear Geoffrey.*

"When did you get back from Rio?" she asked, smiling.

"A few days ago."

"Just in time for the fireworks. Right, dear?"

They looked at each other with the same intense, questioning gaze. Then Geoffrey's face became grim. His voice was level, and there wasn't the slightest hint of a smile. "Tell the truth, Felice, and save us all a lot of trouble. Did you kill the bitch?"

Felice Fallanti threw back her head and laughed. "Of course, but they'll never prove it!"

HONOLULU, HAWAII

May 5, 1985

3:40 P.M.

Quintin Wing closed his eyes and concentrated on the hands kneading his thighs. He tried to believe it was tactile sensation of the highest order, but all he could think was that they were *her* hands and that they were just inches from the towel draped modestly across his crotch. His eyes involuntarily opened, and he saw her long, black hair hanging over him, glossy and fine like a million silken threads. The ends of it nearly touched the towel as she pressed deeply into his muscles with the heels of her hands. The girl's arms were thin, but he felt her strength— the aggressiveness with which she attacked his body.

He had been in Hawaii for a week and hadn't been laid yet, though he'd had a shot at a *haole* or two. But when he was in the Islands, he wanted the local stuff—oriental snatch that didn't regard his Eurasian features as unusual. The women at home adored him because he was big, exotic-looking, but had a Caucasian soul. The girls in the Islands liked him because he was a man and knew what to do with his God-given equipment; that was the difference.

The masseuse paused to pour more oil on her hands and looked up at Wing as she did. Though she didn't quite smile, he read invitation in what he saw—or was it wishful thinking? He studied her profile, deciding she was Japanese. It didn't bother him though, as he had none of his father's Chinese prejudices. To the contrary, he preferred Japanese women, and this one was particularly enticing. She began working the inside of one thigh, just below the towel, in a slow, rhythmic fashion. He felt his cock stiffen with her hands so exquisitely near. He glanced toward the open door, shielded only by a screen.

"Feel free to slide up under that towel, Dee Dee," he said, grinning.

The girl stopped her manipulations and looked at him. "Yeah, sure. You turn out to be a cop and I end up in jail. What for?" Her eyes were flat. "You're cute, but not that cute. And I'm no hooker."

Wing laughed softly.

"What's so funny?"

"As a matter of fact, I *am* a cop, but don't worry, my beat's about twenty-five hundred miles east of here in L.A. And I don't handle vice. I do homicide."

The girl looked at him warily. "I guess you don't look like a cop."

"Why? Because of my urbane good looks or my sophomoric charm?"

She stared at him blankly. "Yeah." Her hands returned to the place just below his loins.

"How about dinner tonight, Dee Dee? Someplace quiet and off the tourist beat."

"When I want to avoid tourists, I eat at home."

"That's fine with me."

Dee Dee laughed. "I don't date customers."

"Hell, think of me as family."

"You don't look like *my* family."

Wing's loins warmed again as she began to ply his thighs in earnest. "Shit, it wouldn't be any fun if I did."

Dee Dee swung her hair back and looked at him, the smile on her face now evident. Wing was ready to bet a week's pay that he'd bag her.

* * *

The seduction had been long and slow because—as she had said—Dee Dee was no whore. To prove his sincerity, Wing had taken her first to Michel's, where she had never been. Then, after a stroll along the beach, they took a cab to her place.

At first they had sat out under the monkeypod tree overhanging the porch, amidst the bougainvillea, hibiscus, and oleanders. Wing had savored the smell of the gardenias and had touched Dee Dee's hair without touching her. He knew the importance of being sincere. He had asked her about her life, then, at the propitious moment, he had taken her to her bed and screwed her exquisitely.

Wing was enough of a connoisseur to understand that a woman was at her best when her expectations of love were understood, if not fulfilled. He understood Dee Dee's expectations beautifully.

They lay for a long time on the narrow bed, her hair a fan of black rice paper on the pillow. He caressed her small but perfect breasts, keeping her nipples erect, keeping her at a low level of arousal. To his pleasant surprise, the girl showed neither any signs of remorse nor the need to justify herself.

"Are you sure you're a cop, Quintin?" she asked, running her fingers over his hybrid features.

"Yeah, you want to see my badge?"

"No, I believe you. It's just that you don't seem like a cop."

"I do it because I like puzzles, not for the money."

"That seems like a strange reason to pick a job."

"Life is not always as it appears."

Dee Dee didn't understand, but it was all right because she liked him and liked his body, which she caressed lightly with her hand. "Do cops on the mainland make so much money that they can come to the Islands and take a girl to a place like Michel's without batting an eye?"

"Not if they're paying on a mortgage, no."

"You rent, then?"

Wing laughed and stroked the girl's head, liking the feel of her naked body against him and liking sex with the innocent, the beautiful, and the unfamiliar. He felt the life returning to his cock. "I inherited a little money, Dee Dee —police work is my avocation."

Her hand had moved to the fringe of his loins. He lightly stroked her nipple with his thumb, hoping to excite her again.

"Was your mother Caucasian?" she asked.

He hadn't expected that question just then. "Yes. And she still is, as a matter of fact."

Her nipple was turgid under his touch.

"Does she have big tits—your mother?"

Wing paused. "I guess she does, yes. Why?"

"I was just wondering. *Haole* women do, mostly. I was wondering if you liked that."

"Big tits?"

"Uh-huh." She pressed closer to him, her fingers rooting between his legs.

"Yeah, I don't have anything against them."

Dee Dee laughed, aware that his cock was standing straight up. "I knew you were big when I saw your nose," she whispered.

Wing swallowed hard, wanting her.

His hand slid toward her pubis, but she stopped him, holding it against the flat of her stomach.

"Quintin," she whispered, "I know we just met and that you couldn't possibly love me, but could you say something nice to make me feel good?"

He smiled in the darkness, knowing what she meant. Wing kissed her temple affectionately, as a lover might. Long ago he had discovered the importance of indulging women's fantasies. The result was always better for him, because it was better for them. Why more men didn't understand that, he'd never know.

It was three in the morning by the time Wing returned to his hotel room. He was exhausted and ready for the sack, but the flashing red message light on the telephone beckoned him. He groaned and picked up the receiver. The operator read him a message from Lieutenant Murdoch of the LAPD Robbery–Homicide Division—Wing's boss.

He looked at his watch. It was just before 6:00 A.M. in

California. He dialed the number the operator had given him.

"Jesus Christ, Wing, what time is it?" Murdoch mumbled into the phone.

"A little before six, your time."

"Shit."

"The message said to call when I got in."

"Don't you even keep decent hours when you're on vacation, for Christ's sake?"

"What do you want, Murdoch? I'm tired."

"God, it must be the middle of the night out there."

"It is."

Murdoch laughed. "What as she—blond, redhead, or brunet?"

"Japanese. In the Islands I tend to go back to my roots."

"Yeah." The lieutenant cleared his throat. "Well, I called because I got a homicide I want you to handle."

"I can't, I'm resigning."

"I know you've been *talking* about that, but this one is right up your alley."

"I'm not talking about resigning. I'm *doing* it."

"Quintin, just let me tell you about the case."

"Quintin? Jesus, you must be serious."

"Truth is, I'm in a pinch. Thomas just went back on disability, and he's the only person besides you who'd be right for it."

"Bullshit. Any good detective can handle any homicide, Murdoch."

"Not this one."

"What's so special that we got it instead of Divisional Homicide?"

"This is a society murder, Quintin, full of classy Hollywood broads. There's going to be a lot of publicity, a lot of big names. The Chief sent it to us and told the captain to treat it like a political thing. Tony Williams is on the case temporarily. His suspect list reads like a *Who's Who*, and it seems that everybody had it in for the victim. This thing's your cup of tea, believe me."

"Who's the victim?"

"Helene Daniels."

"Never heard of her."

"She's been in the movie business. A producer, I think. Anyway, she ran around with that crowd. Her husband was loaded, a millionaire who owned a bunch of department stores."

"What happened to him?"

"Killed in a boating accident in Mexico a couple of months ago."

"Hmm." Wing felt his curiosity rising. "How'd she die?"

"Shot at her house in Bel Air in the middle of the night. She was dressed, nothing missing, no sign of a struggle. Apparently somebody who knew her."

"Do you have the weapon?"

"No."

"Any physical evidence?"

"Bits and pieces, nothing much, yet. That's why I picked Williams. Figured he'd be good on the technical backup for you. I want you in the street talking to these folks, Quintin."

"Shit." Wing knew he was just about hooked.

"Why don't you get on a plane, have a look-see."

A Hollywood murder—he hadn't had one, and Murdoch knew it. The bastard couldn't have planned it better. "Shit," he mumbled again.

"Come on, Wing, you've had enough pussy out there, Japanese or otherwise. Do us both a favor."

BEL AIR

May 7, 1985

Daphne Stephens pulled up behind a Lincoln Continental and glanced at the pond with its flotilla of swans. After turning off the engine, she gathered her purse, slipped her Mark Cross briefcase behind her seat, looked into the rearview mirror at her tired eyes, and opened the door of her Mercedes 450 SLC. The parking attendant at the Hotel Bel-Air, a young man with broad shoulders and blond hair, rushed over.

"Afternoon, ma'am," he said, taking her hand and helping her from the car.

Though she was aware of him admiring her legs, Daphne hardly looked at him. That morning she had attended the funeral, but only because her mother would have turned over in her grave if she hadn't. Ironically, her sister's death created a whole new set of problems.

As Daphne walked to the door, she sensed his eyes on her, though she hadn't felt more unattractive in months. She had a splitting headache and hadn't slept well since the homicide detective had come to the house to question her and Keith. And on top of everything, she was having her

11

period. She probably would have canceled and gone back to the office if Geoffrey hadn't insisted.

"How would it look to be the only one *not* in the drawing room, Miss Scarlet?" he has asked on the phone that morning.

"I haven't a clue."

Geoffrey laughed uproariously, but Daphne decided he was right—she'd better go.

Inside, she stopped by the ladies' room. She was a little early, and since Geoffrey was habitually late, she'd undoubtedly have to wait.

Looking in the mirror, Daphne decided she had to do something about the dark circles under her eyes. It wouldn't do for the doyenne of California fitness and beauty to look like hell. At thirty-seven, she had to be careful; in her business, image was everything. Daphne flicked her fingers through her moussed chestnut hair, determined to look great forever—if Helene didn't get her from the grave first.

She'd been dead four days, but Daphne felt her presence. She knew her sister would haunt her to her dying day.

"Daphne!" Geoffrey exclaimed as she approached the table a few minutes later.

"What are you doing here already? It's only one."

He puckered and she kissed him.

"Hi, Felice," she said to the dark-haired woman seated at Geoffrey's side.

Felice lifted her chin and blew smoke from her cigarette toward the skylight, her mouth moving to a smile. "Welcome to the first official meeting of Ghouls Anonymous."

"Felice," he corrected, "it's *Suspects* Anonymous."

"My version sounds better."

Daphne laughed. "I don't know about the suspect part, but I'm beginning to *look* like a ghoul, that's for sure." The elongated vowels of her soft, southern drawl were noticeable for the first time.

"Of course you're a suspect, darling. Don't be coy," Geoffrey admonished. "That's why we invited you. Feigned innocence will only make you look guilty to the rest of us."

"Whose idea was this anyway?" Daphne asked, looking at the pair and sensing more in the air than simple collegial camaraderie.

"Geoffrey and I hatched it up over a drink on Saturday," Felice said. "But take comfort in the fact that you're in good company."

"Who else is coming?"

"Leslie's suppose to be here," Felice replied, gesturing toward an empty chair. "But as you can see, she hasn't made it."

Felice stared at the chair for a moment. The thought of Leslie Randall as a murder suspect seemed bizarre, yet she had had every reason to kill her stepmother. She pictured the girl's pretty face. Leslie was spirited, but was she capable of murder? Were any of them *really* capable of killing Helene Daniels? Felice glanced at the faces of her friends, realizing she wasn't sure. She wasn't really sure of anything anymore.

Geoffrey was examining Daphne critically. "You know, you're right, darling. You do look tired. It's surely not guilt though—even if you did it."

"Hardly." She turned to Felice. "Have the police been over and talked to you yet?"

"God, I haven't had so many men in the house since the month after Adolfo and I split. I'm beginning to hope one of them has the hots for me, because the alternative's not appealing." She drew on her cigarette, blowing the smoke upward as she had before, looking back and forth at the two of them. "To tell you the truth, though, I wouldn't half mind a tumble with that one detective, the Eurasian with the beautiful almond eyes. I think his name was Wing. He's good-looking and probably kinky as hell."

"Cops make horrible lovers," Geoffrey pronounced dryly.

The two women looked at him.

"Where were *you* the fateful night?" Daphne asked Felice.

She lowered her voice theatrically. "I was in bed watching television, Inspector. I can tell you every guest Johnny Carson had on that night and what they said." She changed her voice. "Do you own a VCR, Mrs. Fallanti?" Felice shrugged. "So when *I'm* the suspect, every cop's got a degree. When it's *my* house that's robbed, they ask, 'What's a Stella?'"

The others laughed.

"Daphne, you do look tired," Geoffrey said, studying her face.

She looked at him irritably. "Lord, you'll have me half dead before lunch is over."

"Don't be bitchy. What are friends for but to tell you these things? Besides, I've got a solution."

"I just need some rest, to get away."

"Perfect! And while you're gone I'll completely redo your place. It's been five years, darling, and it's getting a little outdated—lovely still, but dated. What do you think?"

"Before I've paid you for doing the Palm Springs spa?"

"Why not? Your credit's good. Take Keith and that golden body of his to the south of France or someplace, then come back to a new house." His expression grew wistful. "I know if Keith were mine, I wouldn't hesitate."

Annoyance flickered across Daphne's face. She was well aware how the decorator lusted after Keith, though she had no reason whatsoever to think it was reciprocated.

"Now's not a good time, Geoffrey. Wait until this business about Helene is over."

The waiter came to take drink orders. Geoffrey asked for another martini; Felice, Campari on the rocks; and Daphne, a glass of Chardonnay.

"I wonder where Leslie is," Daphne said.

"Probably visiting her dear stepmother's grave," Felice replied.

Silence hung over the table. Felice began tapping her water glass with her long, sculpted nails. Daphne, staring absently at one of the impressionist paintings across the room, fingered the gold buttons of her white Adolfo suit.

Just then Daphne felt a foot running up her leg. She pulled away and glanced under the table, then at Geoffrey. "What in the hell are you doing?"

"Oh God, Geoffrey," Felice intoned, "not again."

Daphne looked at Felice questioningly.

"He's doing research."

"It's for a book I'm writing," Geoffrey said, taking a small notebook out of his inside pocket.

"A book? What are you talking about?"

Felice laughed with her husky voice. "What's the name of it again, Geoffrey? That's the only good thing—the title."

His eyebrows rose superciliously. *"The Kamasutra of Restaurant Sex."*

Both women laughed.

"My God, where'd you come up with that?"

"I believe that the best sex starts in restaurants, but most people don't know it. It's all a matter of technique."

"I don't mean to disillusion you, dear, but *who's* running their foot up my leg makes a difference. Technique be damned."

"That's not what I was testing." He was writing in his notebook.

Geoffrey scratched out a line or two, but he felt the cracks in his carefully constructed facade widening. He felt their eyes on him—questioning eyes. Though he struggled bravely to maintain his composure, he knew he was holding it together by a thread.

The past few days had been hell—and *these* were his friends! He sighed inaudibly and closed his notebook. It would get worse before it was over. Much worse.

"By the way, Geoffrey," Felice said, "you've been so goddamned good-natured about our little tragedy. Where were *you* last Friday night?"

He forced a laugh. "Watching Johnny Carson. What else?" Geoffrey immediately picked up the martini the waiter had just deposited in front of him. "But I don't remember any of it. You see, *I* don't have a VCR!" He laughed again and took a long drink.

Leslie hadn't come by one-thirty and they were getting impatient. "Where do you suppose she is?" Felice asked.

"Maybe since she's kept us all waiting," Geoffrey said irritably, "we ought to vote her the murderess and be done with it."

"God knows, somebody had to do it," Felice said.

Geoffrey looked toward the door. "It may be too early to

issue an All Points Bulletin, but not to ask for menus. Shall we order and worry about convicting Leslie later?"

"Why is Leslie even a suspect?" Daphne asked.

"The same reason the rest of us are," Felice said. "She hated Helene's guts, and she doesn't have an alibi."

"Where was she?"

"She told me on the phone that she was home in bed at the time Helene was killed," Geoffrey replied.

"Maybe she was."

"Alone?"

"Come off it, Geoffrey," Daphne said. "Leslie's not so bad as all that. Her wild days are over. She's twenty-five now."

"God," Felice intoned, "when I was twenty-five I was just hitting high gear."

Geoffrey laughed. "And now that you're thirty-five, darling, you're in overdrive!"

She extended her middle finger from her fist. "See this perfectly manicured nail . . ."

Daphne laughed. "At least he said thirty-five, Felice, not . . ." Her words trailed off under the other woman's withering glare.

Geoffrey paused with his third martini at his lips. "I must say, though, Leslie does suffer from a dreadful lack of imagination. At least Felice and I came up with Johnny Carson, although *she* had the good sense to buy a VCR." He sipped his drink and turned to Felice. "However, you were too stupid to throw the damned machine into the Pacific before the cops came."

"I didn't throw it in the ocean because I'm not guilty. And if you're so smart, Geoffrey, why didn't you have a VCR?"

"I was hoping my innocence was all the protection I needed, although why that night, of all nights, I didn't go down to Hollywood and pick up a tart, I'll never know."

"Where were *you*, Daphne?" Felice asked. "Watching television, too?"

"No, I was on my way to the airport to pick up Keith."

"God, that's not an alibi," Geoffrey said. "Or do you think that Mercedes of yours is so memorable that every-

body on the San Diego Freeway that night would remember you?"

Daphne sipped her drink. "Unfortunately, Detective
Wing asked me the same question."

After a pause, Geoffrey ceremoniously took the floor.
"Well, what do you think, girls? Shall we decide which of
us did it and get that out of the way, or shall we order lunch
first?" His stomach was a knot that even the martinis
hadn't loosened, but he was determined to carry on bravely—he had to; it was his only hope.

"I think he's serious," Daphne said to Felice.

"Oh, he is."

"Of course I'm serious. You don't think I'm here for the
fun of it, do you?" Geoffrey picked up his glass, trying not
to tremble as he brought it to his lips.

Daphne studied him. "Why are you so damned anxious,
Geoffrey? If you ask me, all this detective work of yours is
a smoke screen. You want the spotlight off you, that's all."

"I just don't want my balls fried in the electric chair."

"They don't use the electric chair in California."

"Yeah," Felice added dryly, "it's too cruel."

"Well, let's not talk about that part," he replied. "I have
no desire to vomit up two perfectly divine martinis."

"Three, Geoffrey."

He looked at Daphne. "So who's counting?" He signaled for the waiter, who arrived with menus.

"Oh shit . . ."

Geoffrey's tone drew their attention. Felice and Daphne
turned. Being seated at a table alone was Detective Quintin
Wing of the LAPD.

"What do you suppose he's doing here?" Daphne asked.

"Probably wants to question us *en masse,*" Geoffrey replied darkly.

"Maybe it's his day off. Maybe he's looking for action,"
Felice suggested.

She looked again in Wing's direction, but he hadn't noticed them—or at least showed no sign that he had. His
serenely handsome face was composed and indifferent in
the way of a man who was used to being admired. His
subtlety fascinated her, and she felt a pang. God, how long
had it been since she'd had a good lay?

"I don't like the smell of it," Geoffrey said under his breath.

"No need to worry about a cop if you're innocent," Daphne said, her stomach tightening at her own bravado.

"Police *do* make mistakes, you know—sometimes on purpose," Geoffrey remarked caustically.

"So that's it! You're afraid of being framed," Felice quipped.

"Well, think about it. He's got to hang somebody. Of the three of us and Leslie, who do you suppose he'd pick?"

"Geoffrey, they can't just *pick* somebody," Daphne said, trying to be reassuring, for herself as much as for him. "They need evidence. District attorneys prosecute cases, not detectives. Besides, somebody other than one of us could have done it. It's just that we have motives and can't prove we're innocent."

"Daphne, since when did logic have anything to do with it? Somebody's balls are going to fry, and my intuition tells me they're going to be mine."

"God knows they won't be mine!" Felice laughed. "But I think you're right about one thing, Geoffrey—what's between that man's legs is just as important as what's between his ears."

Daphne looked at the decorator's ashen face and couldn't help feeling compassion for him. "I'm sure he'd treat you just as fairly as the rest of us."

"I'll bet," Felice added devilishly, "that Detective Wing is every bit as impressed with your dashing sophistication as he is with, say, Leslie's tits."

"Shit," he replied mournfully, "*I'd* bet he's more interested in getting into Leslie's pants than into the question of her guilt or innocence." He took one of Felice's cigarettes, then groaned. A pall settled over the table.

"Detective Wing looks lonely." Felice crushed out her cigarette. "I think I'll go test Geoffrey's theories about restaurant sex." With that she got up from the table and slunk across the room.

Wing looked up from his menu in surprise as Felice Fallanti approached him. He had followed Daphne Stephens to the hotel from the cemetery and had been observing the group quietly. He wasn't sure how they would react to his appearance, but he hadn't expected such a bold response.

"Hello, Inspector. Mind if I join you for a minute?"

"Well, Mrs. Fallanti, good afternoon."

"Let's forget the police academy stuff," she said wryly. "If you don't mind me calling you Inspector, you can call me Felice."

He grinned, admiring her mature beauty. "Please sit down."

Felice slid into the tufted banquette, close enough that her leg went right up against his. "You *do* have a first name," she said in her most sultry voice.

"Quintin."

"Quintin." She savored it. "I like it. It's sexy."

He felt her calf slowly riding up and down his. "To what do I owe this unexpected pleasure, Mrs. Fallanti?"

"Felice."

"Sorry. Felice."

She looked at him through her lashes. "My fellow suspects and I noticed you sneaking around in the bushes and wondered what you were up to."

He glanced over at the table where the others were watching them. "I came here for lunch."

Felice stroked his leg with her calf, liking the mixture of oriental and Caucasian influences in his features. Looking at his face was like looking at an optical illusion that kept playing games with the mind—one instant he looked white, the next, yellow. In any case he was big, and very male.

She liked that he didn't move away from her. He had balls. Felice hated men who denied their balls. "Since when do cops eat at the Hotel Bel-Air?"

He smiled, aroused by her. "Police work is a passion, not a living." Wing couldn't ever remember such a blatant encounter in his life. She had eyed him during their brief conversation the previous day, but this was completely unexpected. He looked at her mouth, liking her game.

"How fortunate for you." She was certain now she wanted to try him out between the sheets. "How did you get your money, then? You weren't in drug enforcement before homicide, were you?"

Wing chuckled. "No, I inherited it. My father's family had money, and my mother is a successful lawyer."

"Your father, I take it, was Chinese?"

"Yes."

Felice smiled into Quintin's soft brown eyes as her hand touched his leg, just above the knee. "We chickens are about to have lunch, so we decided why not invite the fox into the hen house. Would you care to join us?"

Wing didn't flinch at her touch. "You're very thoughtful, but I'm afraid it wouldn't be very professional under the circumstances."

"So ask us some questions. Who knows, you might even solve the case over lunch. Come on, I'm buying." Her hand instinctively slid a few inches up his thigh.

Wing looked at his watch, and Felice knew she had him.

There was surprise and dismay on Geoffrey and Daphne's faces when Felice led Detective Quintin Wing to their table, holding his hand.

"I asked Quintin to join us, gang. If we're going to decide which of us did it, we may as well get his help and advice." She laughed. "Loser buys lunch! What do you say?"

"I think it's sick," Geoffrey said under his breath.

Quintin Wing took the empty chair between Felice and Daphne. He could feel the tension. There was an awkward silence.

Geoffrey fumbled one of Felice's cigarettes from the gold case on the table. "Well, Detective Wing, is there a prime suspect?"

"No." Wing saw a nervous tick at the corner of the decorator's mouth.

"No, there's no prime suspect, or no, you won't say?"

Wing's face was blank for a moment, then it transformed slowly into a smile. "Normally, I don't discuss my cases in public. But since I'm among friends, the answer to your question is that there is no prime suspect, Mr. Hammond."

"God, don't call me Mr. Hammond. The last person to call me Mr. Hammond was an IRS agent, and that didn't end well. Call me Geoffrey."

"Leslie Randall is supposed to be here too, Quintin dear," Felice purred, "but unfortunately she stood us up. By a split decision we've decided she's innocent. What do *you* think?"

"I haven't managed to track down Miss Randall yet, though I'm looking forward to it," he replied dryly.

"Heavens. She hasn't kept her date with us, and now you can't find her. You don't suppose there's a reason for her disappearance, do you?" Felice asked.

"We'll know soon enough."

"Personally, I don't see why we should be pouncing on one another like a bunch of vultures," Daphne said.

Wing saw Felice Fallanti's eyes narrow as she glared at Daphne. "I wasn't pouncing, I was questioning."

"Sorry, Felice. I wasn't being critical of you. What I meant was that we're all in the same boat. The police will see to it that we're divided and conquered." She looked at Wing. "Or am I wrong?"

"The only people we try to divide, Mrs. Stephens, are the innocent and the guilty."

She felt his scrutiny and resented it. "It's no secret that I hated my sister's guts. Unfortunately, I can't prove I was elsewhere at the time she was shot, but I don't have to. So far as I know there's no evidence against me, or any of the rest of us, for that matter. So, with all due respect, I can't help but feel a little resentful of your games, Detective Wing."

"No games, I assure you," Wing replied soberly. "And my apologies for interrupting your luncheon. I only joined you at Mrs. Fallanti's request."

Daphne glanced around the table and realized she had overstepped her bounds. "I'm sorry. I guess I'm just letting the traumas of the past few days get to me."

"I understand." Wing looked at each of them. "It's trite to say this, I know, but I'm simply trying to do a job. I'll do my best to solve the case with as little inconvenience to you all as possible." A hand touched Wing's leg. He turned to Felice Fallanti.

"You know, Quintin, I like your technique. For a cop, you've got bedside manner."

Wing heard clear suggestion in the sultry way she pronounced the words. He looked into her eyes, deciding for the first time she wasn't just a tease. "I try to be discreet." His eyes moved slowly across her breasts, liking her provocative sexuality.

"Hmm," she purred, squeezing his leg. "You're my kind of cop." She contemplated him. "Do you have any Frank Stellas, Quintin?"

Wing nodded. "I did once, but when I had my place redecorated I gave it to my mother."

Geoffrey brightened. "Who did the decorating?"

"A former girlfriend."

"An amateur?"

"No, she was a professional. You probably know her—Meredith Weiss."

All heads turned to Quintin Wing, and Geoffrey's eyes rounded at hearing the name of his biggest rival.

"So, you like Stella!" Felice enthused over the hush.

"I liked the piece I had. Meredith didn't think it went with my colors."

"Not much goes with police blue," Geoffrey mumbled.

"Don't mind Geoffrey," Felice advised. "He's a bit queer."

Geoffrey's eyes flashed. "Better than being a nymphomaniac!"

Felice bristled, withdrawing her hand from the detective's leg.

Daphne took advantage of the heavy silence to call the waiter. "I've got to get back to work. Let's order."

But Felice's fury was building. "This lunch was a mistake," she hissed, her eyes boring into Geoffrey. "I hope they bring back the electric chair in time for you."

"The guillotine would certainly improve your personality..."

The waiter stepped to the table. "Would you care to order now?"

"Yes," Felice said, "I'd like some Rocky Mountain oysters." Then, with a withering glare at Geoffrey, she said, "Well done!"

Geoffrey turned white, looked around the table, then rose to his feet. "If you'll excuse me, I'm going to the men's room."

"Don't get too distracted to return," Felice called after him.

But Geoffrey was already moving at a jog across the floral print carpet.

Daphne looked up at the waiter. "Better give us a few more minutes," she sighed.

Felice turned to Wing, who had listened to everything in bemused silence. "Please forgive our little family spats, Quintin. Geoffrey and I sometimes get on each other's nerves."

"At least you're not a boring group."

"We aren't exactly family," Daphne said in a barely detectable drawl, "but we do have one thing in common. We all hated my sister's guts."

Wing's expression grew serious. "You know, Mrs. Stephens, that's one thing that strikes me about this case — how universally hated the victim was. With all due respect to your sister, the more I look into the matter, the more I get the feeling that the murderer was performing a public service."

The waiter was clearing away the lunch dishes, and Daphne looked at her three companions uneasily. Wing's softly masculine face contained a hint of danger that unsettled her. Though there was a trace of compassion in his smile, his eyes were flat, uncommunicative. The way he looked at her made her uncomfortable. She wished she had gone back to the office or, better still, home to Keith.

"Quintin," Felice said, running her fingers lightly over the detective's hand, "if you're going to solve this case, I wish you'd do it before Geoffrey confesses or they bring the check, whichever comes first."

"False bravado," Geoffrey said under his breath. They were the first words exchanged between them since he had returned from the men's room before lunch.

After brief reflection, Felice chose to let the matter drop.

"As Mrs. Stephens said earlier, you're all innocent until proven guilty." Wing's eyes rested on Daphne.

"What's that supposed to mean?" Felice rejoined. "That we'll have to split the bill?"

Wing smiled. "I'd hate to see an innocent person accused for want of a clear suspect."

"How wonderful to know you've got a conscience, Quintin," Felice cooed. "But I hope it doesn't get in the way of your having a little fun."

"I try not to let myself become too dull."

Daphne reached down and took her purse from under her chair. "I'm sorry to be a party pooper," she said, removing her alligator wallet, "but I've got a business to run." She took a twenty-dollar bill and handed it to Geoffrey. "This is for my share, love."

"I can't take this," Geoffrey said, pushing the twenty back in her direction.

"Why not?"

"I didn't send any flowers to your sister's funeral. I owe you one."

Daphne looked at him. "I didn't either. So keep it." Turning to the others she smiled. "Bye, all."

Wing watched her go, instinctively admiring her nicely shaped ankles and trim figure. Murdoch was right; this case was full of classy broads, and there was still one to go—Leslie Randall.

There was silence for a time, and everyone seemed aware of Daphne Stephens's empty chair. Felice and Geoffrey were thinking the same thing—now that one of their number was gone, she was fair game, but neither of them seemed anxious to take the first shot. They looked at each other for a long time, waiting to see who would bring it up.

Wing glanced at each of them with a knowing smile. "I'm aware of the incident involving the deceased and Mrs. Stephens's . . . friend, Keith Moore."

"Where *was* Keith when Helene was shot?" Felice asked Geoffrey.

"Thirty thousand feet over Kansas."

"Oh, that's right. I forgot."

"I'm afraid that did move him to the bottom of my list," Wing said dryly.

She shrugged. "Personally, I don't think Daphne did it."

"Why's that?" Wing asked.

"Intuition. I don't know why, really. Maybe because she's the obvious one."

"She did look terrible," Geoffrey observed, "for *her*, I mean. Her clothes, her hair, her makeup were perfect, as always, but . . . those dark circles under her eyes."

"She was probably having her period." Felice dismissed Geoffrey's observation with a wave of her hand.

"God," he moaned, "first you declare Leslie innocent . . . and now Daphne. I don't like the trend that's developing." He eyed Wing, then signaled the waiter for the bill. "I've got to go. You're my dear friend, Felice, but it's been a rotten lunch." He handed the waiter his Gold Card.

"Cheer up, Geoffrey. Think how boring life would be if you and I didn't have a spat now and then."

He smiled at her overture, brightening a bit, then looked at Quintin Wing. "I hope you're as good-hearted as my dear friend Felice."

"Geoffrey," she purred, "that's really sweet." She blew him a kiss across the table. "Isn't Geoffrey a sweet man, Quintin?"

"Very."

The waiter returned and handed Geoffrey a small silver tray with the bill and credit card. The decorator added a gratuity to the total and signed the voucher with a flourish.

"Let me pay you for my lunch," Wing said, taking out his wallet.

Felice grabbed his hand. "No, Quintin, this is my treat. We'll find a way for you to return the favor later."

"Really, Mrs. Fallanti, I can't . . ."

"Quintin! You promised no police academy crap. If the chief asks, tell him this was an afternoon of undercover work."

Wing returned his wallet to his pocket.

"Anyway, this has been Helene's lunch. She's been here as much any of the rest of us. Don't you think so, Geoffrey?"

"I can't bear the thought of that woman. Even now." He grunted. "Did anybody see her dead? I mean, *really* dead. This whole business might be a hoax, one of Helene's cruel jokes."

"That would be like her," Felice said.

"Detective Wing, was there a body?" Geoffrey asked hopefully.

"Yes, I'm afraid so."

"Damn!" He thought for a moment, then arched his eyebrows. "Of course, on the other hand . . . good!"

Quintin Wing looked at the man, amused.

Noting the reaction, Geoffrey swished his hand at the officer. "Confusion is more a sign of innocence than guilt, isn't it?"

"Yes," Wing replied, "it is."

"Excellent." He rose to his feet. "On that note, I shall leave."

Felice got up too and went around the table to Geoffrey. Putting a hand on each shoulder, she pulled him against her, kissing him on the cheek. "I wish you'd treat me better sometimes, you bastard."

"If you weren't such a bitch to me, Felice, I would." He kissed her back.

She patted him on the cheek, then stuffed some bills in his coat pocket.

"What's this?"

"Blood money!" she exclaimed with a laugh.

"Oh God."

"Don't worry, Geoffrey. Quintin's a compassionate cop, I can tell. He'll probably close the case unsolved by the time I'm through with him. Besides, you and I didn't see me pay you off. What's the word of one cop against two upstanding citizens?"

The decorator rolled his eyes, then bussed Felice on the cheek again. "I must go before I'm arrested." He nodded to Quintin Wing. "Toodle-oo, Inspector," he cooed and sashayed out of the restaurant.

Felice turned to Wing, her lips parting sightly. "Quintin, I'm a woman of few words. What are you doing at, say, five this evening?"

WESTWOOD

May 7, 1985

3:50 P.M.

Quintin Wing sat at the stoplight where Stone Canyon spilled out of the hills onto Sunset Boulevard. He peered through the smog-tinged air of West Los Angeles in the direction of UCLA and thought—as he inevitably did when he saw the campus—how every year the Bruins creamed Cal in football. As a Berkeley alumnus, he had learned to live with the ignominy, but even from the jaded perspective of his mid-thirties, a little piece of him ached for retribution.

After the light changed, Wing made his way to the campus, humming Cal's fight song about the "Sturdy Golden Bear." He struggled through the second chorus, realizing time had irretrievably blurred the lyrics.

Wing pulled into a parking place near the School of Law. For a brief moment the pangs of youth ran through him again, and he remembered the smell of eucalyptus on the Berkeley campus, the bells of the campanile marking the hour, and the sight from Grizzly Peak of the Golden Gate Bridge towers poking through the fog across the Bay. There had been the long hard hours of study, of course, but

Wing also remembered with fondness the pagan hedonism that had imbued the place.

The first quarter of his senior year, when he battled for the A's he needed to get into graduate school, he had the good—though ill-timed—fortune of finding two girls to share his apartment on Northside. It turned out that Wendy Wexler and Terry Santini both liked to screw as much as they liked to study. At first, they had jockeyed for favored position with him, but they were friends and in the end decided that neither could deny the other the sexual Olympian they had discovered.

The double duty had been a real test of Wing's prowess, but he had regarded it as a once-in-a-lifetime opportunity. The distraction had been nearly catastrophic until he worked out a system whereby he stayed in the library until it closed, then went back to the apartment and fucked his brains out with the girl of the night. But if he could have one each night, he had told himself, why not have both of them at the same time?

Even though he had proposed the idea as a time-saving measure, Wendy and Terry had been offended by his insensitivity. It wasn't until the night before his last exam that they had finally relented. The girls had been celebrating the end of finals over a bottle of wine and a joint at the kitchen table when he had come home from the library, hard and ready for action. God, what a night that had been.

Wing sighed deeply at his nostalgic recollections, then glanced at his watch. His mother was waiting.

The ubiquitous flower was on her desk, the usual work space cleared away in front of her chair, but the rest of the desk—the rest of the office—seemed a nightmare of confusion.

"Another article for the law review, Mother?" he asked after observing the scene for a moment.

Kathryn Wing looked up from the mound of books, files, and papers. "Quintin, dear!" She frowned. "Is it that late already?"

The woman—tall, slender, patrician—lifted the hunter case pocket watch from her ample bosom. She had worn it on a chain around her neck like an amulet for as long as

Wing could remember. Popping it open, she looked at the face through her half frame reading glasses. "Heavens, it is."

She walked around the desk, and mother and son embraced briefly, Kathryn offering her cheek, which he kissed dutifully.

"How are you, Mother?"

"Same as always. Fine. Just fine." She was studying him, much as a master would study one of his own celebrated canvases—with detached admiration. Her hands dropped from his shoulders, and she smiled. "Changed your mind about resigning, have you?"

Wing shook his head. "No, just deferred it for a while."

She gestured for him to sit down. Wing watched her return to her own place. It was a routine played out with generation after generation of students. He sat where hundreds of others had sat, but despite the fact that many of them had gone on to become great successes in the field of law, Wing felt at least their equal in the eyes of the illustrious professor. He was, after all, her masterpiece, and always would be.

"They must have come up with something awfully enticing to bring you back a week early from Hawaii." It was as close as she ever got to directly mentioning Wing's passion for women.

"They found a puzzle I haven't seen before. You know how I am about puzzles."

Kathryn removed her reading glasses and touched the soft waves of her gray hair. "Only that could tear you away from Hawaii, I expect."

Wing knew that deep down his attraction for women was a source of great satisfaction to his mother. She was, in a sense, the creator of it. But during the turmoil of his adolescence, there had been difficult moments for both of them.

As a boy, he had had his father's penchant for scientific discovery, spending long hours in his room with his books and experiments. Kathryn had worried about his lack of socialization, particularly his apparent disinterest in the opposite sex, until she had come home sick from the law school one day during Wing's sophomore year of high school and found him screwing the Filipino maid.

They had had a long talk that evening. Under her persistent cross-examination, it came out that Wing didn't bother with the girls at school, because he was getting all he needed right at home.

The poor little maid was dismissed forthwith, but not without a sizable severance payment. As it turned out, she was three months pregnant. The next week the boy had joined the soccer team and the school paper and was enrolled in a karate course. By the time he had gone off to college, Kathryn had succeeded in rounding him out considerably, but the wonders of the female body had been discovered. Life in the household was never again the same.

"What have they found to capture your imagination this time?"

"A society murder."

Kathryn's eyes widened. "The woman who was shot in Bel Air a few days ago?"

"Yes."

"I read about it in the paper. She wasn't familiar, though I'd heard of her husband. Daniels, wasn't it?"

"Helene Daniels. Her husband died a few months ago in Mexico."

"There are suspects, I assume?"

"A whole drawing room full of them, as a matter of fact." He couldn't help smiling.

"Oh Quintin, you've got a murder case. You're in love again."

Wing was well aware that she would have liked for him to become an attorney—or even a doctor as his father had been—instead of a detective. Criminal investigation had always been, in his mother's mind, on a par with his insect collection.

He looked into her eyes, knowing what she wanted to hear. "It will be my last case, I've already decided."

"Mmm. Have you told Lieutenant Murdoch?"

"Yes, but he hasn't given up on me. Sometimes I get the feeling he arranges these cases to keep me on the hook."

"Well, fate has certainly obliged him."

Wing nodded. "But it's a hell of a case, Mother, a real psychological puzzle."

"Perhaps you should have been a psychiatrist, dear. You'd have had the intellectual stimulation, minus the danger, plus a wonderful income."

"But Mother, that's part of the fun of it."

"Risking your life?"

"No. The high stakes for everyone else involved. Think how the person who killed Helene Daniels must feel right now."

"I wouldn't imagine he or she would be very pleased, knowing you're breathing down his neck."

"Not pleased. But his guts have to be turning, his blood racing." He was beaming. "For once, I may have a case I can sink my teeth into. The usual stuff—husbands killing wives, wives killing husbands—has become a bore."

"There are no jealous lovers in this one, I take it?"

"Not so far. But I've only begun to scratch the surface. I've already decided, though, that Helene Daniels was one hell of a woman."

"Oh?"

"Yeah. She must have been something. Apparently a first class bitch. Everybody hated her. A number of people would have liked to kill her. We've already identified three or four with a motive and no alibi. They're a bizarre group —not your Chevrolet and McDonald's kind of folks, Mother." Wing smiled broadly. "I had lunch with them."

Kathryn's eyebrows rose. "Goodness. How genteel."

"I was hanging around the Hotel Bel-Air when they saw me at a table alone. They invited 'the fox into the hen house,' as one of them put it."

"Hen house? Are they women?"

"Two 'classy broads,' as Murdoch called them, and a gay man. There's another woman, a stepdaughter, whom I haven't met yet. We're trying to track her down. Barring a simple outcome like the stepdaughter skips, or the boys in the crime lab come up with something tangible, I'm going to have to get to know Helene Daniels and her friends so well that I'll be like family before it's over."

Anticipating his next comment, Kathryn asked, "Would

you like some of your mother's home cooking this evening, Quintin? I've got a couple of steaks in the fridge."

"Where's Trevor?" he asked, referring to the man she had been seeing for a few months, Wing's father having died several years earlier.

"At a medical conference in San Diego."

Wing looked at her thoughtfully. "What is it about you and doctors, Mother?"

"I don't know. Probably the same thing about you and 'classy broads.'"

They laughed together.

"Thanks for the invitation, but I have an appointment."

Her look was knowing. "Well, try and come by and see me sometime this week. I've got a new Jasper Johns you'd like."

Wing's eyes brightened. "A Jasper Johns? That's your second. I'm still looking for my first."

"Don't despair, dear. You're prominent in my will."

"I can't wait that long, Mother. Besides, you'll outlive me. Just remember, though, you owe me an important canvas."

"I haven't forgotten. But don't *you* forget, any painting I've got is yours as a wedding present, should that day ever come."

Wing laughed. "And I thought I'd have to marry a Getty to get my Jasper Johns."

"Frankly, dear, I wish you would."

BEVERLY HILLS

May 7, 1985

4:40 P.M.

Wing followed the congested traffic east along Sunset Boulevard, then cut south to Wilshire. He looked for Felice Fallanti's building—her card simply stated her name, address, and phone number. Wing knew she had money, but he wasn't sure where it came from or what she did. He knew he'd soon find out.

The steel and glass high-rise office building was surrounded by lush foliage, palms, and fountains. Most of the occupants were leaving as Wing entered. Several attractive young women were waiting when he got off the elevator at Felice's floor. He paused in the corridor after they brushed by him, savoring the lingering melange of their perfumes, spiced by the faint scent of chewing gum. One of them, a honey blond in a miniskirt, smiled with amusement as he admired her legs. After an instant of mutual appraisal, the door closed between them, leaving Wing alone in the deserted hallway. He turned to look for the suite.

The name was on the door in gold relief block letters. Inside, Wing found a spacious reception area, nicely decorated with several overstuffed couches in cream-colored Italian leather, large potted palms, and an expanse of thick wool carpeting. At the far side of the room an attractive, middle-aged woman with stylish swirls of copper hair looked up from her desk. He gave her his name and sat in one of the leather couches.

Several moments later, a door behind the receptionist opened, and a young man in shirt sleeves and a tie appeared. He had longish sandy-blond hair, deeply tanned skin, and a toothpaste smile. "Detective Wing," he said, walking over, his hand extended, "I'm Eric, Felice's assistant."

The detective took the man's hand, noticing that his crisply starched shirt hugged his frame as closely as a coat of paint. Wing had the amusing vision of Felice doing her hiring from the shirt advertisements in *Esquire* magazine.

"I'm sorry, but Felice is not back yet," he said graciously. "We expect her at any time, though." He turned and gestured toward the double doors in the corner. "Perhaps you'd like to wait in her office. I think you'd be more comfortable there."

Wing followed Eric to the doors, which were opened ceremoniously for him. He stepped into a rather elegant office, unmistakably feminine.

"Please sit down. I'll fix you a drink. What would you like?" He had gone to a small wet bar surrounded by mirrors against one wall.

"Anything wet. Soda water would be fine."

Eric glanced over his shoulder. "Nothing stronger?"

"No thanks."

The young man rummaged around the bar as Wing looked around him, trying to discern what the place told him about its occupant. "Mrs. Fallanti certainly keeps a neat office, Eric. Is she here much?"

He turned and smiled. "Funny you should ask that. Felice is rarely here."

"The place doesn't look used," Wing explained. "She and I have chatted several times but haven't really discussed business. What is it exactly that Mrs. Fallanti does?"

The assistant returned from the bar with a glass of soda water and a twist of lime. "Felice considers herself an investor."

"Is she?"

"Oh, very much so. She has considerable real estate holdings, securities, and so forth, but her first love is films. After she and Adolfo were married, she became very heavily involved. She produces; he directs."

"I was aware that Mr. Fallanti was in the film business, but I hadn't realized she was as well."

"She's not involved in the artistic side—Felice understands the dollar. Adolfo is a genius, but without Felice . . ." He shrugged. "Of course, that was all before the big 'P.'"

"Big 'P'?"

"Prison. You know that Adolfo—"

"Oh yes, that. Sorry, the 'Big P' threw me." He grinned. "I don't watch television, so I'm not up on the latest crime jargon."

Eric laughed. "That's not crime jargon, Detective Wing. It's a little office joke. Felice doesn't like to talk about Adolfo's problems, so we tend to use euphemisms."

"I see." Wing picked up his glass. "Cheers."

"I'd join you, but I've got some letters to get in the mail before I leave." Eric went to the door and stopped. "For future reference, Felice runs half an hour late—almost to the minute. She should be popping in any time now."

He had just returned to the couch after refilling his glass with soda water when the door swung open. Felice Fallanti stood there, her feet slightly apart, her hip cocked provocatively, a Lina Lee shopping bag hanging from her long slender fingers. She had changed from the suit she wore at lunch into a red-and-black silk Valentino dress with a plunging vee neckline. Her open-toed shoes were black alligator, as was her little shoulder bag. Her head tilted plaintively as her eyes met his.

"Quintin, you beat me here!"

"Sorry," he replied ironically, rising to his feet.

"God, I hate punctuality." She pointed a threatening finger. "That's the first thing I'm going to change about you." She walked toward him. "Actually, it's the second. I bought you a tie," she said, lifting the shopping bag slightly.

"A tie?" He glanced at the bag. "From Lina Lee?"

"No, silly boy, I got myself a few things, too. You don't expect me to be completely selfless, do you?" Felice put the bag on the coffee table and looked up at him.

Wing saw the utter sexuality in her look. Her arms slipped around his neck, and she stood watching him with her breasts close to his chest, but not quite touching it. She smiled.

"You don't mind that I bought you a tie, do you?"

He felt her fingertips on the back of his neck and had to repress a tremor. "It's really not proper that you buy me anything, Felice. Lunch was bad enough."

"But Quintin, darling, the tie you have on struck me as one your mother would have picked out for you." She saw something flicker in his eyes and knew she'd inadvertently struck a chord. "It's a lovely tie, to be sure, one you should wear to see her, but when you visit Felice, you should wear something a little ... angrier."

"Angrier?"

"You know what I mean, Quintin. Brooding. After all, I *am* a married woman. And I'm *very* fond of you." The corners of her mouth curled up coquettishly. "Come, let me show you the tie."

She reached into the bag and pulled out a long, flat Bijan tie box. She handed it to him.

"This is my little welcome-to-the-case present."

"Very thoughtful, but unnecessary." He looked at the swell of her breasts, thinking how voluptuous her body was—how she tantalized like a ripe fruit. They smiled into each other's eyes, then Wing opened the box.

"Do you like it, Quintin?"

"Felice, it's gorgeous, but I can't accept this. There are detectives on the force that don't spend this on a suit— even a good suit."

"Now, now, it's not the amount that matters, just the spirit in which it's given." Her hand slipped under his jacket and pressed against his chest. "Why don't you go over to the mirror and put it on? It's not quite right with your suit, but I can see how it goes with your eyes."

He slipped off his suit jacket and went to the bar. After he had put on the tie he returned to Felice, who had kicked off her shoes and curled up on the couch. She was beaming.

"Don't you look wonderful!"

"Angry enough for you?"

"Perfect." Her bow furrowed. "But what's that thing on your hip? A gun?"

"Yes. It's part of the reality of my work. There's always a possibility my day could turn nasty." His expression was indulgent. "Hope you aren't upset, but I *am* a cop, Felice."

"Upset? No, of course not. Every man's got some drawback. I've been around long enough to know there's no such thing as a perfect one." She smiled at him. "But there *are* men who know how to keep their imperfections from interfering, if you know what I mean. As long as you don't sleep with that thing on, Quintin, we won't have any problems."

There was a possessive look in her eyes that amused and excited him. "Can I fix you a drink?" he asked.

"Yes, that would be nice. What are you having?"

"Soda water."

She grimaced disapprovingly. "At least it's not Budweiser."

"Oh, I only drink Bud at home." He laughed. "Or when I go out with some of the boys."

"Quintin! How can anybody with a Frank Stella on his wall possibly drink Budweiser?"

"Actually, I don't drink much at all."

"Hmm," Felice purred provocatively. "Is it true that a man who doesn't drink can keep it up longer?"

"I don't know. But I've never had any complaints."

She reached over and touched his lip with her finger. "Your imperfections don't seem at all obvious. Do you have any?"

"When I was a kid my mother accused me of being oversexed. But I've gotten that under control now."

"What a shame. Any chance of a relapse?"

He grinned. "I try to keep a semblance of professionalism while I'm on duty."

"Hmm. Why don't you fix me a vodka tonic while I consider my options."

Wing went to the bar, mixed Felice a drink, and brought

it to her. She held it to her lips, contemplating him over the rim of the glass.

"Quintin, I've decided we should talk about the case. I know that's what you want to do, so let's get it out of the way."

"I don't want to abuse your hospitality, but that's why the taxpayers are paying me."

"Where do we begin?"

"With the victim. I'd like to know about Helene Daniels."

"Too bad. But then, we can't very well talk about the case without talking about her, can we?"

"She's the most important piece of the puzzle."

"What do you want to know?"

"What was she like?"

"What was Helene Daniels like?" She looked across the room thoughtfully, her elbow resting on the back of the couch. "Helene was like a lioness that hadn't eaten in a week. She was always on the prowl, looking for prey."

"But she was your friend."

"I'm rather feline myself, Quintin, so I understood her. I don't know that I ever liked her, though. I was fascinated by her, as everyone was. Helene could be very charming. Anyone that dangerous had to be charming to survive. In that sense she was like a cobra—mesmerizing, but deadly."

"She sounds fascinating. I would have liked to have known her."

Felice laughed ironically. "In death as in life."

"By that I take it she was attractive to men?"

"Helene used men. She used everybody, but she used men in particular."

"What motivated her?"

"Initially, it was money and status."

"My impression is she had that—at least at the end of her life."

"Yes, that's why I said initially."

"And later?"

"Power. Helene wanted power." She drew on her cigarette. "You see, in the end even her husband, Jed, stood between her and the kind of power she wanted. In a manner of speaking, I was in her way, too."

"What kind of power?"

"Ultimate power over people and situations. Jed gave her anything she wanted, but he was still the giver. Helene didn't like owing anyone. Her big failing was that she lacked subtlety. I abhor people who lack subtlety..."

"So, Helene Daniels was after money and power."

"Yes, that was her history. Maybe her background explains why she was the way she was—though God knows it didn't affect Daphne the same way."

"What was her background?"

"Helene rarely talked about it, but she came from a poor southern family in rural Louisiana. I think she was fairly old before she'd even ventured as far away from home as New Orleans."

"Rags to riches?"

"Yes, but for some reason she figured she had to climb to the top over the bodies of other people, including her own sister. Helene spared no one. Even her husband was just a weapon—a tool to get what she wanted. She was married once before Jed, you know."

"No, I didn't."

"It was the same pattern. An older man, well-to-do, et cetera, et cetera."

"What happened to him?"

"I don't know. She never told me about it and wouldn't talk about that part of her life."

"How do I find out about Louisiana?"

"Talk to Daphne, I suppose."

"Yes, I intend to." Wing contemplated Felice. "Tell me about *you* and Helene Daniels."

"Aren't you going to read me my rights first, Quintin?"

"I already did yesterday, remember?"

"Once is all I get?"

"That's all the Supreme Court says you're entitled to." His look was riveting. "Did you know her long?"

"Only a few years. She and I were in business together —films. It was an intense, passionate, and violent relationship." She could see his eyes widen in anticipation. "Do we have to talk about her, Quintin?"

"If it weren't for her, I wouldn't be here."

"God, the bitch is dead and we're still competing."

"Your relationship was business rather than social?"

Felice laughed. "Is there a difference in this town?"

"When and where did you meet?"

"It was several years ago. Actually, Adolfo and I knew Jed first. He invested in one of our films, and the business relationship gradually became social. Helene really promoted it, I suppose. She had a hunger for the film business and saw Adolfo and me as an entrée. The friendship became a means Helene used to feed her obsession. The power trip I referred to."

"What went wrong?"

"In a nutshell, Helene decided she wanted *everything* I had, including Adolfo. It put a damper on our friendship," she added dryly.

"What's happening with your husband, anyway? I haven't seen anything about him in the papers for several months."

"Yes, the press," she said bitterly. "Bunch of goddamned vultures, that's what they are."

"He's still in Switzerland?"

"No need to be delicate about it, Quintin. Adolfo's still in Switzerland, still in jail." She looked thoughtful. "Funny thing is, I still don't know whether I care. We separated before he was arrested, you know."

"Helene Daniels?"

Felice glanced at him. "Yes, my dear friend, Helene."

Wing studied her eyes.

"What are you looking for, Quintin? Guilt?"

"You do have a motive, like the others."

"Well, I didn't do it — somebody else got to her first." She lit another cigarette. "You want to hear something else?"

"What?"

"I'd bet my ass Helene framed Adolfo."

"I thought she was . . . interested in him."

"She used him, and when his usefulness was over, her attitude toward him changed rather abruptly. What happened was Adolfo stopped cooperating with her, so she tried to destroy him. That's the way she did things."

"But you didn't kill her."

Felice inhaled, then sent the smoke to the ceiling. "What do *you* think, Quintin?"

"I'd like to think not."

She smiled. "Rest assured then, dear."

"Somewhere in these tales of woe, I'm going to find a murderer, Felice."

"I hope it won't be anybody I know."

"Chances are it will be."

"You're sure?"

"I'm only getting started."

"You may as well know you've only seen the tip of the iceberg."

"Are you going to tell me more?"

"You're the detective, Quintin. You ought to have to dig for the juicy stuff." She reached over and caressed his cheek with her long, slender fingers. "But then, the pursuit is half the fun, isn't it?"

Wing felt himself stirring at her touch. He could tell she was without fear, and he liked that. Even the most heartless murderer feared. Felice Fallanti was either the consummate villain, or she was innocent, and he was pretty sure he knew which. "What about Leslie Randall? Is she going to show up, or has she skipped?"

"You would know that better than I," Felice replied.

"If she's guilty, she might have fled."

"If you're asking if I think she did it, I meant what I said at lunch. I doubt Leslie killed Helene."

"Why? She hated Helene bitterly, didn't she?"

"So did we all. I'm not sure hatred is enough."

"What exactly was Leslie's complaint?"

"She was convinced that Helene killed her father."

"*Killed* him? You mean drove him to his death?"

"I mean murdered him."

"I thought he died in an accident."

"Leslie's convinced it wasn't an accident. I think she told Helene as much."

"Hardly calculated to bring stepmother and daughter together."

"No."

"She and her father were close?"

Felice held up two fingers side by side. "Like this."

"But you don't think she killed Helene Daniels?"

She shrugged her shoulders and took a sip of her drink. "No, but who am I?"

"How about Geoffrey Hammond?"

"Geoffrey's my best friend, Quintin. My best girl-friend," she added, smiling.

"I did get the impression you were close."

"The harder you fight, the harder you love. My husband is Italian, that's where I learned that particular pearl of wisdom."

"So you won't hazard a guess whether Geoffrey did it?"

"Sixty-forty against. And it would even be lower except that he does have a temper." She smiled again. "If he had had a guillotine this afternoon at lunch, my face-lift would be in a basket right now."

Wing laughed. "Do you and Geoffrey go back a long way?"

"Years. You were probably still in high school when we met." She sized him up like a mature beauty savoring a young buck. "But not as far as Geoffrey and Helene went back," she continued.

"What was their connection?"

She looked at him coyly. "That's Geoffrey's story. Better that you ask him."

Wing drained his glass. "I will."

They looked at each other again as they had before.

"You like playing detective with your little gun and questions, don't you?"

Wing tried to act blasé, but he knew she had found his weakness.

"This is shaping up to be the most interesting case I've had. Fascinating victim..."

Felice's look became suggestive. She reached up and touched his cheek with her fingertips. "Yes..."

"...fascinating suspects..." Wing saw the creamy flesh of her breast at the vee of her neckline.

"Yes..."

"...the most fascinating interrogation I've ever had."

Felice leaned over and kissed him softly on the lips, then looked deeply into his eyes. "Tell me the truth, Quintin. Have you ever gone to bed with a suspect?"

BEL AIR

May 7, 1985

6:05 P.M.

The two cars snaked their way along the narrow asphalt ribbon past the million-dollar homes that lined both sides of the canyon. Quintin Wing kept his eye on the car ahead, pressing the accelerator in an attempt to keep pace. The rear end of the Maserati ahead of him almost seemed to twitch, like Felice herself. It was funny, he thought, how in the hands of a woman a car could be sexually arousing.

Felice Fallanti was moving at high speed, her sensuous body emblazoned in his mind, luring him. Duty and professional conduct had been consciously brushed aside— her offer was just too exciting, too fraught with danger to reject. She wasn't the killer, he had decided. His only fear was that it was the aching throb between his legs, rather than his reason, that told him so. A serious mistake could prove embarrassing, although it didn't really matter now— it was his last case. He'd already decided he'd do this one his way.

Ahead the Maserati geared down, pulled into the mouth of a driveway, and stopped as an electronically activated gate began opening. Wing pulled up behind Felice, and the two automobiles moved past the massive oaks on either

43

side, around the great sweeping drive, stopping finally in front of the five-car garage.

Wing got out of his car and watched Felice slink toward him. Though she had to be six or eight years older than he, she had an exquisite body, and she obviously knew how to use it. He had no doubts whatsoever that she'd be dynamite in bed.

"Come on, dear," she said in her low, husky voice. Felice led the way up the stairs, letting her nicely rounded ass sway just enough.

Wing enjoyed it every step of the way.

"This is my room," she said, throwing open the double doors. He stepped inside and she closed the doors behind them.

Wing glanced around. The walls were completely covered in a pale apricot moiré. The bedspread and drapes were an apricot, yellow, and leaf green floral print. On the wall opposite the bed was an antique secretaire. A chaise longue was in one corner, and two chairs and a backgammon table were in another. The king-size bed was on a raised platform. Wing studied the painting over the bed. "Matisse?"

"Yes, a wedding present from Adolfo." She smiled. "Between the painting and the ring, he didn't have a cent left. My dear husband was not—is not—a wealthy man."

"Forgive my audacity, Felice, but mind if I ask where you got your start, financially?"

"Quintin, I'm surprised you don't know all about me. I thought my notorious heritage was half the reason I'm suspected." She went to the table by the bed and began removing her jewelry.

He watched her, wondering if she'd undress completely without dropping the conversation. "No, I'm afraid I know nothing about your past, Felice."

"I'll go right to the bottom line, then. My dear, departed daddy was Italian from New Jersey—a very wealthy man with very mysterious business interests. My mother was from a proud, but not too auspicious, New England family that took their heritage and Mayflower connections seriously. They separated when I was about six. I only occasionally saw my father after that, but he provided royally for my mother and me. When he died under mysterious circumstances in either Miami or pre-Castro Havana— there are conflicting stories—I inherited a fortune."

"And you've managed your portfolio ever since?"

"Yes, that's what my tax return says. I'm an investor." Felice had removed her Bulgari gold earrings, matching gold coin necklace, and Adolfo's ten-carat emerald engagement ring, setting them casually on a table by the bed. She was looking at the detective as she began unbuttoning her dress. "As far as I'm concerned, sex begins with foreplay, not seduction, Quintin. I hope you don't mind."

He smiled wryly. "Mind if I take off my coat?"

"God, please do. I can't stand a man who doesn't bother to get completely undressed. It reminds me of the Middle Ages—not mine, Europe's."

Wing went over to the chaise longue and tossed down his jacket, then turned to watch Felice step out of her dress. She flicked it onto a chair and faced him, wearing only a black lace bra, matching panties, and panty hose. She slowly walked toward him. Wing felt himself harden.

Felice stood before him in her stocking feet, seeming to him much shorter without her heels. He had already loosened his tie, and she removed it for him. Then she began unbuttoning his shirt. When he was stripped to the waist, Felice slid her hands over his smooth but muscular chest.

He ran his fingertips along the top of her bra, lightly touching the ivory swell of her breasts. She put her hands around the bulge at his crotch, first cupping it gently, then massaging him through his pants.

"Do you like police work, Quintin?"

His fingers were on the clasp of the bra between her breasts. "I seem to enjoy it more and more all the time."

Quintin Wing stared dreamily at the ceiling, his loins relaxed and spent. The risk he had taken was well worth it, he decided—even if things went badly later.

Felice lay with her Porthault sheets draped casually over her, though the detective at her side was completely uncovered. She admired his smooth skin and muscles that seemed more classical Greek than oriental.

Adolfo's body, like most Italian men's, was a mass of

hair. It could be terribly sexy in its own way, but this Eurasian reminded her of the ancient Mediterranean races that had inhabited the civilized world before the Vandals, Visigoths, and all the rest. Urbanity and sex, she thought, could be a very stimulating combination.

"I figured you'd be good, Quintin," Felice purred, "but I had no idea . . ."

"It's all those months on the vice squad."

She smiled through heavily lidded eyes. "You have a few moves even I haven't seen." She reached over and trailed her fingers lightly over his penis, which—like the rest of him—reclined in mellow splendor. After a minute or so it began to respond to her attention.

He smiled at her, looking more Caucasian at that moment than at any time since she had met him.

"Tell me, Quintin. What does it mean that you went to bed with me?"

"That you're hard to turn down."

"No, I'm not irresistible. I know that. You let yourself do it despite everything at stake. You've given me a great deal of leverage over you, you know. There must be a reason. I'm just wondering if I should worry."

"No, Felice, I have no ulterior motives, if that's what concerns you."

"But this is hardly routine, I'm sure."

"It's not routine at all. It's a first, actually."

"Why'd you do it?"

"First, because I wanted to. Second, because I figure you're not the culprit. Third, because I need a friend—somebody who knew the victim *and* my suspects."

"You want me to help you hang one of my friends?" she asked, stroking him more enthusiastically.

"That's a rather uncharitable way to put it, so let's say our goal is to take the heat off of you and the others who are innocent."

"I'm not a fink by nature, Quintin. I tend to be both loyal and discreet, though you'd have to know me well to appreciate the latter."

"If I thought you were indiscreet I wouldn't be here."

"Then you either know me well or you're more stupid than hell." She laughed and looked down at Wing's swollen cock, which now stood upright in her hand. "What kind of help, exactly, do you want from me?"

"The material evidence in the case is very fragmentary. I don't have the weapon, only the three bullets that were removed from the body. There were no prints, even on the outer doors. No one saw anyone arriving or leaving the house. Whoever killed Helene Daniels knew her—that's a virtual certainty. He was either admitted to the house by the victim, or had a key of his own."

"How do you know the doors were locked?"

"Well, we can't be positive, but whoever killed her bothered to lock the doors on the way out if they were unlocked at the time of entry. It's more likely that they were locked both before and after entry."

"It couldn't have been a burglar?"

"I don't think so. She was killed just before midnight, which makes that a possibility, but there is no indication of anything being taken—no forced entry, and the location and position of the body suggest a known person rather than a stranger."

Felice was running her fingers lightly up and down the shaft of Wing's cock. "How do you know that?"

"There are several things. It's the combination that convinces me. The victim's security system was equipped with a panic button. If she'd heard an intruder, she'd have likely used it, or have been trying to use it before she was shot. And she was killed in the study. The wall safe was open, there were financial documents spread out on the desk—not as though someone had riffled through them, but as though they had been examined in an orderly way."

"Maybe a robber forced her to open the safe."

"Again possible, but they'd have had to gain entrance through a hoax, since there was no forced entry. Also, valuables were not kept in the safe—not even negotiable securities—and nothing was missing as far as we're able to determine."

"So what do you think happened?"

"Helene was still dressed. It means either that she was expecting the killer or that she simply hadn't yet retired. The former works nicely with my hypothesis of the case."

"Which is?"

"That Helene knew her killer. She was expecting the culprit—or was at least not surprised by his or her arrival. She and the murderer went into the study together to open the safe, and possibly examine the documents."

"But why? What documents?"

"Why is the critical question. It will probably tell us who killed Helene Daniels. The *what* is a little easier. Most of the documents on the desk concerned the financial condition of the Daniels's empire—Jed and Helene's holdings. There were balance sheets, records on foreign bank accounts, income statements, and so forth. That would indicate to me the visitor had an interest of some kind in the condition or operations of the family's business and investments."

Felice stopped stroking him and looked Wing in the eye. "Meaning who?"

"Since you seem discreet, and you know me so well," he added, looking down at her hand that was still wrapped around him, "I'll give you my list. The documents on the desk probably affect Leslie Randall more than anyone else. That would have to put her at the top of the list."

"Leslie? But is she smart enough—or stupid enough, I don't know which—to pull off something like that? Somehow I just don't see Leslie doing that, at least not cleanly."

"You may have a point, but she could have been lucky. By the way, we've located her. She'd driven up the coast to get away for a few days. I'll be talking to her tomorrow morning."

"So that's why she wasn't at the lunch." Felice sighed. "I hope you're wrong about her, Quintin. You said she was first. Who else?"

"The safe also contained some of Helene Daniels's personal documents—her will, for example. Daphne Stephens figured prominently in that. She would probably come second on my list."

"Helene's personal papers weren't on the desk?"

"No, but they might have been at the time of the shooting. It could be that the killer switched the documents around afterward, or any of a number of other possibilities. There's something that lends credence to that theory. He found a partial print on the safe that we are fairly certain was not Helene's, but it isn't good enough for positive identification."

"You think Daphne would have shot her sister, then shuffled documents from the desk to the safe?"

"I don't know, but I think she, more than anyone else, would likely be able to do that."

"But she's only number two in your popularity poll. What about Geoffrey and me?"

"As nearly as I've been able to determine, neither of you has a present financial interest in the Daniels, which, if my premise is correct, would eliminate you both."

"Quintin, forgive me, but there's qualification in your voice. Say what you mean."

"I've already told you I think you're innocent, though I can't prove it. On the other hand, I have a funny feeling about Geoffrey. He's hiding something. I'm almost sure of it."

"So he's only number three on the list?"

"Yes, but that's because at the early stages I focus my efforts on where logic, not intuition, takes me. That can change."

"God, let's hope poor old number four doesn't become a rising star."

His fingers gingerly rubbed her erect nipple. "Don't worry, Felice, you aren't even number four."

"No. Who is?"

"I always save a slot for someone who hasn't occurred to me yet. It forces me to keep an open mind."

Her fist tightened slightly on his cock. "For what it's worth, darling, I think number four did it."

Felice gave him a sly look before climbing over him and taking him deeply into her mouth.

PACIFIC PALISADES

May 7, 1985

9:10 P.M.

Wing rang the doorbell and turned to look at the two Labradors that had him nicely cornered in the entry. The large male was growling, his ears back, his bared teeth showing. The detective unconsciously felt with his elbow for his service revolver under his suit jacket, though he knew the dogs would probably tear him to shreds before he could use it.

He pushed the button again and eyed the dogs warily. Finally, the door swung open and a handsome blondish man in his late thirties wearing a pale blue cashmere sweater appeared. Wing instantly recognized Keith Moore from his films, though they'd never met.

"You must be Detective Wing."

"Yes."

"I'm Keith Moore. Come on in," he said, extending his hand.

Wing glanced back at the dogs and stepped in, taking Moore's hand. "I thought for a while your friends out there were going to turn me into hamburger."

"Their bark is worse than their bite. But I imagine you've heard that before." He looked out at the Labradors.

50

"Go on, Rhett! Get back out by the road and keep your eyes open."

The dogs barked and ran back into the darkness. The actor closed the door, grinning.

"Rhett, huh?"

"Yeah, Rhett and Scarlett. I guess my occupational bias shows."

Wing studied the face, which was as handsome as the man's screen image, though Moore looked older and thinner than he did in films. The detective had the strange sensation of dealing with an impostor. "Sorry to be late."

"No problem; Daphne and I were just having a glass of wine." He gestured toward an arched doorway at the rear of the entry. "Come on back."

Waiting on a large couch covered with pillows near the fireplace was Daphne Stephens in a velour jogging suit, a glass of wine in her hand. "Well, Detective Wing. You made it."

"Sorry to be late. I got tied up. Did my office call to let you know?"

"Yes, about half an hour ago. Sit down," she said, gesturing toward the armchairs opposite the couch.

Wing sat, glancing at the small fire burning in the fireplace.

"We have a fire every night during the winter. It's a hard habit to break," Daphne explained.

Keith was still standing. "Can I get you a glass of wine?"

"No, thanks."

"Something else? Coffee?"

"No, nothing. Thank you."

The actor went over and dropped onto the couch next to Daphne, putting his arm around her shoulders. Her hand immediately went to his knee and rested there. Wing noted a protective quality in the man's manner and sensed a genuine regard between the couple.

"I take it you haven't found your murderer, or you wouldn't be here," Daphne said evenly. She seemed to Wing more relaxed than she had been at lunch.

"No."

"You don't really think Daphne killed Helene, do you?" Keith asked.

"I don't know that she didn't. Let me put it that way."

Keith smirked. "Shit, I could have killed the bitch. Anybody could have."

"As I understand it, Mr. Moore, you were on a flight from Europe when Mrs. Daniels was killed."

"Daphne was on her way to the airport to pick me up."

"We believe the victim was shot somewhere between one and two hours before your plane landed."

"But even if Daphne had driven from here to Bel Air, killed Helene, and then driven down to LAX, it would be pushing it."

"In her statement to Detective Williams, Mrs. Stephens said she left the house directly for the airport, but she can't corroborate that because no one saw her leave here at the time she said, or earlier, for that matter."

"Well, nobody saw her at Helene's either, did they?"

"No, that's true. If someone had, she'd quite possibly be under arrest."

Keith looked at Daphne. "I don't like this, honey. Maybe you shouldn't talk to him without an attorney."

"Keith, I've got nothing to hide. There's no evidence against me. There couldn't be." She looked at Wing. "Isn't that right?"

"Yes. That's true."

"You see?"

Keith shook his head. "I still don't like it. Having an attorney is not a sign of guilt."

She looked at the detective. "Why is it, exactly, that you suspect me? I know I can't prove that I was on the freeway when my sister was killed, and it's obvious I hated her deeply, but that could easily be said of several dozen people."

"If necessary, Mrs. Stephens, I'll track down every possible suspect and talk with them as well."

Daphne sighed. "What is it that you want of me now?"

"I'm trying to find out as much as I can about Helene Daniels, and it seems you knew her better than anyone, with the possible exception of her husband, and he's dead. I like to get to know my victims. It's the way I work. And to be quite frank, Mrs. Stephens, I'm getting the impression your sister was a very unusual and interesting person."

"Helene was interesting all right."

"What was she like as a child? What was your relationship like when you were growing up?"

Daphne stared at Wing, her expression vacant. "You wouldn't believe the things she did, even as a teenager..."

"You didn't get along well?"

"Helene was always out for herself. There was a cruel side to her, a hateful side I never did understand."

"You're from Louisiana originally, aren't you?"

"Yes, but Helene would never admit to it—not after she was virtually run out of the state." Daphne's look was as sad as it was bitter. "In those days, Detective Wing, *I* was the victim."

CATAHOULA PARISH, LOUISIANA 1965

June 6

Helene Johnston sat in the dark by her bedroom window, letting the breeze swish the lace curtain across her bare arm, wishing it were Lance Piccard's fingers that caressed her. But he was downstairs on the porch with Daphne, cooing and sweet-talking her. Helene could hear the faint squeak of the porch swing and the murmur of their voices. She thought of Lance's handsome face and wished Daphne were dead.

Over the sounds of crickets and frogs in the soft Louisiana night, she heard Daphne's giggle, the one she used with boys, and Helene knew Lance was probably pinching her sister's nipples or running his hand up under her skirt. Why couldn't it be her? She and Lance had gone through four years of high school together, and Helene had managed to sit next to him in nearly every class their senior year. The thought that he was only interested in her little sister brought tears to Helene's eyes.

Daphne was only seventeen and Lance was twenty—just a year older than Helene. What did he see in her? All she had were big tits and a silly-ass giggle. She was a child, not a woman. Helene knew she'd have to find a way to make him value her instead of Daphne. After all, Lance Piccard was her best, and maybe only, chance at respectability and wealth.

The Piccards were the richest family in Catahoula Parish, and the only well-to-do folks with a son of marrying age. Her only other choice was finding an eligible young man up in Monroe or down in Natchez, but that was like going to the edge of the known world. It was complicated enough getting to either town on a bus, let alone finding a man there. No, she had to get Lance wanting his hands up under *her* skirt, even if it meant getting rid of her sister—any way she could.

Daphne giggled again, and Helene figured Lance was probably hot and bothered. She couldn't stand it and had to find out what was going on.

Their daddy and mama were downstairs in the parlor listening to the radio, so she couldn't eavesdrop from the house. The only thing to do was to creep out on the roof of the porch where she'd be right above them. When they were girls, she and Daphne used to crawl around out there all the time when Mama wasn't looking. It was plenty sturdy then; it probably was now.

Carefully, so as not to make a sound, Helene stepped through the open window. The roof of the porch creaked a little under her weight, so she froze for a second or two before she crept farther out.

"Lance! Stop that! Mama 'n Daddy are just inside. Daddy'd run you right off the place if he saw you with your hand under my skirt."

"You're so goddamn sweet, Daphne, I can't help myself."

"You'd better help yourself if you want to see me again."

"Don't y'all like it when I do this? Huh?"

"Lance!"

"Let me just stick my finger up there for a minute, Daphne."

"What kind of a woman do you think I am, anyway?"

"Damn sweet one. Oh, Lord, so goddamn sweet."

"Don't you go gettin' any ideas. You hear me, Lance Piccard?"

"Just let me rub your leg for a little minute . . . see how good that feels?"

Helene could hear her sister's heavy breathing and felt herself starting to get wet between her legs.

"Oh, Lance . . ."

"Daphne darlin', I sure do want your honey. Goddamn I do."

"Mmm . . . oh, Lance, you better stop that . . . I'm not experienced, you know . . ."

Helene could hear the rustle of Daphne's petticoats and the swing started squeaking. Her sister had stopped him.

"Why don't we take a ride in my car? The top's down. There's a moon. We can go up on the bluffs and look at the water in the moonlight."

"Daddy won't let me go to no lovers' lane with you. I'm only seventeen, you know."

"Ask him if I can take you into town for an ice cream. We'll just stop by the river on the way. It won't be a lie."

"I don't think I should."

"Come on, Daphne. How you ever going to grow up if you're always sayin' no to everything?"

"I don't mean it personal, Lance."

"There's plenty of girls in the parish to say yes to me, you know."

"I'm not like all the others, Lance Piccard, and if that's all you're after, you might as well go on home right now."

"Dammit, that's not what I meant. I know you're the decent kind, but our relationship's got to progress a little, too. There's one hell of a lot we could do without goin' all the way, Daphne."

Helene squirmed, feeling uncomfortable with her bare arms and legs on the rough shingles. She knew exactly what she'd do. She'd let Lance Piccard take her to the bluffs and let him get so damned excited he'd come all over himself. She might even squeeze his thing with her hand so he'd want to put it in her all the more. And she'd let him do that, too—after she got a ring and he had a little talk with Daddy. Daphne was a damned fool.

The porch swing was creaking, and Helene knew her

sister was thinking. She closed her eyes and prayed Daphne'd say no.

"Well, it's not for sure Daddy'd let me go to town with you, Lance."

"For ice cream he would. Sure he would. Go on in and ask him."

"I don't know, Lance."

"Come on, Daphne. You aren't tryin' to tell me you don't like me as much as I like you?"

The squeaking slowed, then stopped. "All right. I'll ask Daddy if I can ride into town with you."

Helene cursed silently. She could hear Daphne walk across the porch. Then the door closed, and there was silence except for the crickets and the frogs in the ditch out by the road.

Helene lay in her bed, listening to the night sounds, wondering where Daphne could be. It was eleven-thirty and she still hadn't come home. Maybe Lance Piccard had gotten to her after all; maybe Daphne let him get her so hot they ended up going all the way. It was a stupid thing to do, if she did. Lance would never marry her after that, which was fine with Helene, but it wouldn't do the Johnston name any good—or her either.

Helene knew it was best if Daphne was cold as ice, that way Lance would eventually lose patience and move on. At his age, all he knew about love was sex. She wasn't sure herself that there was anything else that mattered to a man, but she knew what *she* wanted. She wanted that fine Piccard house. To get his name and all that went with it, she'd have Piccard babies and let Lance do whatever he wanted with her. Besides, she liked Lance. He was the most respected young man in the parish—every girl wanted him. How could she not like him?

Before long Helene heard a car out in the road and went to the window to have a look. It was Lance's Buick convertible. She saw Daphne and Lance jump out and run up the path to the house. Even in the dark she could see terror on her sister's face. Helene didn't know what to hope had happened.

Then she heard her father's voice in the parlor. He'd

been waiting up for Daphne. There was loud talk and apologies, then the sound of the screen door closing as Lance left.

Several moments later the bedroom door opened a crack and Daphne slipped silently into the room.

"Don't bother to be quiet, Daphne. I'm awake."

"Sorry."

Helene watched the silent figure tiptoe across the room. "So did you let Lance Piccard have his way with you tonight?"

"Helene!"

"Oh, don't give me your outraged virgin act." She turned the light on between their beds and stared coldly at her little sister. "His stuff's probably still runnin' down your leg."

Daphne glared. "Why do you always have to be so filthy-minded?"

"Well, I don't hear you denyin' it."

"I don't have to account to you . . ."

"That's what I thought."

"Helene, why don't you just let me be?"

"Because you're my sister and everything you do affects me! I've been careful as I could be with my reputation and you can ruin it all for me."

Daphne unzipped her dress and pulled it down over her shoulders and hips, then stepped out of it. "I haven't ever done anything to ruin our family name." She went to the closet.

"You did tonight. Daddy might be blind to your tricks, but I'm not!"

Daphne spun around. "Helene Johnston, what are you talkin' about?"

"What are all them marks on your neck and shoulders? Mosquito bites?"

Daphne stepped to the mirror and looked at herself. "Lance just got a little rough kissin' me tonight, that's all."

Helene laughed derisively, flipping her long brown hair with her hand. "Bet he kissed you between the legs, too!"

"Helene! What's wrong with you?"

There was a knock at the door, and they both turned. "You girls quiet down in there and go to sleep. It's late."

"Yes, Daddy," Daphne called out. "We will." She glanced warily at her sister and turned her back to her, removing her petticoats and bra. She was taking her night-gown from the hook in the closet when Helene, having slipped up behind her, took her by the shoulders and spun her around abruptly.

"Look at your tits!" she hissed. "Those mosquito bites, too?"

Daphne covered her breasts with her arms, jerking her-self free of her sister.

"You ain't nothin' but a whore, Daphne! Your damned tits still have Lance Piccard's slobber on them."

Suddenly, the bedroom door flew open. "What in hell-fire's goin' on in here?" Wallace Johnston, a ruddy-faced man with a beer belly, came barging in.

Daphne shrieked and jumped into the closet, pulling the door behind her.

"I told you two to go to bed. What're y'all doing up? Daphne," he shouted, glaring toward the closet, "make yourself decent and come out here."

A moment later the closet door opened and she appeared in her nightgown. "Daddy, I was just dressin' for bed."

"There were mighty angry sounds comin' out of this room. Now what's goin' on?"

"Well, I'm right embarrassed, Daddy," Helene said in-dignantly. "My own sister come home from spoonin' with Lance Piccard, and she's got marks all over her. Course, to hear her tell it, they'd be mosquito bites she got skinny dippin' or somethin'."

"What are you talkin' about?" Johnston said, turning to Daphne.

"Oh, Daddy, it ain't nothin'. I just got a couple little bitty scratches on my neck, that's all." She glared at He-lene.

The man went to the door and shouted down the hall-way. "Charlotte, would you come in here, please!" He turned and looked at his daughters, his face getting red.

"Oh, Daddy, it ain't nothin'," Daphne moaned beseech-ingly. "It's just Helene tryin' to make trouble for me like she always does. She's jealous, that's all, Daddy."

"I'm not jealous of you, Daphne Rae. You can marry the

king of England for all I care, just don't go spoilin' my good name."

"That's enough!" Johnston roared. "Both of you shut up till your mama comes in here." He turned to call out the door again when Charlotte Johnston appeared in her night clothes, her long dark hair hanging down her back, her face pinched with concern.

"What's all the fuss about? I went to bed with a head-ache bad enough to kill and now—"

"Charlotte, I want you to look at Daphne. Helene says she's got marks all over her body, and I want to know the truth."

"Marks? What kind of marks?"

"Love marks, Mama," Helene lamented. "I'm so em-barrassed I could die!"

"Love marks? Lance Piccard?"

"They come home late," Johnston said. "I shouldn't have let her go. It was a damn fool thing to do."

Charlotte walked over to Daphne, who was terror stricken. "You girls are goin' to be the death of me before I get y'all married off." She glanced at Helene. "You go out with your pa. I don't need you here."

Daphne started crying as Helene took her bathrobe from the chair by her bed and walked out, her nose elevated in triumph.

"Oh, Mama," Daphne said through her tears when they had gone, "I didn't do nothin'. Honestly, I didn't."

"Well, we'll see. Take off your nightgown."

"Mama!"

"Take off your nightgown, I said. Your pa will want to know, and I never lie to him, you know that."

Daphne began sobbing but managed to pull her gown over her head.

"Come on over by the light," Charlotte said, pulling her by the arm.

The woman looked at her daughter's bare chest and breasts, her face grim. Daphne was crying softly, tears running down her cheeks. Charlotte lifted Daphne's chin and groaned. "Turn around."

Daphne looked up at her mother, her eyes pleading, but Charlotte gave no ground. She turned around, slowly.

"Take down your pants."

"Mama!"

"I have to know because your pa's got to know."

"Mama, I didn't, believe me!"

"Come on, let's be done with it. Move smart, Daphne."

The girl lowered her panties to her knees and her mother peered at her pubis, then checked the crotch of her panties.

"Is that all from you?"

Daphne began sobbing uncontrollably now. "Yes, Mama. I swear it. He came, Mama, but not in me, I swear it! I wouldn't let him. I didn't even take my pants off."

"Well, it does look like a woman's stuff, not a man's."

"Oh, it is! I swear it! Honest to God, Mama," she sobbed.

"I'll tell your pa he mussed you up, Daphne, but that he didn't go in you."

"Oh, I wouldn't let him. I wouldn't let nobody do that, Mama. I only got these marks 'cause he got excited. It wasn't my fault at all."

"It's always the girl's fault, unless she gets raped, Daphne, and even then it's her fault half the time."

"Lance didn't mean me no harm, Mama. He didn't hurt me. He just got excited, that's all."

"Well, you're lucky he stopped. Even if he got you pregnant, there's no way on God's earth we'd have gotten him to marry you—not a Piccard."

"Will you tell Daddy I'm all right?"

"I'll tell him the truth, Daphne. I always do."

"What'll he do?"

"Probably make you stay in for a time."

"But the dance's next week. My senior dance. Lance is takin' me. Daddy won't keep me from that, will he?"

"You can ask him, but I expect he'll keep you in, 'specially since it's Lance Piccard who's takin' you."

Tears started streaming down Daphne's cheeks again. "He'll never want to see me again, Mama. My life will be over!"

"Your pa will do the honorable thing and see that you do, too. Lance will respect you all the more for it."

"He won't understand Daddy's ways, Mama. He didn't

do nothin' wrong, just got a little excited is all! He'll hate me. I'll be the laughin'stock of the parish."

"Your pa will talk with you in the mornin', I'm sure. Now y'all go to bed and thank God you're a virgin. And I hope for your sake you are."

Daphne pulled up her pants, slipped her nightgown back over her head, then fell on her bed in tears.

June 7

Helene Johnston sorted through the packages of seeds on the counter of Mr. Crumbine's hardware store. She looked at the expiration date of each package, dusted off the good ones with a rag, and threw the bad ones in a carton at her feet. She had been working part-time in the store for nearly a year, ever since Mrs. Crumbine had told her husband she wanted mornings off for bridge.

There wasn't a soul in the store. Mr. Crumbine had gone over to the bank across the square, and Helene worked steadily to fight the boredom. The only good thing about her job—apart from the money—was waiting on customers, and that was only because faces were more interesting than a piece of pipe or a sack of nails.

She was thinking about Daphne sitting at the breakfast table that morning, tears running down her cheeks, after Daddy had told her she couldn't go to the dance with Lance. From the way Daddy was talking, Daphne hadn't let Lance go all the way—that was good for Daphne, but bad for her.

Helene agonized as she mindlessly worked with the seeds. How could she get Lance's mind off Daphne and on to her? If she could get Daphne interested in somebody else, that'd do it, but she was so damned sappy over Lance Piccard it wasn't likely. Why couldn't the Piccards have two boys—a younger one for Daphne?

The image of Daphne crying at the breakfast table was a gratifying one, but Helene was still bitter that Lance had picked her younger sister over her. Helene probably intimidated Lance—that was the problem—but as he got a little older and saw she was still a virgin, he might realize that she would make the best wife of any girl in the parish. She sure hoped so, because she'd kill herself before she'd spend the rest of her life dusting seed packages in a hardware store.

Helene was starting to work herself into a blue mood when the bell over the main door of the store rang. She looked up and, to her utter surprise, saw a young man in uniform—a sailor. It took her a second to recognize Raymond Wicks, a classmate from high school.

"Hi there, Helene."

"Ray Wicks! What y'all doin' here? Last I heard you was in the Indian Ocean or someplace like that."

He strolled over to her. "That was last winter, since then I got me another stripe..." He grinned and pointed proudly at his shoulder. "...and I'm home on leave."

Smiling prettily, Helene looked Ray up and down. He appeared rather dashing with his white cap tilted down so it nearly touched one eyebrow.

"I heard you was workin' here in the hardware store, so when my ma said she needed light bulbs I thought I'd come over and say hello."

Helene smiled again. "That's mighty thoughtful of you, Raymond." She looked him over again. "You sure have changed since high school—bet you've got a girl in every port." The grin on his face told Helene he'd seen a bit of the world since leaving Catahoula.

Helene's ego was touched by Ray Wicks's unexpected appearance, but she was smart enough to know that a sailor was poison. There was no way she'd let this go anywhere.

Although he was nice looking, he had always been on the wild side, pulling pranks, getting into trouble. There was even a rumor he'd gotten his little cousin over in

Winnfield pregnant just before he went into the navy, but nobody knew for sure.

"Helene Johnston, how come you ain't married? I always thought you was the prettiest girl in the class."

"Thank you, Raymond. The truth is, I will be gettin' married soon."

He frowned. "Oh, really?"

"Yes, not many folks around here know about it though —I mean it not bein' official yet and all . . ."

"Who is he?"

"Oh, a rich young man up in Monroe. We're keepin' it secret 'cause he won't be of age for a few more months and he gets a big inheritance when he's twenty-one."

"Must be nice," Ray replied sourly.

"Yeah. I'm very happy, Raymond."

He sighed. "Well, congratulations, Helene."

"Thank you, Raymond." She could see he was disappointed, which was exactly what she had intended, but Helene needed to hear him say it. "Y'all don't seem very happy for me."

"Well, actually my ma don't need no light bulbs. I just come over to the hardware store to see you, Helene."

"Whatever for, Raymond?"

"Like I said, I always thought you was the prettiest girl in the class, though you was a little stuck-up when we was in high school."

Helene grimaced.

"Not that y'all are now, Helene," he added hastily. "You growed up to be a fine lady, I can see that all right."

"So you came all the way over to the hardware store just to say hello?"

"No, I was hopin' you'd go out with me on a date, since I was home on leave."

Helene smiled to herself, knowing just what Raymond Wicks had in mind. He'd been with girls all around the world and now he thought he was man enough for a real lady at home.

"I surely appreciate you thinkin' of me, Raymond, but under the circumstances I couldn't go out with you. You know I was always very fond of you when we was in school . . . and I do respect what you're doin' now in the service and all . . ."

He brightened, not quite certain where Helene's change of tone was leading.

". . . I can't go out with you, but I've been thinkin' about my sister, Daphne. Y'all remember her, don't you?"

"Sure I do, but I heard she was sweet on Lance Piccard."

"Well, she is and she isn't. I'm afraid that's turned out to be a tragic love affair, Raymond."

He frowned. "What do you mean?"

"It's a long story but—"

The bell over the door rang, and Helene turned to see Mr. Crumbine enter.

"Lordy," she exclaimed, moving around the counter. "I'll be in the square in an hour, Ray," she whispered, "if you'd like to talk about Daphne some."

He nodded. "All right." Then he turned and headed for the door, casually touching his hat in salute to Mr. Crumbine. "Mornin', sir."

Helene watched him leave, sensing that he was somehow the solution to her problem with Daphne and Lance Piccard, though she didn't quite know how.

"Goddamn," Ray said, picking up the Coke bottle sitting on the bench next to him, "I forgot how boring this town is." He glanced at Helene, who sat with a brown paper sack flattened on her knees and half a sandwich opened on top of it.

"Well, seein' the world as you have, Ray, I'm sure it's been like a fireworks display. I know this town is like a glass of lemonade, but if the day's hot enough, even a glass of lemonade can be welcome."

He looked at her quizzically. "Helene Johnston, you're talkin' like you was still in English class. What're you gettin' at?"

"Raymond, you and I have been sittin' here talkin' about every damn thing in the world for half an hour, but we both know what it is you're interested in. Thing is, neither of us has come out and said it."

Ray sat up straight, understanding Helene's tone of voice better than her words. "What's that, Helene?"

"You want to get laid, Ray Wicks," she said, her eyes meeting his boldly.

The sailor smiled. "You're more growed up than I thought, Helene."

"Well, don't go gettin' any ideas about me, Raymond. I'm engaged, like I told you."

"Then what . . ."

"I'm thinkin' about my sister Daphne. She might be just your cup of tea."

His eyebrows rose in surprise. "What do you mean?"

"You're a man of experience, Ray, that's plain to see, and more important, this town doesn't mean nothin' to you. I figure you can do my sister a turn, and maybe she can do you one at the same time."

"Yeah . . ."

"I want y'all to swear to God and all that's sacred to you that you won't ever tell anybody what I'm about to tell you—not even Daphne."

"All right." Ray's mouth had dropped open a bit in anticipation.

She looked around the town square that was deserted except for a couple of old men on the bench opposite the barbershop. "My sister, bless her soul, is the sweetest, nicest girl you can imagine. She's grown a lot since you've seen her, Ray. Pardon my French, but she's got the biggest, nicest tits you'll ever see."

He grinned at Helene's unexpectedly frank vocabulary.

"Well, she's a senior this year," Helene continued, "a grown woman for all intents and purposes. She's graduatin' this week."

"Yeah . . ."

"Well, the problem"—Helene rolled her eyes toward the heavens—"Lord forgive me, is that she lost her virginity last summer and not a soul knows about it, except me."

"So?"

"Well, Daphne's a good girl, and I love her dearly, but she's been goin' through hell the past year. Everybody thinks she's inexperienced and a virgin, and 'course, she's got to act like she is, because in her heart she's pure as the snow. The truth is, though, she's a woman who's had it, and God knows she wants it some more. But she can't, not if she wants to keep her reputation. You know, Raymond, she has her heart set on marrying Lance Piccard."

Ray Wicks scratched his head. "I don't understand what you're sayin', Helene. If Daphne's so pure like you say, how come she's done it?"

"That's the tragedy, Ray—family tragedy actually. You see, we've got these relations that live over in Jefferson County, Mississippi, near Fayette."

"Yeah?"

"Well, Daphne and I had this cousin, Bobby Joel, who's just crazy over sex." Helene lowered her voice and looked around again. "Ray, he even does it with the barnyard animals. I've never seen him, mind you, but he told Daphne and me about it."

"So he was the one that fu—that did it with Daphne?"

"Oh Ray, it was so sad." Helene's face was full of pain. "Bobby Joel gave Daphne some of the stuff they give cows to make them want to do it with the bulls . . ."

"He did?"

"Our whole family was over there visitin' our relations and my mama 'n daddy went off with my aunt 'n uncle and Bobby Joel's little sister to a church social and left me and Daphne at home. Bobby Joel was supposed to be visitin' at a friend's, but he and his friend came over to pester us girls."

"So what about the stuff—the Spanish fly?"

"The what?"

"That's what they call it, Helene—the stuff for the cows."

"Oh. Well, to make a long story short, I run off Bobby Joel's friend, who was near as bad as he was, but Bobby Joel had gotten Daphne off in the barn. He must have put the stuff in her lemonade or somethin' because by the time I sneaked out to the barn it was too late, my poor little sister was crazy as could be. She liked to do it to old Bobby Joel before he could do it to her."

Ray was grinning from ear to ear, and Helene could see the buttons bulging at his crotch. She couldn't remember feeling so good, not since she let Lonnie Watkins touch her breasts her junior year.

"So, that's how Daphne did it."

"Yes, Ray, but don't you tell nobody, hear? You swore an oath to me."

"I won't tell nobody, Helene. Who would I tell? Nobody in this town means nothin' to me."

"Well, that's exactly why I told you. Because of that and because I love my sister and think you can help her."

Ray looked at her anxiously. "Me? What's this got to do with me?"

"You might know about women, Ray, with all your experience and all, but I doubt you know very much about a real lady."

"What d'you mean?"

"I mean proper ladies mostly want it as much as the other kind. And, of course, when they're married they get it. But if a proper lady's had it once—sort of accidentally like Daphne—but can't have it again 'cause she's not married, it can be mighty difficult. I imagine like a sailor when he's out at sea for months at a time."

"So?"

"So imagine poor Daphne bein' out with Lance Piccard makin' out, but she can't go all the way because she's a proper lady with a reputation to maintain and all. It's sort of like if you was on your ship in the middle of the Indian Ocean and one of your girls is in the next bed, but you can't do nothin' about it."

"Yeah . . ."

"Well, here Daphne is a virgin in her mind but not in her body. She can't go out and do it with any other boy because of her reputation. If you was Daphne and your body was screamin' for it and all of a sudden this handsome sailor come to town, and he was experienced, knew how to keep his mouth shut, and was only going to be around a short time anyway, wouldn't you consider that to be an opportunity?"

"You mean me, Helene? You think Daphne'd want to fu—do it with me?"

"Well, not in her head, because in her mind she loves

Lance Piccard, but as a proper lady, I can tell you her body would just love it."

"Well, what good does that do? She'd have to say yes."

"Don't you see, Ray, if her mind had an excuse—just like that time with Bobby Joel—then she'd still be a lady in her heart, but her body would get what it's been beggin' for since last summer."

"So, what are you sayin'? I should get some Spanish fly and come a callin'?"

"Well, I was thinkin' that if I could help my poor little sister with that terrible frustration she's sufferin', I would do it. I always thought I wish I knew a man who could keep his mouth shut and who didn't live around here. Then there you was this mornin', Ray, big as life standin' right in Mr. Crumbine's hardware store."

"I'll admit, Helene, I'd be happy to oblige you and your sister, but I still don't see how I can do it."

"Let *me* figure that out, Ray. The question is whether you would be willin' to do us a favor, keep your mouth shut about everything I've said, and be content goin' back to your ship havin' had a little fun for your trouble."

"I suppose so, but . . ."

"And maybe more than anything, the question is, could you quietly find some of that Spanish stuff?"

"I don't know; that might not be so easy."

"Well, I tell you what, Ray, I'll think about a way we can arrange to help poor Daphne, and you check around and see if you can find some of that stuff. We can meet here in the square tomorrow at lunch and see what each of us has come up with."

Ray Wicks beamed. "You know what, Helene? This town ain't as boring as I thought it was!"

June 13

Daphne Johnston sat on the divan in the parlor wearing her best summer dress and feeling as if she'd died and her soul was already in the hell Reverend Harley had preached about so fervently that morning. The senior dance had been the night before, and Daphne was the only one in her class that had been at the service that morning. Doubtless there had been plenty going on in the backseats of cars after the dance, yet Daphne alone had to hear about hell.

She had sat on the hard wooden pew, listening to the Reverend's fearful words about all manner of sin, and wished that Helene were dead. Daphne hadn't spoken to her sister for ten days—not since that night—and she wouldn't ever again if she could help it.

Mama was standing in front of the hall mirror pinning her hat back on, and Helene was next to her, wearing her white dress that Daphne had always thought so contradictory to her character. Helene might be a virgin—but if she was, it was in body only. Her heart and soul were as corrupt as the worst slut on God's earth.

"Now your pa and I might not get back until after supper," Charlotte said, "so if you get hungry, fix yourselves somethin' to eat." She turned and looked into the parlor at Daphne, who was staring out the window, her face somber.

"Don't you worry about us," Helene said. "We'll be just fine. You and Daddy have a good time."

Charlotte Johnston was still looking at her younger daughter. "Now I know you're upset, Daphne Rae, but that dance is over now, and there's no point in frettin' about it. These things happen in life. You've got to learn to put it behind you and go on."

Daphne glanced up at her mother but said nothing. She didn't blame her, or even her pa, though she didn't feel much charity for either of them. Helene was the one she blamed. She hated her sister for what she did and would to her dying day.

Outside, the horn of Wallace Johnston's pickup truck sounded impatiently and Charlotte sighed. "You girls make an effort to get along while we're gone, hear?" she said over her shoulder. "I know neither of you is feelin' very kindly toward the other, but this house'd be a lot more pleasant if you'd all make an effort."

Charlotte caught Daphne's eye before she went out the door, and the woman's imploring look touched her. Daphne knew her mother's heart was always in the right place, even if she always did what Daddy wanted her to.

Helene had gone out on the porch, and Charlotte turned a final time to Daphne. "Goodbye, honey."

"Bye, Mama," she mumbled, not having it in her heart to hurt her mother.

As soon as the screen door slammed, Daphne went upstairs to the bedroom, took off her dress and lay down on the bed in her slip. A few minutes later she heard Helene coming up the stairs; she dreaded seeing her.

The door opened and Helene entered. Daphne stared at the ceiling, not willing even to acknowledge her sister's existence.

"Daphne," she said, "I know you hate me, and I know I'm probably the last person in the world you'd like to talk to just now, but there's somethin' I'd like to say, and I hope you'll do me the kindness of hearin' me out."

Daphne was surprised at Helene's words, but she was resolved not to let them affect her—at least not until she figured out what Helene was up to. She continued to stare at the ceiling.

"When I put Daddy on to you last week," Helene continued, "I thought I was doin' the right thing, Daphne, I really did. Bein' a little older and all, I thought you didn't understand what a mistake it was to be gettin' so intimate with Lance. I was just sure as could be that you'd go get yourself in trouble and spoil your dreams."

Daphne sensed her sister was being sincere but she was still suspicious.

"But seein' how it turned out—you missin' the dance, I mean—I come to see that what I done was wrong."

Daphne looked at Helene, unable to resist a comment. "What would you care if I missed my senior dance, Helene Johnston? Since when have you ever given a damn about me? Besides, if you're so worried about me ruinin' myself by bein' intimate with Lance, how would missin' the dance change that?"

"Well, whether you believe it or not, I do care about you, Daphne. I care for your sake, but I admit I care for my sake, too—the family reputation and all."

Daphne rolled her eyes, still skeptical of what Helene was up to. "You were glad, Helene, and you know it!"

"I'll admit to bein' jealous some, Daphne. It's not easy bein' damn near twenty and havin' nothin' to look forward to in life but workin' in a hardware store. You don't know how lucky you are to be young and havin' marriageable young men around you."

"Helene, you're talkin' crazy. To hear you, you'd think you was an old maid."

"Would you care to name me one young man I'd want to see, let alone marry?"

"There's lots."

"You think I want to be a farmer's wife or married to somebody who works in a gas station or at the feed store?"

Daphne looked back up at the ceiling, unable to feel sorry for Helene.

"Anyway, feelin' bad about gettin' you in trouble like I did, I took it upon myself to do somethin' for the both of us."

Daphne sensed Helene was finally coming to the point.

"I invited a guest over to visit us this afternoon," she continued.

"Who?"

"Raymond Wicks."

"Raymond Wicks? I thought he was in the navy."

"He is, but he's in town for a while on leave."

"Why'd you invite him over? You know Daddy won't let us have boys in the house when him 'n Mama's not here."

"I know that, Daphne, but it's sort of a gift to make up for what I done to you."

"Helene Johnston, what on earth are you talkin' about? I don't care about Ray Wicks, and if you invitin' him here is another of your tricks, you can just forget it. I'm not interested."

"I can understand you feelin' bitter towards me still, Daphne, but it might be in your interest to be sociable to Ray."

"Why?"

"'Cause him and Lance have gotten to be kind of friendly during this visit of Ray's."

"Lance Piccard and Ray Wicks?"

"Ray has changed. He's gotten's promotions in the navy and has settled down to be a real gentleman."

"I can't believe Lance and him would be friends."

"Well, I happen to know with Lance not bein' allowed on our place, he was mighty anxious to have Ray come and see you. I don't know that for sure, but I'm suspicious that's what's behind it. I seen Lance and Ray in town together a couple of times before Ray come to talk to me, so I got my suspicions."

"You sweet on Ray?"

"That might be puttin' it a little strong. I find him kind of interesting. Who knows? When he's out of the navy and settles down, he might make some girl a mighty fine husband. Point is, I took the chance in inviting him over here. If you don't want to find out whether Lance's behind him comin', that's your privilege. Actually, I couldn't blame you if you used this against me and told Daddy. Anyway, my purpose is to make amends to you, Daphne."

"I don't think I'm interested."

"Well, that's up to you. If you want to come down and have lemonade with us in the parlor, you're welcome. Ray'll be here in about a half an hour. If not, I'll find out what I can for you about what Lance's up to."

Daphne watched Helene leave, uncertain, but intrigued.

Ray Wicks seemed strangely nervous sitting in Wallace Johnston's chair, and Daphne wondered why Helene thought he had become so interesting. The sailor uniform did give him a certain appeal, but he still struck her as a little wild and impetuous.

"You sure growed up to be a pretty woman, Daphne," he said, unconsciously fingering his sailor cap.

She smiled weakly and looked toward the kitchen where Helene had gone to get the lemonade. "Thank you, Ray."

"You was just a kid, a sophomore, the last time I seen you."

Daphne nodded, and felt uncomfortable the way he seemed to stare at her breasts. If Lance had sent him here, it was to test her, not to reassure her, that much was certain.

"Helene!" she called toward the kitchen. "You need some help?"

"No, thank you, Daphne, I'm about done. I'll be right out."

A moment later Helene reappeared carrying a tray with a pitcher of lemonade and three glasses filled with ice. "Here we are, Ray, some good old-fashioned Louisiana lemonade. I bet you don't get much of this on your ship."

"Ain't that the truth," he said, grinning, but he was watching Daphne, not Helene, as the older Johnston girl filled the glasses.

Daphne felt strange under his gaze.

"Oh, darn," Helene said. "I forgot the cookies. Daphne, would you mind goin' into the kitchen and puttin' some of Mama's sugar cookies on a plate?"

Daphne was glad for the excuse to leave; maybe Ray would switch his attentions to Helene and get himself worked up over her for a while. Leaving the parlor, she still had trouble believing Helene could be interested in Ray Wicks—something was up, but she wasn't sure what.

Before she had gathered the cookies and some paper napkins, Helene came through the door. "I must have totally misread the situation," she whispered. "That man is just nuts over you. I'm sorry, Daphne."

"Well, let's try and get rid of him. There's no point in us getting into trouble with Daddy for the sake of a visit that don't mean nothin' to us."

"Okay, but I think we ought to be polite. Let's have the lemonade, talk a spell, and then we can start hinting. 'Course, there's still a chance somethin' about Lance might come up, too."

"I doubt it. I think you were wrong about Lance and Ray, Helene."

"We'll see. No point in offending him just because he's hot for you."

"I have trouble thinkin' about men bein' after me, Helene. Even Lance scares me, and I *love* him." She picked up the plate of cookies and headed for the parlor. Helene was right behind her.

When they entered the room, Ray was sitting in his chair, spinning his sailor cap on his finger and looking rather impatient. Daphne put the plate of cookies on the coffee table. "Help yourself, Ray," she said, dropping back down on the couch where she had been sitting. She picked up her lemonade and took a sip, immediately noticing a funny taste. She made a face and looked at Helene, who was watching her.

"Why, what's the matter, Daphne Rae? You have the strangest look on your face."

"Does the lemonade taste funny to you?"

"Why, no." Helene looked at Ray. "How about yours, Ray?"

"No, tastes just fine to me."

Daphne took another sip. "It's never tasted this way before."

"Have you been drinkin' much lemonade lately, Daphne?" Helene asked.

"Not especially, no."

"I'll bet it's one of those vitamin deficiencies, from not eatin' enough lemons and oranges and such like."

"Why would that make it taste funny?"

"I don't know, but seems like I read that someplace. You've heard of that, haven't you, Ray?"

"Oh, yeah, happens all the time on the ship. The only cure is to drink a bunch, then the taste goes away."

Daphne looked at the glass in her hand and took another sip. "Are you sure?"

"Yeah," Ray said. "Take a big sip."

Daphne did, but it tasted just as bad. She grimaced, then leaned back as Ray Wicks started talking. There was still a funny taste in her mouth, and she wondered how she could have gotten a vitamin deficiency. Her period wasn't due for a couple of weeks, so it couldn't have anything to do with that, though the curse sometimes did odd things to her appetite. However, she did notice a strange sensation in her stomach. It wasn't exactly like indigestion or gas or cramps, but it felt mighty funny.

Daphne felt her mouth sort of spontaneously twist into a smile and she looked at Ray, who was talking and watching her all at the same time. She thought he looked awfully funny in her daddy's chair, which made her giggle in spite of herself, and she had to clamp her hand to her mouth.

Ray looked at her strangelike, and Helene did too, but he just went on talking, and Daphne leaned back again, sipping her lemonade and feeling sort of giddy. A few minutes later, she felt a tickle in her abdomen. She grinned at Helene.

"You feelin' all right, Daphne Rae?"

"Just as sweet as you please," Daphne replied, then laughed and drank some more lemonade.

"Your eyes are lookin' kind of funny. Are you sure you're feeling well?"

"Except for my head and my stomach and . . . between my legs, I feel just fine." Daphne looked at Ray, not knowing why she said what she did, but he was smiling like he was amused, so she did, too.

"Would you like a glass of water or an aspirin or somethin'?" Helene asked.

She nodded, not exactly sure what Helene had asked, but knowing she felt mighty bizarre. Helene left the room and Daphne looked at Ray. His eyes were on her breasts.

"Ray Wicks, you've been lookin' at my tits ever since

you come over here this afternoon. What's the matter with you?"

"You got a nice set, Daphne," he said in a low voice, "that's all."

She laughed, feeling really silly. "You like my tits, do you?"

"Goddamn if I don't," he muttered.

"Lance Piccard likes them real fine. He likes to lick them, you know."

Suddenly, Ray stood up and came around to sit down next to Daphne on the couch. She laughed. Things were getting stranger and stranger now, and Daphne wondered why Lance was acting so funny.

Ray touched her thigh with his hand.

"Lance Piccard, my daddy doesn't like you doin' that, you know." The room started spinning and Daphne felt a hand going right up under her skirt. She giggled.

"Don't you want to go out and get some air?" She heard the voice imploring her, but she had trouble forming words in reply. "Come on," the voice was saying insistently, "let's go outside for a while. You'll be just fine." Daphne felt herself rising to her feet, her stomach burning, her head spinning.

Lance kept pulling on her, and Daphne wondered if he meant to put marks all over her again. She walked and stumbled across her front porch while the voice at her ear repeated things about her tits. She was half-dragged across the lawn to a car. She felt the ground spinning under her feet and bumped her head as Lance pushed her in the car. What was Lance doing in a sailor suit, anyway?

Daphne's head was on the back of the seat and her eyes were closed. "Oh, Lord God," she moaned, "I feel sick, like my stomach's on fire."

Daphne felt someone pulling on her breasts and squeezing them so hard it hurt. She shrieked once, then started laughing uncontrollably.

"Goddamn, I want you," the voice said.

In her misery, Daphne couldn't see anything, but she heard the engine roar to life, then she felt the car lurch forward as they took off down the road. Daphne felt Lance grasp her wrist and press her hand between his legs. She felt a warm, taut bulge and then heard more talk about her tits. Lance was talking fouler than he ever had. Oh God, how sick she felt.

Her hand was momentarily pushed away from Lance's bulge and a second later brought back again, this time to grasp the flesh protruding from the gap in his cotton pants. Despite the blur that faded in and out of her head, Daphne knew what was in her hand.

"Suck it. Suck it!" the voice insisted, but she knew she didn't want to, no matter what.

An unseen fist took the hair at the side of her head and roughly pulled her down till her face was pressed into the warm, moist place between his legs. "Oh Lord," she moaned, but the strong hand on her head forced her mouth down.

The pungent smell made Daphne nauseous, and she turned her head away despite the pain of the fist on her head. Then the car jerked sharply to a stop, knocking her temple against the steering wheel. A moment later she was dragged from the car and through the tall grass while her legs managed only every third or fourth step.

When they came to a large sycamore tree, he let her fall into the grass. Daphne rolled from her side to her back, and looked up at him through half-open but unseeing eyes. He was a blur, towering over her. She saw the white pants drop.

"Oh, Lance," she groaned, but somehow she knew it wasn't Lance.

He kicked her ankles apart so that she was lying spread-eagle on the ground, like a pinwheel on a stick. She felt her skirts and petticoats being pulled up over her face, and a pair of rough hands grabbing at the band of her panties.

"No . . ." she moaned instinctively.

Daphne felt the bite of fingernails on the skin of her belly and thighs as her panties were ripped over her hips and down her legs.

Daphne felt sick all over. Her mind was forming thoughts of flight, but her body just wouldn't respond. Finally, she felt the large body drop down on her. Her skirts were over her face so she couldn't even see the tree. Her arms were at her side on the moist ground, but she couldn't move. She felt his distended member pressing between her legs. Daphne cried out, but the pressure against her increased, hurting her.

"No. Oh please, no," she cried, summoning resistance from the depths of her awareness.

But he pushed further into her until she felt a terrible tearing.

"God, you're a virgin," the voice cried with dismay through the petticoats. "Helene said you wasn't no virgin!"

"Helene, Helene," she murmured, her mind clinging to the only familiar thing in the swirl surrounding her.

"Bitch!" he shrieked, and he drove hard into her, impaling her on the boggy ground. An instant later he started heaving and pitching on top of her body until his pelvis rocked a final time and his loins spewed their contents into her.

Seconds later he got up. "Jesus, sweet Jesus," he said as he pulled up his pants, his face twisted like he was going to cry. "I thought you was experienced, Daphne. I didn't know you had your cherry." He emitted a sound that was half sob and half a cry of anguish. "I swear to God I didn't!"

Daphne heard the words. She heard the voice more clearly than she had during the entire nightmare of confusion that had enveloped her. Even without the pain between her legs, she knew her body had been violated.

At the periphery of her vision, Daphne could see him wringing his hands. She could hear the voice moaning as though something precious had been taken from him too, but she couldn't imagine what.

"Oh Daphne, what are we going to do? I thought you wanted it. Honest to God, I thought you wanted it." He knelt down beside her for a moment, but he could see she was off in some other world. It wasn't just the delirium of the drug, he could tell. Why hadn't he known? He'd gotten so hot he couldn't think straight, and now here she was, blood running out from between her legs.

Ray Wicks knew what they'd say—she was a virgin and nothing else would matter. Helene must have tricked him for spite, but he'd never know why. No one would believe Helene Johnston had put him up to it. No one would believe he thought he was doing Daphne a favor. They'd send him to prison—no doubt about it. His only chance was to get away before they came looking for him.

He bent over and looked at Daphne's glassy eyes and wondered if she might die. Oh God, what would the navy do? Was he better off with the sheriff or the navy? God. Neither! He wondered if they'd put him in the electric chair. They'd all want to kill him for this.

Ray Wicks chewed his fingernails. He shivered, then gathering himself, ran to the car, leaving Daphne in the cool grass, under the boughs of the sycamore tree.

June 14

The sounds of the Louisiana night carried through the screen door to where Charlotte Johnston and Helene sat waiting in the parlor. Even though it was past midnight, the air was warm, thick, and sultry. Charlotte stared straight ahead with a vacant look. Helene thought it was like a vigil for the dead.

When neither Daphne nor Ray had returned, everybody had begun to fear the worst. Helene knew that only Ray could implicate her, and she'd already anticipated the scene. It was just his word against hers, and there was no doubt who'd win in that contest of credibility. The only unknown was what Daphne would remember.

"I just feel terrible, Mama. It's all my fault. I shouldn't have invited Ray Wicks over for lemonade."

"The question is why she would go off with him like she did. Your pa thinks it was to spite him because of the dance, but I don't think Daphne would do a thing like that. And wild as that Ray Wicks is, I can't believe he'd force her."

"Me neither, Mama. He was bein' polite as you please

before I left the room. Only thing funny was how Daphne got sick drinkin' the lemonade."

"None of this makes sense to me, Helene. I can't imagine what happened."

"I pray the Lord, she's all right."

"That's all we can do."

They sat in silence for a time listening to the crickets, when they heard the sound of a vehicle coming down the road. Charlotte looked toward the door. "Maybe that's your pa."

When it was apparent the vehicle had turned in the drive, Charlotte went out onto the porch. Her husband walked toward her in the darkness.

Helene listened expectantly. "We found her," she heard her father say. "A deputy found her wandering down a track out in the swamps."

"Praise God. Is she all right, Wallace?"

The man climbed the steps and stood with his wife under the porch light. "She'd been violated," he replied in a low voice. "Sheriff said there was blood still runnin' down her legs when they found her."

"Oh, dear God," Charlotte moaned.

Helene felt sick and wondered if Ray Wicks would accuse her.

"I was out to the other side of town when the word went out, so I come right over here to get you, Charlotte. The deputy took her to the hospital." He turned and looked through the screen door and saw Helene standing there. "Your sister's alive, so you can go to bed," he said bluntly.

"Did they find Ray?" Helene asked.

"No, and he'd better hope somebody finds him before I do. He ain't showed up and his ma's car is still missin', so the sheriff figured he'd hightailed it. They got a bulletin out. They'll get him."

Helene's stomach knotted. Her mind turned back through the events of the past few days—the conversations, the plan. No one could implicate her but Ray. She peered at her parents through the screen. "You want me to come with you, Mama?"

"No, honey, you just go on to bed. There ain't a thing you can do."

"You'll be alone in the house," Wallace added, "so lock the doors. I don't expect he'd come back this way, but there's no point in bein' unprepared twice."

Helene watched as her parents disappeared into the darkness. She thought about Daphne and wondered what it would have been like if she had died. Sad as it would have been, it might have been better for everyone, even Daphne.

The way things were, her sister would either have to go away from home or become an emotional cripple. Helene hoped she'd go, leave Catahoula Parish and—praise the Lord—Lance Piccard.

Events during the next few weeks turned out better than Helene could possibly have hoped. Daphne didn't remember much of anything after Helene had left the parlor, except vague impressions of what had happened to her. Ray Wicks seemed to have disappeared from the face of the earth. His mama's car was found three days later down in Alexandria. And, in addition to the sheriff and the state police, the navy was looking for him, too.

Helene figured the longer Ray was on the run, the better it'd be for her. His credibility alongside hers wouldn't amount to anything by the time they caught him.

When news of the crime got around the state, a veterinarian over in Winnfield reported that his assistant had sold a drug used in cattle breeding to a young fellow fitting Ray's description, and the authorities soon figured out what the funny taste was in Daphne's lemonade. The time the girls had spent in the kitchen getting the cookies had given Ray the opportunity to doctor her drink, the police concluded, which was precisely the way Helene had planned it. Since she never saw the stuff, Ray was out there on the limb alone—just the way she wanted him.

When they finally brought Daphne home from the hospital, she didn't say much to Helene. She just looked at her in a funny, vacant sort of way. Mostly, though, she spent her time crying.

For a while, nobody was sure how news of the Johnston

family tragedy would be viewed in the community. More critical to Helene was how Lance Piccard would view it.

Fortunately—or unfortunately, she wasn't sure which —Lance left within days of the incident for Europe with his family. The trip had been planned long before, but Helene figured that Olivia Piccard was glad to be gone from the parish just then. Her son's past association with Daphne couldn't have been welcomed at that point.

Daphne had a very slow convalescence. She stayed in bed until Charlotte made her get up, get dressed, and go into town with her about a month after the rape. After that, she'd get out of bed without much trouble, but she never left the house unless forced. Usually, she'd sit out in the porch swing, though she didn't often move. Helene couldn't help thinking Daphne did it to make her feel bad, so she started resenting her sister for her attitude.

By the end of August, the Piccards had returned from Europe, and Daphne seemed to be going from bad to worse. The doctor told Charlotte that what she probably needed was a change of scene. There wasn't money for a fancy sanitarium, so Charlotte called her sister Edris, who had been living out in Bakersfield, California, for ten years. They discussed Daphne's situation, and it was agreed that the girl would be put on a bus for California to visit a spell.

The whole family drove up to Monroe in the truck to take Daphne to the bus station. It was a solemn ride. The only one who talked much was Charlotte—she was giving advice to Daphne right and left, and the closer they got to Monroe, the faster she talked. Helene had the feeling her mama was packing advice for a lifetime into one drive, and then it occurred to her that was exactly what was happening.

When they were all saying their goodbyes on the sidewalk in front of the Missouri Pacific Trailways bus station on Hall Street, Helene realized she'd never see Daphne again—at least not in Catahoula Parish. Mama realized it too, judging by the way she started crying. Daddy looked a little sad, but Helene could tell that he was relieved. He always said that having unmarried daughters was hell for a man. Sending Daphne to Bakersfield wasn't quite like sending her to the altar, but the effect was near the same.

Charlotte Johnston insisted on waiting till the bus pulled out, so they all stood around and waited. Helene passed the time looking at the bus schedule with all the towns on the route. Even the first city, Shreveport, sounded awfully exotic, and it was still in Louisiana. Helene didn't even contemplate what places like Dallas, Phoenix, and Los Angeles would be like. She smiled to herself at the irony. Maybe she had done her sister a favor, after all.

When the three of them got back into the pickup truck, it was more spacious than it had been on the ride up. She hadn't realized how much of an imposition Daphne had been until she was gone. Now it was like it had been when she was a toddler, before Daphne was born—just the three of them, Daddy, Mama, and her.

Helene sighed with relief and looked out the window, admiring the fine houses of Monroe. She took comfort in the fact that there was a big house waiting for her back home. It belonged to Lance Piccard's family.

Olivia Piccard—tall, patrician, handsome, with skin like ivory and a head of luxuriant black hair—was like no other woman in Catahoula Parish. Her clothes were from New Orleans, if not New York or Europe, and she spoke nice and sweet and refined. Helene always wished she could talk that way, but she was cursed with the dialect of her backwater origins—unlike Olivia, who was from Virginia and who had gone to the best schools as a girl.

The expression on Olivia's face was decidedly superior as she sat across from Helene pouring tea. Helene felt more inadequate than at any other time in her life.

"Your little note, dear, was very sweet. To be honest, I didn't think there were any young ladies in the parish with the refinement to do such a thing."

"Thank you, Mrs. Piccard," Helene said, struggling to emulate the elegant speech of her hostess. "My parents certainly aren't as wealthy as they'd like to be, but they did bring my sister and me up to do the things proper folks do." Helene had spent a whole afternoon at the library reading etiquette books, trying to figure out how a proper young lady might approach the family of a proper young man. She had eventually settled on a note asking if she might pay a social visit to Olivia Piccard.

Helene was smart enough to know that the gesture wouldn't mean a hill of beans to Lance, but to get anywhere with him she'd need Olivia's support, if not approval. She started by securing an invitation to tea with the lady of the house.

Helene's comment about her upbringing must not have been the right thing to say, because she immediately detected a hint of a smile on Olivia Piccard's mouth.

"Tell me, dear, how is your sister, Daphne? I was so upset to learn of her tragic experience."

"Thank you for askin' after Daphne, Mrs. Piccard, but I'm afraid to say that the experience was a devastatin' one for her. My parents decided to send her to live with my aunt and uncle out in California. They're quite well to do, you see. Sad as it is to say, Daphne bein' in her present condition, so to speak, it would be very hard for her to find a future in a place like Louisiana."

"Hmm . . ." Olivia sipped her tea.

"My sister asked me to pay a visit to your family, Mrs. Piccard, to express her regret at not bein' able to say her farewells personally—bein' a friend of Lance this past year and all."

"That's very thoughtful of you both, Helene. I know Lance was very fond of Daphne and was saddened by the news of her . . . experience."

"I do hope I'll have occasion to express my sister's regrets to Lance personally." She sipped her tea with her little finger sticking out just like Olivia Piccard.

"I told him about your visit today, dear, and he said he'd drop by the house while you're here."

"I appreciate that. I do hope to write Daphne a little note sayin' I've done my duty by her." Helene smiled politely and sipped her tea. "I understand your family had a European trip this summer, Mrs. Piccard. I do hope it was an enjoyable one."

"Thank you, Helene. As a matter of fact, it was very pleasant."

"Did you go to various countries, or did you just stay in one place—if I may ask?"

"We traveled a little, dear, but most of the summer we were in Greece, on Corfu, actually."

"That is nice. I understand it's very pretty there."

"Yes, I've always liked Corfu."

"It must have been quite a treat for Lance."

"It was a special time for him, Helene—very special."

"Oh?"

The smile on Olivia Piccard's face indicated there was a good deal more. "You may as well be the first to know, dear. Lance started the summer as a carefree bachelor; he's ending it as an engaged man."

"Engaged?" The words struck Helene like a brick against the side of her head. Her mouth dropped open and she looked at Olivia in disbelief.

"Family friends from Virginia rented the villa next to us," she explained, "and the young lady of the family caught Lance's eye. She was just a child the last time the families were together. Now she's a woman and . . . well, Lance fell in love."

Helene was speechless. How could it be? Her brain started reeling with confusion. Then her eyes began moving around the elegant sitting room of the Piccard house, which seemed, like her dream, to vaporize before her very eyes.

The shock of Lance Piccard's engagement was such a blow that Helene fell sick and took to her bed for several days, wondering how, after all she had been through and done to get the man, fate could trick her that way. Though Olivia could hardly have known of her interest in Lance, Helene blamed the woman and conjured up a powerful hatred for her.

In one fell swoop, Helene's dream had been laid to waste. For the first time she understood Daphne's depression. Unfortunately, Daddy and Mama wouldn't see her own circumstance as sufficiently tragic to send her to California, so if she was to escape the hardware store, Helene knew she would have to arrange it herself.

But before she could deal with the future, another problem presented itself. Raymond Wicks had been arrested by the FBI in Atlanta.

The night after the news came out Helene slept in a cold sweat. She was sure it wouldn't be long before the sheriff came to the house. She told herself over and over how important it was to act surprised when he told her about Ray's accusation of her involvement. She practiced what she'd say in her mind, but she also realized she had to sound spontaneous when she said her piece.

The next few days were hell. The sheriff didn't come, and Helene had to continue on with her life as though nothing were amiss.

Then one evening the whole family was sitting in the parlor listening to the radio when they heard a car pull up outside the house. Daddy was surprised, but Helene knew sure as anything it'd be the sheriff and a deputy.

Wallace Johnston was standing at the screen door, looking out into the dark, when they came up onto the porch.

"Evenin', Sheriff. What brings you out here on a Friday night?"

"Evenin', Mr. Johnston. Toby and me's doin' a little follow-up investigatin' on the . . . incident involvin' your daughter, Daphne, and we wanted to talk to the family a little more about it, if we might."

Johnston pushed the screen door open. "I don't know what there is to talk about, but come on in."

Helene looked up at the sheriff, a slender gray-haired man with steel-rimmed glasses. She had pictured him coming like this countless times, so she did what she had planned. She smiled in a friendly way, but looked a little surprised and wary, too.

"Evenin' Mrs. Johnston, Helene," he said politely, holding his hat in his hands. "Excuse us for bargin' in and interruptin' your evenin'," he said as Wallace Johnston brought a couple of straight-backed chairs over from the dining table, "but Toby and me have some questions we'd like to ask Helene, since she's the only witness in this case."

Charlotte nodded, her face solemn, suspicious.

"What sort of questions?" Wallace asked, sitting in his

chair—the same one, Helen remembered, that Ray Wicks had sat in.

"It's about the Wicks boy, Mr. Johnston. Y'all may have heard that the Feds picked him up in Atlanta at the beginnin' of the week..."

"Yes..."

"Well, I haven't talked to him personally myself—prosecutin' attorney's tryin' to work out the extradition issue with state of Georgia and the Feds—but we've had word that he's tryin' to implicate Helene here."

Helene's mouth dropped open.

"Implicate Helene?" Wallace exclaimed.

"Me?"

The sheriff grimaced, sort of embarrassed. "I know it sounds crazy, but the boy concocted this wild story—I guess bein' a fugitive so long gave him time to think—and the FBI asked us to investigate further."

"How in God's name can a girl be an accomplice to a thing like he done?" Wallace asked, his face turning red.

"Not to the act itself, Mr. Johnston. But if you don't mind, I'd like to ask Helene a few questions." He turned to her, looking apologetic.

Helene's heart was rocking in her chest, but she could tell by the sheriff's face she'd have a sympathetic ear. Her own expression was a balance of dismay and incredulity.

"Helené," he sad, "before Ray come over here to the house that day, you had several conversations with him, didn't you?"

"Yes, sir."

"What was it you talked about, exactly?"

"Just the usual sort of stuff, Sheriff. We was classmates in high school, you know. We talked about some of the kids. And Raymond told me about the navy and all the places he'd been, and such like."

"Where was it exactly that these conversations took place?"

"Well, the first time Ray come into the hardware store where I work for Mr. Crumbine."

"What was his purpose, Helene?"

"He said he needed to buy a light bulb for his mother, but then he sort of admitted it was just an excuse to see me 'cause he heard I was workin' there. He said he wanted to ask me out on a date."

"Did he?"

"Well, yes sir, in a roundabout way he did. He was hintin' pretty broadlike, but I didn't want to see him on a romantic basis, so I told him I was engaged."

"When and where else did you talk to Ray?"

"I saw him that same afternoon in the square. I usually have a sack lunch there."

"So you seen Ray that same afternoon in the square?"

"Yes sir, he just come by and sat on the bench and we talked a spell."

"What about, Helene?"

"About the same things. Only he did ask me about Daphne. I guess bein' a sailor and all he was mighty interested in seein' a girl, 'cause when I told him I was engaged, he changed his tack and started askin' me about my sister. It was probably pretty foolish of me, Sheriff, but I told Ray that Daphne and Lance Piccard's romance wasn't goin' too good and that she was kinda unhappy and lonely. But I never thought that he'd ..."

"That's all right, Helene. Let's just stick to what he said and what you said. Is that when you invited him over to the house?"

"No, I never even thought about that until later. You see, Daphne was mighty unhappy because Daddy had kept her in from the senior dance ..."

"She was out neckin' with the Piccard boy, Sheriff," Wallace Johnston explained. "I don't take to my girls doin' that sort of thing. So I kept her in. We raised these girls to be ladies. And they are. Both of them! And no goddamn little—"

"Hold on, Mr. Johnston," the sheriff said, cutting him off. "Don't get excited. This is an investigation, not an accusation. Wicks is obviously tryin' to cover his ... excuse me, Mrs. Johnston ... he's tryin' to protect himself by implicatin' Helene. But we have to check out his story, nonetheless. That's why I'm here." He turned back to Helene. "You was sayin', honey ..."

"Well, 'cause Daphne had to stay in like my daddy says, I was feelin' real bad for her. You see, Sheriff, it was my fault that Daddy made her stay in over Lance. I told on her, thinkin' it was the thing to do."

"And it was," Wallace said.

The sheriff nodded.

"Anyway," Helene continued, "I love my sister, and her bein' so unhappy and all, I thought it might make her feel good to see a new face and maybe hear about all the exotic places in the world we'd only seen in books and movies."

"So you invited Ray over to the house."

"Yes," Helene said with a quivering voice. "I know now it was the wrong thing to do. I hope God will forgive me someday, seein' what come of it. But I did, Sheriff. I invited that terrible man to come and visit my little sister and me." Helene's face crumpled and she began sobbing softly into her hands.

Charlotte put her arms around Helene's shoulders. "I'm sorry, Sheriff, but I surely don't see the point of this. The family has suffered enough without this, too."

"I'm sorry, Mrs. Johnston, I don't like this any more than y'all, but I have to. I won't be much longer."

Helene cried, hoping her tears would soften the sheriff's heart.

"Come on, honey," Charlotte said soothingly, "bear up and let's be done with this."

Helene managed to get control.

"Helene," the sheriff said with a weighty tone, "in all your conversations with Ray Wicks, did the subject of Spanish fly ever come up?"

"Sir?"

"Drugs for . . . sexual stimulation."

"Oh, no sir. Never."

"You and Ray never discussed the possibility of givin' your sister a drug to stimulate her?"

"Lord as my witness, Sheriff, Raymond Wicks and I never discussed such a thing. Is that what he's sayin' about me?"

"Words to that effect, Helene. Yes."

"My Lord, why would I want to do a thing like that? I love my sister."

Wallace Johnston was at the edge of his chair. "Why in God's name would Helene do somethin' to hurt her own sister? That's the damn stupidest thing I ever heard. Are they goin' to send that little bastard to the chair?"

"We'll see, Mr. Johnston. Right now, the navy's got him. But we're workin' on it, believe me."

"Let me ask you folks a question, Mr. and Mrs. Johnston. Do you have relations over in Mississippi, a nephew about the age of your daughters?"

"Yes," Charlotte replied. "My sister and her husband live near Fayette. They've got a son a few months older than Helene, and a daughter that's ten. Why? What do they have to do with this?"

"Just a minute, ma'am. Helene, did you discuss your cousin with Ray Wicks?"

"Yes sir, I believe I mentioned him. Why?"

"Could y'all tell me in what connection he was mentioned?"

Helene let her cheeks color, and she acted flustered. "It's kind of embarrassing, Sheriff."

"It might be, Helene, but I think it best you tell me."

"Well, it was in the square. Ray had been talkin' about his travels around the world and . . . well, he begun talkin' about ladies in different places and such like."

"Yes . . ."

"One thing led to another and we was talkin' about . . ."

"About what, Helene?"

"About . . . virginity, Sheriff." Helene dropped her eyes to the carpet. "I know I shouldn't have done it." She looked at her daddy imploringly. "I'm sorry, Daddy. I'm real ashamed."

"What did virginity have to do with your cousin?" the sheriff asked.

"Ray was sayin' that sex was so good he didn't see how anybody could be a virgin once they got to a particular age. I know I shouldn't have let him talk that way, but I did, and I'm awfully sorry."

"And . . ."

"And so he asked how Daphne and me could stay virgins with a whole world of men out there."

"What about your cousin?"

"Ray asked me if Daphne or me didn't even have any boy cousins we fooled around with. I told him about

Bobby Joel and that I thought maybe Daphne and him had kissed and a few other little things in the barn when she was fourteen . . ."

"Helene!" Charlotte exclaimed.

"I'm sorry, Mama. I had no idea when I said it what Ray would do. I'm awfully sorry." She turned to the sheriff, her face twisted with torment. "Is that what Ray said, Sheriff —that I told him about Daphne foolin' around in the barn, so he figured she wasn't a lady?"

"No, that's not it, Helene. He said you told him your cousin had given Daphne some . . . a sex drug and she lost her virginity."

Helene clasped her hand to her mouth.

"He what?" Wallace Johnston bellowed.

"I take it, then," the sheriff said, "that Daphne wasn't involved with your nephew in such a way and that there hadn't been an incident involving a drug?"

"Lord-o-mercy, no!" Charlotte exclaimed.

"It sounded outlandish to me," the sheriff admitted, "but I had to ask." He turned to the deputy, who had been hunched over on his chair listening with rapt attention. "You have any questions, Toby?"

The deputy rubbed his chin. "The only thing that puzzles me, Sheriff, is how Wicks came over here and knowed he'd have a chance to put the stuff in the lemonade."

The sheriff turned to Helene, and she felt her stomach drop. She struggled to keep an innocent, concerned expression on her face.

"Did you tell Ray there'd be lemonade, Helene?"

"Why yes, Sheriff. He made a point of it. Askin' if there'd be lemonade because he never got it on the ship, and my mama's sugar cookies are known far and wide in the parish."

"As I recall from when we talked last time, both you and Daphne was in the kitchen at the same time. How'd that happen?"

"Daphne went back in the kitchen to get the cookies after I brung out the lemonade. Then Ray says to me, 'I sure would like to take Daphne out on a date. Do you suppose she'd go out with me?' I said I didn't know, and he asked me to go ask her privatelike. So I went to the kitchen."

"That explains it," the deputy said, nodding his head.

"Yeah." The sheriff rose to his feet. "Mr. and Mrs. Johnston, we've imposed long enough. I'm satisfied, and I'm mighty sorry to have to put you and Helene through this. The FBI gave us certain information and ... well, when there's Feds involved, you got to be a little more formal than you otherwise might be."

"Well, I hope the FBI is as worried about sending the little bastard to the chair," Wallace Johnston said, "as it is about accusin' my daughter of helpin' him with his crimes."

"They ain't accusin', Mr. Johnston, they're questionin'. But don't you worry none. Wicks's story don't make much sense, and most important of all, Helene here don't have a motive for doin' what he says she done." He nodded his head toward Helene, a sympathetic look on his face. "I sure am sorry to put y'all through this, honey, but I don't expect to have to trouble you again."

Helene wiped the corners of her eyes with her fingers and smiled weakly. Then she sat passively as her father walked outside with the sheriff and the deputy. Though her face was grim, her heart soared with joy.

Charlotte patted Helene's hand sympathetically. "The nerve of that boy," she murmured, "accusin' you of doin' somethin' like that."

Helene closed her eyes to pray—the first time the urge had struck her in years. What she saw though, in her mind's eye, was Olivia Piccard's superior expression and the vast wilderness that her hometown now represented.

The sheriff hadn't even left yet, but Helene had already decided on her next move. There was no future for her in Catahoula Parish. Ray Wicks being captured had dragged her into Daphne's tragedy, and her reputation would always be suspect to one degree or another.

Lance Piccard and that house were lost to her for good, but Helene had come to realize that there was a whole world of nice, big houses and rich men out there waiting for her. She remembered the homes she had seen when they took Daphne to the bus and decided that Monroe was as good a place to start as any.

PACIFIC PALISADES

May 7, 1985

10:05 P.M.

Keith Moore pulled a handkerchief from his pocket and handed it to Daphne, who dabbed her eyes and blew her nose.

"I'm sorry, Detective Wing, I haven't cried over my family in years. I didn't realize I still carried all that pain inside."

"What you went through would have been rough on anyone," Wing replied. He was a little embarrassed at the depth of feeling his questions had evoked.

"I'm glad I wasn't around at the time," Keith said, his eyes on Wing. "If I'd known Daphne then, I'd probably have killed Helene on the spot, and you wouldn't have to worry about her murderer now."

"I still marvel that Helene was my sister. There was something in her that was alien—completely different from the rest of the family. There was nothing in my parents that could have created someone so twisted. My daddy could get a mean streak at times, but nothing like Helene."

"Have your parents passed away?"

"Yes, my father died soon after they came out to California. And Mother died just a few years ago, of cancer.

She had a painful, slow death, poor thing. Helene never went to see her even when Mama was dying. It would have been easy enough for her—she was just up in Bakersfield —but Helene wouldn't go."

"I take it you didn't have any contact with Helene after you left Louisiana?"

"Not until she moved out here in '72."

"What exactly did Helene do in Louisiana between the time you left and when she came to California?"

"Helene left home and went to Monroe, a town north of where our family lived. She married a rich older man named Latrobe. My parents only saw Helene once after she left when they were on their way to California. They stopped in Monroe, apparently much to Helene's embarrassment, from what my mother said."

"Helene didn't even invite her parents to her wedding," Keith added.

"My sister had money for the first time in her life, and she thought she was Mrs. Astor. She wanted to forget her past."

"I take it things didn't work out well for her, though."

"Oh, no. The marriage ended in some sort of disaster that nobody knows about. At least Helene never told me about it. She wanted it a mystery, and that's the way it stayed. I'm sure there was more of her dirty work involved, though."

"So she came to California from Monroe?"

"No, she spent a few years in Dallas in the clothing business. That's where she met Jed and Geoffrey Hammond."

"Did something go wrong there, too?"

"You should talk to Geoffrey about that, Detective Wing," Daphne replied darkly.

"Look, we could go on all night," Keith said, looking at his watch, "but I've got to be on the set early tomorrow morning, and Daphne's got to be at the office. Is there anything more we can tell you, Detective?"

Wing looked at his own watch. "I've imposed enough, and you've been most cooperative." He rose to his feet. "I've got a busy morning myself. We've located Leslie Randall."

Daphne looked surprised. "Not fleeing justice, I hope."

"No, she was visiting friends in Santa Barbara for a few days."

Daphne and Keith walked Wing to the front door. "I know this business is hard for you," he said sympathetically. "Hopefully, it will be over soon." He started to go, then stopped. "You know, Mrs. Stephens, the period in Helene Daniels's life between when you left Louisiana and when you saw her again in California intrigues me. I intend to speak with Geoffrey Hammond about Texas, but who might I talk to about her life in Monroe?"

"I really don't know."

"Perhaps Mr. Latrobe?"

"You can try, I suppose — if he's alive."

Wing's eyebrows rose.

"I'm not sure why, because I don't recall Helene even mentioning him, but for some reason I have the impression the man is dead."

MONROE, LOUISIANA
1970

July 18

Helene Latrobe looked at the thin beam of sunlight penetrating her bedroom through the gap in the heavy damask overdrapes. She had already gone to his room in a filmy negligee to awaken him before returning to her own room to close the curtains. Through experience she had learned that Claude was best able to get an erection in the mornings, but that he preferred doing it in the darkness.

Helene lay on the pink satin sheets, her gown pulled up to expose her pubis and breasts. Her legs were apart and her hand was between them. Claude had walked into her room several minutes earlier, looked at her nude body, then retreated into her bath. The pattern was always the same.

He had been in there for five minutes, so she could count on him staying there at least five minutes more. Helene had decided to overwhelm him with the most diverse array of her undergarments yet, leaving virtually everything she had in there for him to feel and touch and fondle himself with.

The previous two Saturdays he had failed to get it up, so in desperation she had practically turned the room into a Chinese laundry, swearing to herself that if it didn't work she'd cut off his balls. In four years of marriage he had made certain she'd had no opportunity to get any else-where—without risking everything she'd worked for—so for sex she had been totally dependent upon him.

Helene heard the commode flush, though she knew he hadn't used it. Knowing there wasn't much time before he'd be out in one of two conditions—either anxious or defeated—Helene began working herself more vigorously. She closed her eyes and lapsed into one of her fantasies, her current favorite involving the young, lean tennis in-structor Claude had hired to help her with her game.

Helene was just starting to moisten when she heard the bathroom door open. She glanced over and saw that Claude had succeeded in getting it up. She kept her eyes closed and kept rubbing herself, just as he liked. It was always done just as Claude wanted, but Helene didn't mind, con-sidering the weekly ritual little enough hardship for the life it had earned her.

For several minutes, he silently stood beside the bed watching her. It was the only part of sex Helene found stimulating, knowing that a man who owned a good part of Monroe would be standing at her bedside watching her work herself into a fever of excitement.

Sometimes, she'd open her eyes a little and watch the desire growing on his face as he reached under that belly of his and played with himself. Then, as always, he sat down and began running his hand over the satin sheets for a min-ute or two before he touched her.

Helene continued until he commanded her to put the pillow under her ass. Then he crawled with difficulty on his arthritic knees until he was between her legs. She looked up at him then, his fat face florid, his mouth open and breathing hard from the exertion.

She felt his belly press against her. Helene opened her legs farther. As Claude eased inside of her, his mouth fell on her breast and he began rocking his pelvis and sucking her earnestly with his lips. After thirty or forty seconds, she heard his warning gasp, followed by the final thrust.

Helene waited, bearing his weight as long as she could before forcing him to roll off of her so that she could breathe. The last part, having his rubbery old flesh on her, was the worst.

When she didn't come, which was most times, she was especially resentful. She felt doubly denied that morning, first because it had been nearly a month, and second because it was even briefer than usual.

Claude Latrobe, Monroe's leading banker, and at sixty-five enjoying the pinnacle of his powers in the community, stopped at the door to look at his young wife, her pelvis gently rocking on the bed under the pleasure of her own touch. It irritated him that she didn't wait until he was gone, but seeing her eager told him she hadn't managed to find a way to get it somewhere else. And that pleased him —better her finger than someone else's cock.

"When you finish, Helene, come on down to breakfast. I want to talk to you about the party tonight," he said and turned and quietly left the room.

Claude was sitting at the table in the garden eating his usual Saturday morning breakfast of waffles with strawberries and cream when Helene joined him. She was dressed in a pair of plum-colored raw silk slacks and a wild, geometric print silk blouse.

Claude's attention was on his paper, and he didn't bother to look up as Helene approached. He was wearing his sun visor, a polo shirt, and his favorite forest green golfing slacks. The sight of him after they'd had sex always disgusted her, especially when she didn't come.

"You aren't going to play golf today, are you?" she lamented upon seeing his outfit.

"Yep, I have to—it's business," he said, without looking up.

He didn't see the contempt on her face, and she had learned not to let her voice betray her feelings. This morning, however, it was a struggle. Even her fantasies had left her unsatisfied. Sex again was at least a week away, so despite her best efforts there was an edge in her voice.

"Claude, your son's coming this afternoon. Can't the business wait until Monday? This is his first visit to the house in the four years we've been married."

"This is important, Helene," he said, finally looking at

her. "You know how much I get done playing a round of golf? More than the whole rest of the week."

"You'd think, just this once—"

"Dammit, Helene, it's important!" He colored at her insistence. "I hired you all the help you could possibly need to put on a dinner party. What do you want me to do, vacuum the sitting room?"

Helene's eyes flashed. "I don't think it's right that I greet André alone. I've only met him once in my life."

"The boy's in business himself, Helene; he understands. Besides, I'll be seeing him tonight, tomorrow, and however long he cares to stay."

She sat down and poured herself some coffee. "You said you wanted to talk to me about the dinner party. . ."

Claude looked up at her through his bifocals, his visor casting a greenish hue over his face. "Yes," he said, gathering his thoughts. "Who was it you said was coming over?"

"I invited Faye Kimbrough. She's been wanting to see André ever since our wedding, and I thought he might enjoy her. She's attractive and all."

Claude snorted. "Unless he's changed, André'll be coming to Louisiana to get away from women, not to find them."

"You always make him sound like Don Juan."

"You know how many girls he got pregnant here in Monroe when he was a kid? Three! Not one, not two, but three! If I hadn't shipped him away to college he would've had half the female population of the city pregnant. Lord, I'd paid for two births and one abortion before he got his high school diploma."

"Well, he's thirty-four now, not eighteen."

"Thank God."

"So, is that all you wanted to know about the dinner party—who's coming?"

"No," he said, putting down the paper. "I was wondering if I might have a couple of the bank's customers come by, too."

"With family here?"

"Well, they'll only be in town for a couple of days. They're leaving tomorrow."

"Lord, you don't have to invite them to the house, do you?"

"I can't take them out, can I? You're already upset because I'm playing golf. Want me to miss dinner, too?"

"How about if you just invite them over for a drink before dinner? Who are they anyway?"

"People wanting a big operating loan for a farming and lumber business in Central Louisiana. They have a nice assortment of accounts they'll be bringing to the bank. They're from down your part of the country—where your folks is from, I mean."

"What's their name?"

"Piccard. Widow named Olivia Piccard and her son. Do you know them?"

Involuntarily, Helene gasped. She hadn't heard the name Piccard since she'd left Catahoula Parish five years before.

"I knew them," she said, recovering. "The Piccards were the wealthiest family in the parish."

"When shall I tell them to come by?"

Helene's curiosity had been aroused and she was intrigued at the thought of seeing them again, now that she was their equal. "Have you ever mentioned me to the Piccards, Claude?"

"Why no, I don't believe I have. Why?"

"Well, do me a favor and don't say anything before they come. I'd like to see Olivia's face when she sees me in this house."

"What're you up to, Helene?"

"Nothing, just a woman's pleasure at seeing an old friend."

"All right. When should I tell them to come by?"

"Let's see, André's due at three—tell them five-thirty. Oh, and Claude..."

"Yes?"

"Are you beholden to the Piccards, or are they beholden to you?"

"If their operation's financially sound, I'd like their business, but I *am* the banker. I've got the money, and they want to borrow it."

She beamed. "That's what I thought, dear." She got up,

went around the table, and kissed him on the temple. "By the way," she whispered, "you made me feel mighty fine this morning."

Claude Latrobe reached up and patted Helene's cheek with his beefy hand. "If I didn't have this important golf date, sugar, I'd take you upstairs and show you some more."

Helene kissed him again and stood up, smiling at the prospect of the day ahead. She watched him leave, going down the steps of the great white house that was set in a private park of large shade trees and lawns; a house with a pool and tennis court. Minnie, the housemaid, came hurrying out from the kitchen to clear away the dishes, and Helene Latrobe knew that she would tolerate Claude every morning if need be.

Billy Sanders leaned forward, then arched upward, his body extended, his arm thrust toward the sky as he released the ball. "You see what I mean, Mrs. Latrobe?" he asked, catching the ball without hitting it. "Wait until your arm is fully extended before releasing the ball."

He returned to the ready position as Helene watched. Her eyes, though, were on the firm, tanned flesh of his thighs.

"Okay, y'all try it," he said, turning and handing her the ball.

Helene stepped to the baseline, and he moved behind her. She leaned over in the ready position, realizing that her ruffled sport panties were showing under her tennis skirt. Then, unable to resist, she bent over and slowly re-tied her sneaker, knowing the boy had to be ogling her, speculating on the wonders that lay under the skimpy little bit of fabric shielding her from his eyes.

Helene finished with one shoe, then switched to the other, wondering if the sight of her was making him hard. And wondering if there was any way she could possibly find to get him to take advantage of her.

"Well, that's quite a sight she's showing you, son."

Not recognizing the deep voice, Helene stood up abruptly. There at the side of the court, behind Billy, was a handsome man in shirt sleeves, his tie loosened at his neck, his hands on his hips, a crooked grin on his face.

"Who . . . what . . ." Helene stammered.

"What's the matter, Mama?" he said with an exaggerated drawl. "Don't you recognize the prodigal son?"

"André?" She frankly didn't recognize him, having only a vague recollection of his dark, good looks from the day they'd met four years before. "I didn't expect . . ."

He laughed, then smiled at Billy. "That's the impression I had."

Helene turned red, fully realizing what had happened. "Billy's giving me a tennis lesson. He was state champion." She gestured an introduction. "Billy Sanders, André Latrobe, Mr. Latrobe's son from New York."

"How do you do, Mr. Latrobe, sir."

They shook hands and André smiled at the boy. "Sorry to interrupt your lesson, son."

Helene knew exactly what he was implying. She glared at the man.

"You want me to go now, Mrs. Latrobe?" Billy asked awkwardly.

"Our time's about up," she replied, "so you may as well. Thank you, Billy."

The boy gathered his gear, then headed off across the yard. Helene placed the cover on her racket and glanced at André Latrobe, who was still grinning at her.

"That was very impolite," she said casually. "You embarrassed the poor boy."

André laughed, his white teeth gleaming, his expression completely irreverent. Helene suddenly understood the problem Claude had had with him as a boy. The combination of his manner and good looks could weaken a woman instantly.

"Sorry, Helene. You have such a shapely ass, I couldn't resist commenting."

Her eyes flashed, but he dismissed it with a curl of his lip.

"Come on now, don't tell me you were sticking it up in the air by accident."

"I was tying my shoe."

He snickered. "I could use a cold beer. Will you join me?"

"I'll ask Minnie to bring us some," she said, then she headed for the house.

A few minutes later they both sat at a garden table as the black maid poured the beer, then returned to the house.

"I thought you weren't coming in till this afternoon," Helene said, looking at him over the rim of her glass.

"I got on an earlier flight." He glanced around the yard. "Place looks the same," he said. "Only thing that's changed, I guess, is that Daddy's got himself a little fire-cracker now."

"Are you referring to me, André Latrobe?"

He lifted his shoulders casually. "If the shoe fits . . ."

"I wish you wouldn't talk to me disrespectful like that. If your daddy was here, you wouldn't talk that way."

"And if my daddy was here, you wouldn't be teasing that boy's prick either."

Helene narrowed her eyes. "I told you I was tying my shoes."

"Are you fucking the kid, Helene?" he asked evenly.

She sat upright. "Why you foulmouthed . . ."

André waved his hand at her. "Save your righteous indignation. If you aren't balling him, or somebody else, you're a fool."

"What a terrible way to talk to the wife of your very own father. You've been up North too long, André. You're no gentleman."

"Mama, dear, if I were a gentleman and if you were a lady, this would be a very dull conversation."

Helene's mouth dropped open. Then, despite herself, she smiled and finally laughed. He was too outrageous to be taken seriously. She could see there was no point in protesting further.

They both drank, and Helene felt his ankle against hers. Then it began slowly running up the inside of her calf.

"Tell me the truth, can the old boy still get it up?"

Helene moved her leg away from his. "You must not think very much of your daddy to say a thing like that."

"As a matter of fact, I don't."

"Then why y'all here?"

André sipped his beer. "Family business."

"Is seducing me part of it?"

"I hadn't planned on it, but when I saw you with the boy, I realized what desperate straits you were in."

"Meaning?"

"Meaning whatever you want it to mean."

"Well, I'm not desperate, André Latrobe."

"Then you've got a lover."

Helene's eyes flashed again. "That's not true. Not that you have a right to know, but I was a virgin when I married Claude, and he's the only man I've ever been with "

"You're kidding?"

"I'm not."

"Jesus Christ."

"What's that supposed to mean?"

"It means you've never been properly laid."

Helene turned her head away in disgust. "How would you know? You have no idea what your daddy's like."

He laughed. "How old is he now?"

"Sixty-five, but that don't mean nothin'."

"Is he still fat?"

"He's a mite heavy."

"None of that indicates a likely Casanova, Helene, but the best indication of all is what's going on between *your* legs."

Helene felt her knees spontaneously clench together. "You're disgusting!"

"Save your act for him, Helene, I'm a friend."

She turned away in disbelief.

"Don't you know it's obvious? And not just to a trained eye like mine. Half the able-bodied men in Monroe would probably love to get you alone in a barn."

"Oh, go to hell," she said bitterly.

"Sorry, I didn't mean it personally. It was a comment on your circumstances, not your character."

"Speaking of trained eyes and character, from what I hear, you've single-handedly sired half the children in this town."

André nodded. "I confess to sowing a few wild oats."

"If Claude's so bad and you're so accomplished, who'd you get it from. Your mother?"

His eyes grew dark. "As a matter of fact, Helene, that's how I know my father couldn't satisfy a woman to save his soul."

"Your mama told you?" she asked incredulously.

"Not exactly. I found out at sixteen, when my mother was dying. She was upstairs, bedridden for more than a year. Claude had a nurse stay with her while he was at the bank. He'd come home on his lunch hour to see my mama —at least that's what everybody thought, including me. By accident one day I found out he'd been meeting the nurse in the downstairs bedroom for a nooner."

"Claude?"

"I'd always leave before he'd arrive, and I'd tell the nurse I was going to the swimming pool or something. Then, I'd spy on them, sometimes I'd be in the closet, a time or two even under the bed." André laughed. "I used to time the old fart with a stop watch—keep charts on him. He'd never last more than a minute or two at the most, and that was twenty years ago."

"You did that? You watched Claude with another woman?"

"Every day."

"Every day?" Her eyes rounded and her hand went to her open mouth.

Seeing her, André Latrobe threw back his head and roared with laughter.

Helene turned scarlet.

"Like I was saying, he can't satisfy a woman. Lord Almighty, Helene, you've never really been fucked!"

Helene stood in her slip looking out her bedroom window at André Latrobe strolling about the grounds of his boyhood home—*her* home. Helene had met some mighty impressive men in her life, but she never recalled one who intimidated and aroused her like André. It was incredible that the first man to truly move her since her marriage should be her husband's son.

She decided André was probably motivated by a desire to hurt his daddy, but it didn't dampen the effect he had on her. He was undoubtedly right that she had never had a real, first-class sexual experience, and the fact that they both knew it only exacerbated the effect that he was having on her.

Helene had withdrawn to her room immediately after the beer in the garden. She had asked Minnie to make André some lunch and to bring her up a tray. Isolated in her room, she tried not to think of the man downstairs, but it wasn't easy. André had put her in a difficult position. He had robbed her of what little respect she had for Claude, and at the same time made it easier for her to justify her own wayward tendencies. Helene couldn't help wondering if that had been his intent.

When Claude got home, Helene was lying on her bed. She heard him mount the stairs and knock softly on her door. Without waiting for a reply, he entered. "Hi, sugar," he said, smiling broadly. "Didn't wake you, did I?"

"No, Claude, I was just resting."

He walked over and sat on the edge of the bed next to her. Helene saw that he was perspiring heavily. His hair and brow were moist and his shirt soaked around his belly.

"I see that André got in all right."

"Yes, we chatted briefly, but I was tired so I've been up here most of the afternoon."

"That's what he said. Y'all feeling all right?"

"Yes."

Claude grinned. "Maybe the nookie this mornin' was a little too much for y'all, sugar." He let his moist palm drift across the satin fabric covering her stomach before resting on the mound between her legs. "If these Piccard folks wasn't comin', I might tire you out even more." He gave a self-satisfied laugh, then rose to his feet. "I'd better go have a shower and get dressed."

Helene's eyes narrowed with disdain as she silently watched him leave her room.

July 18

Helene Latrobe crossed her legs and ran her fingers lightly over the lacquered surface of her hairdo, which she had cut precisely in the style of Jackie Onassis. She smoothed the skirt of her indigo silk cocktail dress and glanced around the room, looking at it through Olivia Piccard's eyes.

After their marriage, Claude had given Helene free reign to redecorate the house as she pleased. Most of the antiques she had kept—not because she liked them but because she knew that they had value. She considered the hardwood floors to be old-fashioned and had covered them with white shag carpeting, adding matching gold love seats and chairs in the sitting room. What she saw pleased her as she looked around, but the anticipation of seeing Olivia's face when Claude introduced her as his wife would please her even more.

Before she had come down, André had borrowed the keys to Claude's Fleetwood for a drive around town and promised to return before Faye Kimbrough was to arrive at seven. Helene was glad as she did not want any distraction while Olivia was there.

Arriving a polite ten minutes after the appointed hour, Olivia and Lance Piccard were shown into the sitting room by the maid. Claude rose to greet them in courtly fashion. Then, taking Olivia by the arm, he brought her across the broad expanse of white carpeting to where Helene was sitting. With her heart beating excitedly and her mouth chiseled with a smile of triumph, Helene slowly rose.

While Claude babbled, Helene watched Olivia's face turn from composed serenity to curious uncertainty, and finally to aghast recognition. However, Olivia composed herself, and her practiced expression returned to serenity.

"Helene," she said, extending her hand, "how well you look. I knew that Claude Latrobe was a clever banker, but I had no idea he had the good sense to marry one of *our* young ladies."

Helene took the proffered hand, her smile unbroken. "I know so little about Claude's business, Olivia, it's good for a change to know a customer and be able to offer an opinion of the people."

"Hello, Helene," Lance said, as she turned her brittle smile on him. "You're lookin' mighty well."

"How are you, Lance?" she said, taking his hand. "Claude, honey, would you believe that Lance Piccard and I went to high school together? Now here he is, a big businessman and all." She looked at her guest and savored the awestruck expression on the man's face. "Was it in English or Algebra we sat next to each other, Lance?"

"Both, I believe."

"Was it really? I do declare." She smiled at mother and son, knowing the Piccards would at last be giving Helene Johnston her due.

Helene and Claude sat on the porch in air heavy with the scent of lemon verbena. In the shrubbery at the boundaries of the property a chorus of crickets formed a background to the doves cooing in nearby trees. Beside her, Helene heard the tinkle of ice cubes in Claude's glass as he swirled it.

"Think I'll go in and fix me another nightcap," he said softly. "Can I bring you something, sugar?"

"No," she said. "Thank you." Helene didn't look at him. Her eyes were fixed instead on the couple moving about the shadows in the garden, strolling in the pleasant hush of the Louisiana night.

She strained to see what they were doing, whether he touched her. Helene had intended that Faye would have a chance one day at André Latrobe, but now that it was happening she hated it. She wanted him for herself.

Helene had met Faye five years earlier at Mrs. Potter's boarding house on South Grand Street and, though their backgrounds were vastly different, they had become friends. Faye's family was well-to-do, and with her help Helene found a job in Monroe and, eventually, Claude. It was at Helene's wedding that Faye and André Latrobe became acquainted. She instantly fell in love.

Unfortunately, André spent little time in Monroe, having a theatrical agency in New York that kept him occupied. But Helene had given Faye her oath that when the opportunity arose, she would see that they got together. Helene owed everything she had to Faye Kimbrough, but now her promise was one she bitterly regretted having made.

Peering into the darkness, Helene heard Faye's laughter drifting across the grounds of the Latrobe estate. André was being charming, and Faye was giving it her all.

Behind her, the screen door quietly opened and closed, and Claude moved through the obscurity across the porch. He silently sat beside his wife. "André and Faye still out walkin'?"

"Yes."

Claude chuckled. "Judging by the way she was lookin' at him at supper, I'd say André was going to get a piece tonight."

Helene filled with hatred at her husband's words—hatred for him, hatred for Faye, even hatred for André, whose arms she wished she were in at that very moment.

"As much a problem as that boy was for me when he was young, I gotta say, he does inspire a body." Claude reached over and touched Helene's arm with his hot, moist palm.

Without thinking she pulled her arm away. Hearing his snort, she looked at him apologetically. "It's awfully warm, Claude dear."

"Yes, it is."

She saw him leering at her in the dark.

"I imagine those satin sheets of yours would feel real cool now, sugar."

"I'd like to sit a while longer."

Faye's laughter drifted through the darkness, piercing Helene's heart. Strangely, though, it was Olivia Piccard's face that popped into her mind. "Are you going to give Olivia her loan?"

Claude was taken aback by the unexpected question. "We still have to review their finances and check out the collateral, but I'd say there's a good chance. Yes."

"Isn't there a way you could turn her down?"

Claude looked at her with surprise. "Of course, I could say no, but why should I?"

"Would it be that much of a loss for the bank to turn the Piccards down, Claude?"

"Helene, are you tryin' to tell me you don't want me to make that loan?"

"I don't like them."

"Well, I'm right sorry to hear that, but I can't run the bank dependin' on who my wife likes and doesn't like. This is business, Helene."

She fell silent, knowing it would be that way. A few moments later they heard the sound of Faye's car starting around the side of the house.

"Well, sounds like they're going to get laid," Claude said matter-of-factly.

Helene's stomach tightened. "I think I'll go to bed now."

The lace curtains of her bedroom window moved ever so slightly in the gentle breeze of the night. Helene looked at them through half-open eyes, her hand lightly caressing her mound. She could never remember feeling such an intense craving for a man.

Though her thoughts were far away, Helene heard the faint sound of her bedroom door opening, and she turned her head. By the bulk of the shadowy figure filling the doorway, she knew it was Claude.

"Are you awake, sugar?" he whispered.

For an instant Helene considered feigning sleep, but then she decided against it, curious about what he might want. "Yes, I'm awake."

She watched the figure move quietly toward the bed. Claude wore a bathrobe, which was hanging open over his body, and nothing more. In the darkness she could see the stub of his penis.

"What's the matter, Claude?"

"Nothing," he said, sitting on the edge of the bed.

"Can't you sleep?"

"No . . ."

"Why?"

"I've been thinkin' about André balling that Kimbrough girl and . . . well, I started thinkin' about your sweet little body, sugar."

"Now, Claude?" she said in disbelief. "Just this morning, we . . ."

"I know, but I just started thinkin' about it." He reached over and slipped his hand under the sheet, running it along Helene's thigh.

She trembled under his touch, not expecting the overture or being prepared for it. Claude rolled onto the bed, his bathrobe falling off his rounded torso. Brushing the filmy fabric of her gown off her breast with his hand, he lightly pinched her exposed nipple between his fingers.

"I even got hard a while ago thinkin' about you, sugar," he said, his voice indicating a trace of his own wonder.

Helene was so caught by surprise that she didn't know what to think. She had been aroused herself, but the thought of Claude revolted her. For the first time in their marriage, excuses for rejecting his initiative went through her mind.

Claude brought his face close to hers, the smell of bourbon strong on his breath. His lips grazed her cheek. "Would you like to do something a little different tonight, sugar?"

Helene heard a faintly ominous ring in his words. "What do you mean *different*, Claude?"

"Do you know what it means for a woman to go down on a man, sugar?"

"No . . ." She did know what it meant but hoped a posture of innocence might end the conversation.

He hesitated, then kissed her on the cheek. "You wait here. I'll be right back," he said, rolling to the edge of the bed and getting up.

"Claude, where are you going?"

He was at the door. "A picture is worth a thousand words, sugar. I'll be right back."

Helene groaned to herself, expecting the worst.

Several minutes later Claude returned. She could see something in his hand in the dark.

"Let me turn on the light for a second," he said, reaching up under the lamp.

The light came on, and Helene blinked at the intrusive brightness. "Claude, what on earth . . ."

In his hand was a magazine-sized book—*The Illustrated Guide to Oral Sex.* He handed it to her.

"Claude! What kind of trash is this you're showin' me?"

"Just look at the pictures," he said. "I'm going to the bathroom."

Helene watched him walk across the room. She hadn't left any of her things in the bath for him to fondle, and she wondered what he'd do in there without her underwear.

When he had closed the door, Helene looked at the book. The photographs were of men and women engaged in various forms of oral sex.

It was clear to Helene that Claude hoped the pictures would either educate or stimulate her—perhaps both. But what drew Helene's attention were the lean, firm bodies of the men. If Claude had known how poorly he fared in comparison, he might not have shown it to her.

Visualizing herself and Claude doing some of the things she saw in the picture made Helene sick. Although he was obviously serious about trying it, Helene knew she didn't have it in her—not with Claude Latrobe.

She heard the commode flush. Helene quickly closed the book and turned off the light, not wanting to have to see Claude's face when she told him no.

The bathroom door opened. "Hey, what'd y'all turn off the light for, sugar?"

"Claude Latrobe, I looked at your disgusting book, and I don't ever want to see anything like that again."

"Helene, there's nothing so terrible about that, not nowadays," he lamented.

"It's disgusting. It's a sin."

"A sin?" He walked to the bed and sat down beside her. "When did you become religious, Helene?"

She detected the irritation in his voice. "I couldn't do that, Claude," she said, letting her voice quiver.

He reached over and fondled her breast. "Oh, come on, sugar, it might not be so bad. You might like it."

"No, Claude."

"Please . . ."

"If you want that, you'll have to go see a hooker, Claude Latrobe."

"What do I need a hooker for when I've got a wife?"

"Claude!"

"I married a young woman because I thought you'd be like the young folks."

"I thought you married me because you loved me."

"I did, sugar. I *do* love you."

"Then how could you possibly ask me to do something like that?"

"Please, Helene. For me?"

His insistence surprised her, and she knew she had to be firm.

"No. I'm sorry, but no."

Claude's hand tightened on her shoulder, almost to the point of being painful, then he released it, caressing her lightly. His fingers ran over the nape of her neck, first softly, then grasping her firmly with his large, fat hand. He had never been rough with her before, and she wondered if he might try now.

"Y'all remember that emerald dinner ring you've been talking about, Helene? Maybe if you're inclined to cooperate with me a little tonight, we might just go down and pick it out for your birthday."

"You sayin' I got to go down on you, Claude, if I want that ring?"

"No, I didn't say that. I just was thinkin' that if a wife

expects a present that's real expensive like that, she ought
to cooperate with her husband's desires, that's all."

"I don't want the ring that much."

Claude's hand tightened on the back of her neck, hurting
her. Although he didn't say anything, she could feel anger
in him. "Is there anything you want that much?" he finally
hissed, trying to contain his temper.

The image of Olivia Piccard came to mind. She knew
how hard it would be for Claude to turn down the loan
when business dictated that he make it, but she also knew
how good she'd feel to be the cause of Olivia and Lance
Piccard's failure. Helene toyed with the idea, thinking it
would only be worth it if Olivia found out the loan had
been denied because of her.

She closed her eyes and sighed, wishing life were different, wishing she could force a man to go down on her in
exchange for a favor. "Claude, dear," she said to the anxious man at her side, "would you go get me a drink first—
a stiff one? I think there *is* something I'd like—something
I'd like very, very much."

All day Sunday Helene stayed in bed. The headache she
had was the result of the bourbon she had consumed, but
she preferred to have Claude think it was from the shock of
her experience with him. She had succeeded in arousing
him much more than she had liked, and she was determined that he wouldn't get any ideas about making it a
habit.

Monday morning Claude left early for the bank, as was
his custom. When he was gone, Helene went down to have
her breakfast in the garden. André was not anywhere to be
seen.

"Where's young Mr. Latrobe, Minnie?" she asked the
maid as she poured her coffee.

"I don't know, ma'am. I thinks he's still asleep."

"Hmm. When he comes down, tell him I'd like him to
join me for breakfast."

"Yes, ma'am."

Helene sat drinking her coffee and wondering about
André. She knew instinctively that playing with him was
dangerous, but that it could be a rewarding, satisfying ex-

perience—*if* she could interest him, that is, and *if* Faye Kimbrough hadn't already frozen her out. The thought that he might care for Faye made her want him all the more.

"Mornin', Mama." She looked up to see him standing handsome and tall beside the table. "You looked like you were off in Never-Never Land," he said with a grin.

"Good morning," she said, smiling. "As a matter of fact, I was."

He sat down beside her, his tanned arms and neck set off by a green polo shirt that matched his eyes. "Seeing that expression on your face, I think I'd like to have been the guy."

Helene gave him a level look. "You're into incest?"

"So, that *was* what you were thinking about!" He grinned. "Daddy must have been *bad* last night."

"André," she said, fighting back a blush, "you've got a one-track mind."

"At least . . ."

". . . it's on the right track," she said, finishing the phrase for him. "Believe it or not, that one's made it to Monroe."

André poured himself some coffee. "Be honest, Helene, don't you get bored?"

"No. I like my life."

"Do you?"

"Most of it, yes."

"I won't embarrass you by asking which part is lacking."

"Well, that's a surprise. I'd have expected you to tell me in glowingly explicit terms."

"Do you want me to?"

"Here," she said, pushing a tray of pastry toward him, "have a sweet roll."

André smiled wryly and took a large bite of pastry. "What are we going to do today?"

"Oh, is this *my* day? What about Faye?"

He laughed. "Helene Latrobe, are you jealous?"

"Jealous?" Her eyes narrowed, but she realized she hadn't been subtle in the least. "Faye Kimbrough happens to be my very good friend."

"Since when did that ever matter to a woman, Mama?"

Helene gave him a dirty look. "I wish you wouldn't keep callin' me Mama. I ain't your Mama."

"Sorry, but your suggestion about incest does intrigue me, I must admit."

"It wasn't a suggestion!"

"But doesn't the thought put a little fire in your loins?"

She gave him a disgusted look out of habit. "What about Faye? Or is she already another victim of your love-'em-and-leave-'em philosophy?"

"My, but you're hard on me," he complained mildly, "and you sure are curious about Faye and me. I do think you're jealous."

"Think what you wish."

André drank his coffee. "How about if we begin with a set of tennis?"

"Begin what?"

His smile was positively devilish. "Why, our games for the day." He reached over, took her hand, then rising, pulled Helene to her feet. "I left my calendar completely open for you. I surely hope y'all done the same." He led her toward the house, his hand tightly clamped around hers.

At the far side of the court, André Latrobe threw the ball in the air, much as Billy Sanders had done, but when he brought his racket down, hitting his serve into Helene's service court, she knew he was holding back, giving her a chance to put the ball into play. They had been playing for about forty-five minutes in the pleasant morning air, managing long rallies, neither of them taking a winner when it was offered, preferring instead to volley.

After a while, Minnie brought a pitcher of lemonade and some glasses out to a courtside bench, and they broke for refreshment.

Helene tried to act indifferent as they sat side by side, but his tanned, firm thighs so close to hers immediately aroused her. She felt his eyes penetrating her, drawing out every feminine impulse she possessed. He didn't say anything, he just looked at her. She stared back frankly. Then he put his hand on her thigh, just above the knee, squeezing it slowly, gently. She didn't flinch. Then André began drawing his hand up her leg, rotating it slowing toward the inside of her thigh. Helene didn't move until she saw that he meant to go all the way up under her tennis skirt. She finally pushed his hand away, picking up the pitcher of lemonade and pouring them each a glass.

They drank for a minute without speaking.

"You know, Helene, that body of yours is totally wasted on Claude. How do you do it?"

She didn't look at him. "I . . . I love Claude."

André gave a little laugh. "You mean you love his money, don't you?"

Her eyes flashed at him.

"Don't be so goddamned self-righteous," he said casually. "It's obvious. Even Claude knows it. He's got the money to pay for what he wants, so why not?"

"You're callin' me a whore, André Latrobe."

He sipped his lemonade. "We all are, Helene, one way or another."

"What do *you* sell yourself for?"

He thought. "I don't know. Power and independence, I suppose."

"If you're so independent, why are you back here in Monroe?"

"Claude hasn't told you anything, has he?"

"Anything about what?"

"The bank."

"What about the bank?"

"Claude controls the bank. You're aware of that, surely."

"Yes."

"Did he tell you that fifty-five percent of the bank's stock, which he's been voting, is mine?"

"Yours?"

"Yes. Mine."

Helene felt her heart in her throat. "If it's yours, why's Claude voting it?"

"Fifty-five percent of the bank was my mother's, which she had gotten from my granddaddy, Claude's original partner. The stock went into a trust for me when my mother died, but Claude's trustee. That's how he's been able to be kingpin. He owns thirty-five percent in his own name, with the balance owned by the employee pension fund."

Helene sat stunned, not knowing exactly what it all meant. "But André, you're of age. Why is Claude voting your stock, and not you?"

"He won't be for long. I'll be thirty-five in two weeks, at which time the trust terminates and the shares go into my name directly." He grinned at her and pinched her chin. "You see, darlin', that's why I'm here. I'm deciding how I want the bank run."

Helene felt shaken. "What about the house?" she asked, glancing at the great white mansion—*her* house.

"I'm afraid that's mine, too."

"Yours?" Helene felt as though her guts had been wrenched from her. "You mean in two weeks . . ."

André laughed. "No, Claude has a life estate, exclusive use of the house for his lifetime."

"His lifetime?" Helene asked mournfully.

"That's right, darlin'." André rubbed Helene's leg again. "I enjoyed the tennis. What do you say we go have a shower?"

Helene got to her feet, not knowing whether to scream or cry. She stared off into space, picturing Claude's fat face and them in bed together. "The bastard!" she seethed under her breath.

"Come on, little lady. After all this bad news, you're deservin' of a treat."

July 20

Helene Latrobe slipped off her bra and panties, then looked at her nude body in the bathroom mirror. She had been shaken by André's revelation and felt insecure. Claude, the house, her status in the community, everything seemed suddenly on tenterhooks. In the midst of it all, her husband's son had propositioned her. He suggested that after her shower she come to his room.

For two days Helene had been craving him, almost to the exclusion of every other consideration, but now his news had stunned her. If what André said was true, Claude was still a wealthy man, but not nearly so wealthy as she had thought. And the house—the house that was to be hers the rest of her life—was simply on loan from André, and then only as long as Claude lived. Before, the thought of him dying was of no great importance as far as her personal financial situation was concerned, but now it would mean the end.

Helene was about to turn the water on in the shower when she heard the door open. She spun around to see André standing there in a terry cloth robe, his mouth twisted into a broad grin. Shrieking at the sight of him, she grabbed a bath sheet from the counter and held it up to her, fumbling to get it over the critical places. "André! How dare you walk into my bathroom! Please get out!"

"Get out? But Helene darlin', this is *my* bathroom. The whole damned house is mine."

"Not yet."

"Oh, it's mine. I've just got tenants, that's all." He stepped toward her. "You see, I came to Monroe to look over what's mine, to see what's here that I like, and what I don't like." He inched closer. "You want to know what I've found that I like best of what my daddy has?"

Her look was wary. "What?"

"Why little darlin', it's what's under that towel." He reached up with his hand and grasped the top of it, slowly pulling downward until she stood totally naked before him.

"That *is* a sight to behold," he said, letting his eyes move over her.

Helene tried to be as bold as he, though her body was shaking imperceptibly. André took the end of the cotton belt around his waist and pulled on it slowly so that it untied and the robe fell open.

She stared at him for a moment, not believing the size of his penis, which was easily twice the length of Claude's— the only other one she had ever seen. André, noticing the shock on her face, laughed.

"What's the matter, haven't you ever seen a real man before?"

André was looking at her breasts and hips, savoring the voluptuous curves of her body. "Since this is all among family, darlin', I'll tell you a dark family secret. Claude ain't my daddy—not my real father. My mama told me before she died. There was somebody else, but Claude don't know. He don't know a thing."

The words were unexpected, but they didn't really faze her. Helene was totally preoccupied with his body.

"Lord, honey," he said, removing the bathrobe and throwing it down, "you're in for a treat."

He grabbed her arms and pulled her abruptly against his body. Then he covered her mouth, taking it forcefully, hungrily.

"Oh, Lord," she gasped when the kiss ended.

"Baby, you ain't seen nothin' yet. Come on," he said, taking her by the arm, "let's wash up, and I'll show you some fun."

Moments later Helene stood under the pulsing stream of water. He was behind her, his arms wrapped around her. One hand manipulated her between the legs—as expertly as she could herself. She closed her eyes and moaned at the sensation.

"Oh Lord, I'm goin' to come, I'm goin' to come," she groaned.

His teeth bit gingerly into the soft flesh of her neck. "You just do that," he murmured. Helene felt her body convulse once, then fire ran like lightning in every direction.

"Lord God," she cried out, and her knees buckled under her. She sagged into André's arms.

The next thing she knew he was helping her from the shower. She felt too weak to stand, so he let her slip down onto the thick mat. The last of the orgasm was still coursing through her body as she looked up at him, his swollen member above her, pointing at her ominously. But now she wanted it, wanted it more than anything imaginable. As she lay on the bathroom floor, her legs apart, her body his for the taking, André knelt down between her knees and began caressing her with his hand.

Just when she thought that there was no other sensation left to experience, Helene felt André's breath on her thigh, then his lips. Slowly, incredibly, his tongue slid up her leg, moving to the inner flesh. The photos in Claude's book flashed into her mind.

"Oh God, André," she said, her voice quivering with anticipation.

An instant later his tongue found her, and her entire body shuddered at the touch.

"I want you, André. I want you now."

He grinned. "You really want me, don't you?"

"Oh, please."

"Where do you want me?"

"In me. Oh, in me. Please, André."

"Where?"

"Don't do this to me, André. Please."

"What'll you do?"

"Anything you want?"

"Here I come then, Mama."

André drove mercilessly into her. His rhythmic lunges were determined, vigorous, and Helene felt her control slipping away. Then, suddenly, he exploded, his frenzy igniting her. Somewhere in the back of her mind she heard her own screams of pleasure.

André lay dead upon her for a long time. Finally, he stirred, moved from her and got to his feet.

"Did you enjoy that, little lady?" he asked in a hoarse whisper.

Helene barely managed to nod.

André grinned. "You ain't a virgin anymore, Mama. You can consider yourself fucked." Stepping over her he picked up his bathrobe, slipped it on, and left the room.

From her bed Helene stared out the window at the familiar landscape, but somehow the world had changed. She knew for the first time, the possible pleasures of the flesh and enjoyed the ecstasy. But Helene realized that André Latrobe was not hers to possess and enjoy—at least not yet. Before he could be, Helene would have to know his mind and understand his desires.

It had been half an hour since André had left her, but her body was still glowing. She wanted him more desperately than she thought possible, as if her very life depended on it. After contemplating the future for several minutes, Helene picked up the phone to call Faye Kimbrough—hoping she might have some insight into André.

"Faye, honey, how y'all doing?"

"Helene, I've been meaning to call and thank you for the delightful supper. It was a wonderful evening. It truly was."

"I'm sure my table had little or nothing to do with that. How was André after all these years of waiting? Was he what you expected?"

"André's a delightful man, Helene. He's a fine gentleman."

Helene smiled at Faye's term, thinking it signaled more restrained behavior by André than she had expected. "I'm happy to hear that. I was afraid all those years up North might have corrupted him . . ." She waited.

"Well, I don't know what he'll be like as time goes on, but he was as respectful as he was affectionate."

Helene grew impatient with the conversation. "Lordy, Faye, don't we know each other better than this? What you're saying is, he didn't take you to bed, isn't it?"

There was stunned silence for a moment. "Well, yes, Helene, if you must know."

"I'm not prying, Faye. It's just that I love you and I don't want to see you hurt."

"Thank you, Helene. You are a true friend."

"Naturally, I'll keep my eyes and ears open, but based on what I've seen, I do have a bit of advice for you."

"Yes . . . ?"

"Go slow, Faye. Keep a little distance. Turn him down if you get a chance. It'll make him want you more."

"You think so?"

"Well, nothing is for certain with men, mind you, but he's been having his fill of them Yankee girls, and he doesn't know what it's like to be around a real lady."

"Don't you think we're a mite old for those kinds of games?"

"Well, I can tell you his daddy wasn't too old for that game. I'd say the colder the better, Faye."

At four-thirty that afternoon Helene heard Claude's car coming up the drive. She went to the front window and watched as he mounted the front steps, looking hot and red-faced from the heat and exertion.

"Howdy, sugar," he said, dropping his briefcase on the hall table. "You're lookin' mighty cool and nice." He walked into the sitting room, but stopped when he saw the hard expression on her face. "Don't tell me y'all are still upset about that little incident the other night."

"I want to talk to you, Claude."

He blinked at the tone of her voice, knowing something was up. "Can I go to the toilet and then fix myself a cocktail first?"

"Yes, I'll be on the porch."

While she waited, Helene burned with hatred at the

thought that he had probably deceived her about his financial situation. She didn't know whether to hope André's story had been a lie or that André had told the truth, and if she played her cards right, she might end up with both André and the house.

Claude finally came out with a glass of bourbon in his hand. He had removed his suit coat and tie, but he wore the same shirt. He grinned at her uncertainly. "Would you like somethin' to drink?"

"No, thank you," she replied curtly.

"What was it you wanted to talk about, sugar."

"I had a terrible shock today, Claude, and before I get myself too worked up about it, I thought we ought to talk."

His expression was wary. "What is it, Helene?"

"I asked André this morning how it felt to be visiting his family home, and he replied it felt just fine and he was anxious to be living in it again. Naturally, I asked him exactly what that meant."

Claude's eyes dropped and his expression grew dark.

"He assumed that as your wife I knew your financial situation." She glared at him. "Apparently, I don't."

The banker grimaced, staring down at the glass of bourbon in his hand.

"Is it true that this house is his—that it'll never be mine, Claude?"

"Well, it's yours as long as I'm alive, Helene. It's mine for life."

"Yes, that's what I understand," she replied icily. "I can live here for *your* lifetime, not mine."

"Helene, sugar, that don't matter," he said plaintively. "I've got my interest in the bank. I don't know that André is really that interested in the house. He might even be willing to trade some stock for it."

"I also learned today that you don't own that bank, Claude, you just have a minority interest. After André's birthday, he'll be controlling things, not you."

His fat face was a blend of irritation and contrition. "I still own plenty. I *am* a rich man, Helene."

"Not so rich as you led me to believe."

"Well, did you marry me for my money or because you loved me?"

"I married you for the man you *appeared* to be. It would clearly be an understatement to say the appearance was deceiving. You apparently aren't even a man of integrity — duping a poor, innocent girl. I was deceived, Claude," she said, raising her voice, "and that doesn't please me one little bit!"

"I'm in good health, sugar. And besides, I can make other arrangements for you before I go . . . there's plenty of time."

"I want this house!"

"And you will have it. You will, if I can make the arrangements."

"If? *If?* You expect me to live on that kind of a promise? No, Claude Latrobe, I expect you to arrange something with André before he leaves town. I want to know this house is mine!"

The next morning Claude's car had no sooner pulled out of the drive than André appeared at Helene's bedroom door. She smiled a silent greeting.

"Oooeee, Mama," he said, strutting toward her, "you sure must have put the fear of the Lord in Daddy. He come to me last night wantin' to buy this house."

"I mean to have your house, André Latrobe, one way or the other. And I'll do anything I have to do to get it."

André gave a low laugh. "You know, darlin', that's the kind of talk I love to hear." He made a low sound, deep in his throat, as he climbed onto the bed, right above her.

Every morning that week after Claude left, André appeared at Helene's bedroom door, and they spent the next hour or two in bed. She accepted the pleasure he offered gladly, but insisted on knowing the things that he desired too. Then she put every ounce of her energy into doing what he wanted — better than anyone had ever done before.

Between her conversations with André and Claude, Helene knew that they were negotiating, but neither would give her any indication of what was happening. She figured the worst that could happen was that she would end up with Claude and thirty-five percent of the bank, and no house after he was gone. The best was that she'd end up with André, fifty-five percent of the bank, and the house.

As it turned out, Claude had to leave Thursday night for a meeting with the state banking examiners in Baton Rouge, and did not plan to return until Saturday. At André's suggestion, Helene gave Minnie all day Friday off, and the two of them planned a day-long orgy that would take them to every room of the house.

André bought four bottles of champagne and put them in the refrigerator Friday morning. They started with breakfast in bed, which included champagne and orange juice, whipped cream spread over Helen's body, and fruit carefully placed in the cream, which André plucked away with his teeth.

Once they had worked their way through lunch, and a long afternoon nap, André announced the plan for the evening. They were to begin with a nude candlelight supper in the dining room, followed by a surprise game. Helene questioned André insistently about the game, but he was adamant about keeping it secret.

Helene sat at the dining room table feeling pleasantly high from the champagne and satiated by the rich meal André had prepared. He sat at the far end of the long table, bare chested in the candlelight, and she wondered if there was no end to his talents.

"Ever done this before?" he asked, sipping his champagne.

"With Claude? Are you kidding?"

He contemplated her for a long moment. "Well then, you about ready for your little surprise game?" He got up from his chair and walked to where she sat.

"First," he said, taking the napkin from where it lay on her naked lap, "we've got to add a little suspense." He folded the cloth and tied it as a blindfold over her eyes.

"What are you doin' that for?"

"It's part of the game." He took her by the hand. "All right, stand up and come with me."

"André . . ."

"It's okay, don't worry."

He held her arm and Helene let him lead her out of the room. "Where're we going?"

"Never mind. Just come with me."

She felt her way along, knowing they were crossing the sitting room and heading toward the hall. "This is silly," she giggled.

"Careful, there's a step."

She felt with her toe, knowing they were at the staircase. "We going upstairs?"

André didn't say anything. He led her up the stairs then down the hall. Helene calculated they were at about where Claude's room would be when they stopped.

"Claude's room?"

"Could be."

They went in. Helene rarely was in the room herself, never having been in Claude's bed. Their conjugal encounters were always in her room.

"Now stand still for a minute."

She heard him pulling back the bedding of the big mahogany four-poster.

"André, here? We're going to do it here?"

"You bet. Frankly I've thought about having you in Daddy's bed ever since your wedding."

Helene's heart warmed at his words. He'd been thinking about her for a long time. That was a good sign.

André led her to the bed, then gently pushed her down on her back, and, before she could object, bound her hands and feet to the bedposts.

"Can I take this off?"

"No, not yet. The fun is just about to begin."

He ran his fingers lightly over her stomach, sending a tremor through her. "First, I think we need some more champagne. I'll be right back."

Helene waited, feeling the excitement between her legs building with anticipation. Several minutes later he returned, and Helene heard the rattle of the ice bucket. She heard him removing the foil wrapper on the bottle, then a moment later the loud pop as the cork shot out. André silently poured the wine, the only sound the hissing effervescence of the liquid. Helene took several big gulps, choking a little as the champagne ran down the corners of her mouth. André bent over and lapped away the rivulet with his tongue, pausing to kiss her on the lips.

"Oh, André," she whispered, "you do such wonderful things to me." Then she felt his tongue tracing the rim of her nipples, bringing them quickly to erection. She moaned.

He moved to the edge of the bed and got up.

"Where are you going?"

"I'll be right back."

Helene waited for several minutes, wondering what could be next. When he returned he silently sat on the edge of the bed. She twitched her nose. "What's that I smell. Is something burning?"

"I'm smoking a joint."

"A joint? You mean marijuana?"

"Yeah. Want a drag?"

"I don't smoke."

"Never tried pot?"

"In Monroe, Louisiana?"

"I see what you mean. Here," he said, pressing the thin, rolled cigarette to her lips.

Helene hesitated, then took a drag, choking on the acrid smoke.

"Let's go back to champagne, then," André said and gave her another drink from the glass.

"When do you take the blindfold off?"

"Not until later."

"When?"

"After I get you good and hot."

There was silence, then Helene felt André's fingers running lightly over her skin, from her shoulders to her stomach, to her knees and toes. "Lord, I'll die if you don't fuck me, André."

She felt the joint at her lips and sucked on it again, this time choking less. The fingertips lightly coursed her body. More champagne. Then another drag on the cigarette. More caressing. Helene was really feeling lightheaded and there was a throbbing deep up inside her. When André sucked her breasts she got so excited she thought she might come just like that. "Woo," she cooed, smiling, "the room's starting to spin, and I can't even see it."

"How do you feel?"

"Lord, I feel good. Read good."

He gingerly nibbled at her breast with his teeth. "You taste real good, too."

Then Helene felt his tongue on the inside of her thigh. "Oh, Lordy."

André's lips and tongue moved up her leg and she trembled. "Take off the blindfold so I can see, please, honey."

"Not yet," he mumbled, "not yet."

Helene felt André shifting on the bed, over her, when there suddenly was a loud sound from downstairs—a door slamming. "What was that?" she whispered, lifting her head blindly.

"A door, I think." He listened. "Oh shit! It must be Claude."

"Helene!" came a voice from the foot of the stairs. "Where the hell are you? What are these candles doin' burnin' in the dining room?"

She frantically pulled off the blindfold—but realized there was nowhere to go.

Claude walked down the hall, and she heard him knocking on the door to her room. "Helene? Where are you?" The door down the hall opened, then closed. The footsteps moved closer. Then the door creaked open. Silence.

"What in God's name . . ."

"Well, Daddy, what a pleasant surprise." André's voice was calm, his tone ironic.

"André, what in hell . . ." The rotund old man stared at his son, seated in the elder Latrobe's armchair, a glass of champagne in his hand. Then he turned to the bed. His mouth sagged open.

"Why Daddy, Helene and me was just havin' a little fun. To be honest, we didn't expect you . . ."

Claude looked at Helene, then at André, his eyes round in disbelief. "Have you been fucking my wife? You goddamn sonofabitch!"

"Now calm down, Daddy. We was just havin' a little harmless fun . . ."

"You goddamn fuckin' bastard!" Claude shouted. "Wearin' *my* bathrobe, drinkin' champagne in *my* bedroom, fuckin' *my* wife, in *my* bed!"

"Calm down, Daddy. I'm just samplin' some of your

wares, that's all. Don't forget, you and me's in the middle of a negotiation."

Claude was huffing, his face red, his little eyes round beneath his bifocals. He headed for André with blood in his eye. The younger man stood up abruptly, holding off his father by pushing his hand against Claude's chest. "Take it easy, old man, or I'll set you down on your ass."

Helene watched them fighting and screamed to make them stop. Claude stepped back and glared at his son, his eyes narrowed in hatred. "Get out of my house, you fucking sonofabitch. I never want to see you again."

André smirked and moved past the man toward the door. "All right; it's yours for the time bein'. You won't be seein' me again, if you don't want to. But my attorneys will be in touch. After my birthday, we'll be makin' arrangements to take over control of the bank. You won't be president anymore." He grinned. "See you around, Daddy."

Helene couldn't believe what she was hearing. André couldn't be leaving her. "André," she called, her voice pleading, mournful.

He stopped and looked at her. "Thanks for the hospitality, Mama. It's been great fun. Sorry we couldn't finish the party tonight." He glanced at Claude. "If you think you can get it up, you old fart, you might try going down on her first." He grinned. "She really likes that."

Helene watched the door close. She couldn't believe it. One moment ecstasy with André, now this. He had left her—with Claude. What would he do? Oh God, what would he do? "Claude?"

He barely snorted in response, his breathing heavy.

"Claude?"

Helene heard a zipper opening. "Oh Lord, Claude." She bit her lip, her mind turning frantically. "He tried to rape me, Claude. I'm your wife."

"You're no wife, Helene. You're a goddamn whore."

"No. I did it for you, Claude. He promised me he'd sell you the house if I let him have me. I did it for you."

Claude snorted.

"Don't you hurt me!" she warned. "I'll report you to the police. I swear I will. Both of you."

He removed his pants.

"Claude, I'll divorce you. I swear it."

"I've been payin' for the whorin', Helene, but you may as well see me get my money's worth, now that everybody else's had their turn at the trough."

"What are you going to do to me?" Helene looked down and saw him stroking his stubby penis with his hand.

"I'm goin' to take what's mine, what I paid for, one last time—before I toss you out into the street where you belong."

"Claude, we've got an agreement. It's on paper in the lawyer's office."

"Well, you just go on down to the lawyer's office in the mornin', sign up for a divorce, get your ten thousand, and good riddance. But tonight, I'm gettin' mine."

"You stay away from me, Claude Latrobe!" She looked at his florid face, then at his penis, which was still limp in his hand.

"You bastard..." she seethed, her voice trembling with hatred. Claude climbed onto the bed. "André!" she screamed at the top of her lungs. "You'll pay for this! I'll get you if it's the last thing I ever do!"

MALIBU

May 8, 1985

The Coast Highway was bathed in a layer of light fog as Quintin Wing drove up to Malibu. He found Leslie Randall's house, a tiny place wedged between two larger, million-dollar homes on the beach. Despite its modest proportions, Wing was sure that it was ten times more expensive than most people Leslie's age could afford. He went to the porch and rang the bell.

As he waited, Wing looked back across the road at the hillside where grayish white pockets of fog lay against the slope, obscuring it to the point where its top was nearly invisible. When Leslie didn't respond he began to grow suspicious. He pressed his ear to the door and heard a faint, high-pitched whistle over the noise of the highway. There was also a continuous thumping. His mind began moving quickly over the possibilities, alert for evidence of danger or trouble.

Wing listened again. The high-pitched sound continued, but the thumping had stopped. He moved to the windows but couldn't see through the drapes. Pressing his nose to the glass, he thought he detected the smell of some sort of gas fumes. He tried the doorknob, but found it locked.

135

The space between the adjoining houses was fenced, but on one side Wing found a gate secured by a rusty, light-weight chain and padlock. He shook the gate and could see that the chain was barely holding together. Stepping back, the detective raised his foot and kicked it as hard as he could. The chain snapped and the gate flew open.

Wing moved slowly along the passage, his revolver in his hand. He crept to the back of the house and stepped onto a large open deck overlooking the beach, fifty feet below. Beyond the sand was the Pacific, shrouded in vaporous layers of fog. Over the sound of the surf, Wing heard the high-pitched whistle clearly now, as though the sound were coming through an open window or door.

Cautiously, he peered into the first window and saw the kitchen. The room was empty, but there was a tea kettle on the stove, steaming and whistling violently—the sound he had heard from outside the front door. If Leslie Randall was in the house, she had overlooked the kettle as well as his knocking.

Wing moved further along the deck until he came to an open sliding door. He looked in on a small living room. It was empty, but protruding from a side room were the bare feet of a woman lying on the floor, motionless. The detective carefully tested the sliding door, and finding it unlocked, entered. As he moved toward the body, his ears were alert for the sound of anyone in the house. When he came to the body, Wing quickly straddled the outstretched legs while pointing his gun into the room. He looked down at the woman, his mouth slowly opening in surprise.

The face was angelic, blissful even, as though in wonderful slumber. The beautiful visage held his eyes, even though the body was naked except for a pair of panties. The arms were extended over the woman's head as though they were bound there, but they weren't. Covering her ears was a set of headphones.

It wasn't until Wing's eye slid down to the full softness of the woman's breasts that he saw her chest rise, then fall. She was breathing.

At that very instant her eyes opened and she let out a bloodcurdling scream. Before he could move, she brought her leg sharply up between his, and her foot caught him squarely in the scrotum. He crumpled under the blinding pain, only vaguely aware of her rolling away from his slumping body. There was the fleeting image of thrashing naked limbs, then a flash from nowhere as a heel caught him in the temple. The next thing he felt was the floor as his cheek crashed into it.

Wing felt an envelope of cold wetness on his forehead and a trickle of water running down his temple and into his hair. He opened his eyes and saw the same angelic face he had seen before, but this time it was hovering over him with tawny hair swinging freely at the sides of the face. The lower lip was full, poised somewhere between petulant and sensuous. Leslie Randall smiled.

"You must be Detective Wing."

He groaned and tried to lift his head, aware that he was lying flat on the floor. She was kneeling over him, her torso covered by a tight-fitting tee shirt.

"I'm awfully sorry about hitting you, but you startled me," Leslie explained. "I didn't mean to hurt you—it was just a reflex reaction."

"Goddamn," he mumbled. "Some reflexes."

She moved the wet cloth from his forehead to his cheek. Wing realized then that his entire head was throbbing.

"What were you doing coming into my bedroom with your gun drawn, anyway?"

Wing moaned and tried to get up, but his brain was still swimming. He eased his head back down onto the floor. "I thought you were dead, or hurt, or something."

Leslie laughed. "I was resting after doing my sit-ups. I exercise for twenty minutes every morning."

Wing saw the amusement at the corners of her luscious mouth. "Who do you use for a kicking dummy when I'm not around?"

"Twice a week I practice at a karate studio."

"I'm not surprised."

"Are you all right? Your eyes look a little blurry."

"I think my whole head's out of focus."

"Well, forgive me, but you deserved it. Your badge doesn't give you the right to invade the privacy of a lady's bedroom."

"It was a well-intended mistake." Wing explained the tea kettle, the knocking, the fumes, the feet extending into the hallway."

"Well, you scared the shit out of me."

Wing grinned. "Yeah, and you nearly ended the Wing dynasty right on the spot."

Leslie looked down at his crotch. "Sorry. Are you all right?"

"I'll live." He sat up, the room pitching and rolling under him. Seeing his service revolver on the floor, Wing picked it up and holstered it. "Sorry about the gun, but I wasn't sure if your assailant was still in the house. We're trained to be cautious."

"They ought to train you to be careful where you put your legs."

"Yeah, I won't take any corpses for granted in the future." Wing was aware of Leslie Randall's large breasts as she knelt beside him. He glanced down at them, seeing her nipples under the thin fabric. She had slipped on a pair of shorts as well, but her legs and feet were bare. When his eyes met hers, he could see sympathy in them.

"I guess it was a series of accidents that led to this," she said apologetically. "I like to listen to loud music while I do my exercises, and my stereo in the bedroom has the headset. The slider was open because I like the ocean air. I forgot about putting the tea kettle on."

"What about the fumes?"

"Fumes?"

"The window by the door, coming from that room. I thought I smelled fumes—kerosene, turpentine, some sort of petroleum product."

"Oh, it must be my oils. I keep them in there."

"Oils?"

"Yes, I'm a painter."

He was looking at her eyes, feeling as though he were peering directly into her soul. Was it the blow to his head or was he seeing something he had never seen before? He stared at her, unable to help himself, and saw the mixture of beauty and bemusement in her wonderful eyes. They were mustard colored, with flecks of burnt sienna and forest green.

He knew he was staring, that's why she was smiling. He couldn't help himself, though. The crack on his head had left him dizzy, or was it her?

"You paint?" he asked, catching the question as it passed through his brain again.

Leslie laughed. "I think you're a little groggy. Would you like something to drink, or would you like to lie down for a few minutes?"

"Oh, I'll be all right." Wing climbed to his feet, Leslie helping him. He looked at her, the room spinning about them, but her pretty face perfectly in focus. He felt weak.

"Are you sure?"

"You really paint?"

She nodded. "I think you should sit down. Come on into the kitchen and we'll have a cup of coffee."

"You *are* Leslie, aren't you?"

She laughed. "Who else would you walk in on nude in this place?"

Wing followed along, reaching out to the wall to steady himself. Leslie still held his arm. He looked down and saw her feet. The nails were painted, the toes long and thin. He loved her feet—already.

She helped him into a chair by the window. The foggy Pacific was fifty yards away, the horizon invisible, the world confined to the room he was in. He turned and looked at the woman who was facing the stove. She seemed real enough to him, though so wondrously beautiful that it made his stomach ache.

"Maybe you should have a doctor look at your head," she said, turning around.

"I think I'm all right," he mumbled in the direction of the vaguely pouting mouth, the wonderful, full breasts.

"You don't look all right."

"Tell you what, I won't sue you if you won't sue."

Leslie smiled. "I don't know . . . the City of Los Angeles has a deeper pocket than I do. I'll have to think about that." She was putting instant coffee in a couple of mugs. "Besides, it was your fault."

Wing sighed. "Yes, I suppose it was."

"Well, Detective Wing," she said, picking up the tea

kettle, "I don't suppose you came here this morning to save me."

Wing remembered, for the first time, the reason he had come to see Leslie Randall. She was suspected of killing Helene Daniels.

BEVERLY HILLS

May 8, 1985

5:20 P.M.

Geoffrey Hammond's shop was just off of Rodeo Drive, where he could rub shoulders with Giorgio, Gucci, Hermes, Ralph Lauren, Van Cleef & Arpels, and Bally without enduring their rents. He sat in his private office in the back of the shop at his Louis XVI black-and-gold-lacquered desk, nursing his late afternoon hangover and surveying his job list for the month. The decorating side of the business had shown a resurgence during April, but sales in the shop were down for the second month in a row. Geoffrey knew the problem was inventory—he needed new things—but he had been traveling too much to do the necessary buying and trading.

The decorator was rubbing his temples, cursing his headache when he heard the bell over the front door to the shop jingle. According to his watch, it was nearly five-thirty. He hoped it wasn't a regular customer because Richard, the shop boy, would be wanting to go home in a few minutes, and a regular would expect personal attention from Geoffrey. Why did he have to choose a business where he had to kiss people's asses and smile when he'd rather be home in bed with the comforter pulled up over his ears?

Geoffrey sighed. Maybe whoever had come in was just a tourist who had wandered off Rodeo by accident.

"Excuse me, Mr. Hammond. There's a gentleman to see you."

Geoffrey looked up at his clerk, a thin young man with a trim mustache and soft blue eyes. Even though his lisp sometimes annoyed Geoffrey, the decorator tolerated him because Richard knew antiques and was willing to work for a pauper's salary, which was all Geoffrey was willing to pay. "Who, Richard, who?"

"I don't know, Mr. Hammond, I didn't ask his name."

Geoffrey scowled.

Richard stepped to his employer's desk and whispered. "He's oriental, if that helps."

The decorator's eyes widened. "About thirty-four, thirty-five, tall?"

"Yes."

"Shit."

Richard looked dismayed. "Shall I tell him you're not in, Mr. Hammond?"

"Yeah, tell him you haven't seen me since yesterday after lunch when I rushed back, packed a bag, and caught a plane for South America."

The clerk started to turn away.

"No, you silly ass, I was just joking."

Richard looked perplexed.

"Never mind, I'll go out. You close up and go home." Geoffrey got up from his chair and led the way back into the shop.

Quintin Wing was studying some porcelain in a Chippendale curio cabinet when Geoffrey entered. The detective turned and looked at him, smiling as the decorator approached.

"Well, Detective Wing, doing a little early Christmas shopping?"

"Hello, Mr. Hammond. Hope you don't mind me dropping in on you."

"Of course not; I've told every other cop who's been in

today that I wouldn't buy tickets to the Policemen's Ball from anyone but you."

Wing grinned. "Protection's a nasty business, isn't it?"

"Cheap insurance when your balls are on the griddle," he said dryly. Geoffrey's expression changed as he examined the detective's face. "Ouch! Nasty-looking eye you have there, Inspector. Did you run into the proverbial door, or did somebody take exception to your subtle methods?"

"The latter."

"Thank God there are fellows like you out there protecting those of us in the taxpaying minority."

"Yes."

Geoffrey could see it was not a subject to be pursued. "What can I do for you?"

"I was admiring your Chinese porcelain. How much for the tureen and platters?"

"For you, a special price."

"You mean you'll only charge me the nineteenth-century reproduction price?"

Geoffrey's eyebrows rose. "You don't believe they're original?"

"I'd think anything late Ming of this quality would be in a museum, or at least in a wired case. You're talking tens of thousands of dollars."

"Mmm. Very impressive, Inspector. Where were you when I had that burglary three years ago?"

"Already working homicide. Why? Didn't the detective on the case have any bedside manner?"

"Let me put it his way, I'm surprised he didn't piss in the eighteenth-century chamber pot I had in the shop at the time."

"Well, I don't mean to defend mediocrity, but there are two ways to look at something like that. In whose interest would it really be to have a detective knowledgeable about antiques, yours or your insurance carrier's?"

"You have a point." Geoffrey looked Wing up and down. "Well, what'll it be—the porcelain, or do you want to talk?"

"May is a little early for Christmas shopping."

"I was afraid of that. Okay, come on back."

Wing noticed the tremor in Geoffrey's hands as he

folded them on the desk. He sensed the decorator was not in the mood for more small talk. Their eyes met.

"Helene Daniels?" Geoffrey pronounced glumly.

"Yes."

"What do you want to know?"

"The background of your relationship, I suppose."

"It's not enough to know that I hated her—you have to know why, too?"

Wing shrugged. "It's my job."

Geoffrey's fingers fluttered nervously before he leaned back and dropped them out of sight onto his lap. "Where do you want me to begin?"

"When you met."

The decorator lifted his chin and looked past Wing, gathering his thoughts, turning his mind back in time. "It was in Dallas," he said evenly. "Twelve years or so ago. Nineteen seventy-two, I believe."

"Dallas? You lived in Dallas then?"

"No, I was already out here in California, but I had gone back to take care of my sister's affairs. I'm a Texan originally, you know."

"No, I didn't know."

"Yep, born and bred."

"What happened to the accent?"

"Let's say it doesn't serve what I'm doing these days."

"I see."

"As a matter of fact, when Helene and I were still friendly, we used to lapse into the patois of our origins occasionally. We were kind of a pair, actually. Lots of polish on the surface—glamour, maybe—but there was dust from the chicken yard between our toes. If there was a difference between us, it may have been that she was less willing to admit it." Geoffrey laughed. "In other words, I had pretensions. Helene was a phony."

"So how did you meet?"

"Through—or I guess because of—my sister, Rina. After Helene left Louisiana, she went to Dallas and managed to hook up with Rina. It was because of Helene Daniels that my sister has spent a dozen years in a mental institution. The irony is that I didn't find out until years later that the bitch was essentially the cause."

"What do you mean?"

"Rina was virtually catatonic for nine years before she started coming out of it. When I visited her about three years ago, she managed to relate to me the gist of what happened with Helene. Much of it's still hazy, but there was enough to make Helene's involvement and responsibility clear."

"How did they meet?"

"Soon after Helene arrived in Dallas, Rina ran into her at a modeling agency. Rina owned a chain of dress shops—rather exclusive boutiques, actually. She was a very successful businesswoman. Unlike me, she had our father's backing and support—you see I was disowned by the old man. He didn't approve of my life-style, so Rina became his only child. He adored her—at least until Helene came along.

"Anyway, my sister apparently took a liking to her and sort of took her under her wing, helped her get on her feet."

"She gave her a job?"

"Eventually, but at first Helene was more like a house-guest. She stayed with Rina in her penthouse in Dallas. Rina sent her in for beauty treatments, turned her into a blonde, introduced her to tasteful, sophisticated fashion. Through Rina, Helene got a glimpse of the high fashion business and the people in it. Rina was good to the bitch—that was her mistake."

"What kind of a relationship did they have?"

"I wasn't there, but I have no doubt Helene was using her from the very beginning. My sister had class, Detective Wing. Helene was always drawn to classy people, classy things, and she emulated those she was attracted to, but only with partial success. She never got past being a phony. The bitch had no trouble taking from people. She could bleed a person dry, then kick them for running out of blood."

Wing watched him closely, Geoffrey's hatred evident. "You haven't mentioned Jed Daniels. Isn't that about the time Helene met him?"

Geoffrey turned scarlet before the detective's eyes. "Yes."

"How did he fit in?"

"It . . . it was his money that made Helene queen."

The detective stared at Geoffrey for a long time, watching him struggle to keep his composure. "I'd be very interested to know about Helene's life during the years she was in Dallas," Wing said. "What can you tell me?"

DALLAS, TEXAS
1972

September 30

Helene Latrobe tossed her bra on Rina's bed and stepped out of her panties, which she flipped onto the quilted spread. She peered out across the terrace at the hazy skyline of downtown Dallas in the distance. The warm sun was beating down, and she knew it would be hot out on the terrace, but it would feel good on her naked flesh. One of the things she had liked best about Rina's penthouse was that she could lounge around practically nude without a care in the world.

It had been over a year since Helene had been there, but she had never given back her key, and Rina had never asked for it—a symbolic gesture on both their parts. Helene smiled to herself. She knew Rina would be pleased to come home and find her there.

She considered whether she ought to put on a suit rather than sunbathe nude, as she had in her early days in Dallas, while waiting for Rina to come home from the office. Going through Rina's dresser looking for a bikini, she found a leather-bound album. Curious, she opened it, and was surprised to see page after page of photographs of women, all either nude or in some degree of undress. With each photo there was a name and a date. She realized she had found a chronicle of Rina Chandler's sex life.

Helene's mind spun back to the days she had spent with Rina—trying to recall if there had ever been a camera and wondering whether she would encounter herself on the pages. Toward the end she came to two pictures of a flat-chested girl named Beth, whom she recognized to be a model she had seen around some of the fashion shows. The date was December 1969, eight months before Helene had arrived in Dallas.

Flipping over the final pages, she found a number of loose photographs. To her horror she discovered a picture of herself—her hair mousy brown, her makeup overdone. She was nude astride a straight-backed chair, her legs spread in a most unladylike fashion. She was holding a thinly rolled joint in one hand, a bottle of bourbon in the other.

As Helene stared at the photo, the occasion came back to her, although she didn't remember Rina taking any pictures. Looking down at her dowdy image, Helene felt humiliation and resentment. She didn't like the thought of being part of Rina's collection—or anyone else's, for that matter.

Among the other loose photos were some of Rina in the naked embrace of another woman. On an impulse, Helene took a number of the cruder pictures of Rina, along with the photo of herself, and put them in her purse. Then she put everything back together and returned the album to the drawer.

Out on the terrace, Helene spread a towel on the lounge chair and, settling down on it, stretched her long legs and basked in the caress of the sun. She thought about the photos, and while she resented Rina she also felt vaguely aroused. Then she remembered the fight they had had at the office that morning and her reason for coming to the penthouse to make amends.

"Helene, what's the matter with you?" Rina Chandler had worn the disapproving look of an irate mother. "Is it me? The work? The time of the month? What's wrong?"

Helene crossed her legs, trying not to be intimidated.

"Just because I'm only Executive Vice President, I don't see why I can't have a few ideas of my own."

Rina straightened her long slender frame slightly and fingered her pearls. "*Only* Executive Vice President, Helene? Barely two years off a bus from some swamp in Louisiana and you're complaining because you're *only* Executive Vice President? Most girls in your shoes would still be behind the lingerie counter."

Helene sat in stony silence, bouncing her leg.

Finally, Rina gave a little shrug. "All right, let's forget all that, sorry I brought it up. What I'm having trouble understanding is why you think it's so goddamn important that we expand."

"It's important because we have an opportunity to grab the market by the throat. With Fortney's on the ropes, Texas is wide open now. I was hoping we'd beat everybody else to the punch—lead, instead of follow."

"So that's what you think of Rina's of Dallas—that we got to the top of the heap by following everybody else?"

"I didn't say that, Rina."

She stared at Helene, liking the swell of her breasts under the baby blue Missoni she wore and the flattering look of her blond hair that was more her doing than God's. At times, Rina marveled at what a wondrous and awful creature she had created. She had come from nowhere in Louisiana to Dallas with a head for business and a hunger for power and money. Rina was impressed by how quickly she'd developed. "You know I didn't mean to be unkind. You're where you are in this firm because you're good, and you know it."

"I'm sorry, too," Helene said.

She remembered again the early days she had passed at the penthouse waiting for Rina to come home, waiting for the next lesson on sophistication. Helene had learned her lesson well, and now she too was sophisticated, and just as smart as Rina—maybe smarter. The difference was she didn't have a daddy with millions of oil dollars in the ground. Rina's pa had found oil under his West Texas chicken farm ten years ago, whereas her daddy was sitting on nothing but red Louisiana clay.

But that little trick of fate wouldn't stop her. Brains and

guile had got her what she wanted before, and they would again. It was time now, at twenty-seven, to find a man with money who was good in bed and would treat her right.

Helene luxuriated in the early autumn sunshine. She knew what would happen to Rina when she came home and found her like that. Despite everything, Helene couldn't help smiling.

Jed Daniels stepped out of Rina Chandler's Mercedes as the doorman held the car door for him. Rina got out from the driver's side and walked around to join him.

"Eddie, I just have to run upstairs for a few minutes, so I won't bother to put the car in the garage. I left the keys in the ignition, so you can move it if necessary."

"Yes, ma'am, Miss Chandler."

Rina brushed on ahead of Jed and he followed her into the building, noting the woman's femininity, but not trusting it.

"I do apologize for appearing so disorganized, Mr. Daniels, but had I known you wanted to go to the Pyramid Restaurant this evening, I'd have changed before picking you up." Rina pushed the button on the elevator.

"I'm sorry my secretary didn't make things clear. You're sure you don't mind me coming up?"

"Heavens, no—if you don't mind having a drink alone while I change. I would have driven you directly to the Fairmont, but it would have meant coming all the way back here."

"No problem. I'm sorry for the imposition."

The elevator came and they went up to Rina's penthouse.

"If you don't mind," she said, opening the door, "I'll call my associate, Helene Latrobe, and see if she'd care to meet us for dinner this evening. You haven't met Helene —she's joined my executive staff since your last visit to Dallas—but I'm sure you'll find her full of wonderful ideas." They stepped into the living room. "Every organization needs new blood from time to time, Mr. Daniels, don't you agree?"

"Yes. That's why I'm interested in bringing Rina's of Dallas into my family of companies."

She smiled at him, but without warmth. "You're a persistent man, Mr. Daniels."

"Only when the prize is worthy."

Rina showed him the bar. "You'll find just about everything that's legal in there."

"Scotch is all I need."

"There's Glenlivet, Johnnie Walker Black, and several others, and the ice is underneath the counter."

"Don't need ice, Miss Chandler. I drink my Scotch straight."

"Oh?"

"A habit I picked up in Korea twenty years ago. I was assigned to a British unit for a while. The Limeys drank their whiskey warm and straight, and so did I. Still do."

Rina smiled again. "Well, I certainly do have warm Scotch, so help yourself."

While Jed Daniels made himself comfortable, Rina went to change. She looked out at the terrace that wrapped around to her bedroom, and spotted Helene.

"Jesus Christ, Helene, what are you doing out here?" Rina was standing in her slip.

"I just came by for a little sun."

"Well, get in here. I've got a guest with me. A man! He's in the living room."

Hearing the anger in Rina's voice, Helene rose and joined her in her room.

"What are you doing bringing a man here, anyway?" she asked.

"We just stopped by so I can change. He wants to go to the Pyramid Room, and I'm not about to waltz in there in just any old rag. Damned Californians are as bad about haute cuisine as easterners."

"Who is he?"

"Jed Daniels, the guy from L.A. with all the department store chains. I told you about him."

"What does he want?"

"He always comes to see me when he's in Dallas—been talking about buying me out for years. He's probably heard about the expansion plans you've been pushing."

"Nothing's been said publicly, Rina. Besides, you've scratched it."

"These boys know everything." She glanced down at Helene's body for the first time and smiled warmly. "It's been a long time since you've come by."

Helene shrugged. "I felt badly about this morning at the office." She gave a coquettish grin. "I thought I'd make amends."

"I intended for you to join us for dinner. I called your place, but got no answer. You can imagine my surprise when I looked out and there you were."

"You wanted *me* to join you for dinner?"

"Don't worry, precious, Mr. Daniels won't be in Dallas long enough to get into your pants. Besides, I like your company—you know that." And the look in her eyes as she again glanced over Helene's body was one of deep hunger.

Helene smiled, eager for the night ahead.

Rina had been doing most of the talking, but Helene paid little attention to her. She had been eyeing Jed Daniels almost, but not quite, as much as he had been eyeing her. She watched the shadows from the single candle play on his face, the corner of his mouth bend in a way she found provocative, interesting. His expression didn't exactly say he wanted her, but it betrayed something intimate and it intrigued her.

"What do you think about the Gatsby look, Helene?" Jed asked, interrupting Rina's monologue.

"I'm sure the flapper thing's going to be big, and I'm not talking fad."

"There's no need to rush into anything like that, though," Rina said defensively. "If it turns out that way, we'll just do it better."

Helene didn't look at her, nor did Jed Daniels.

"We'd be smarter to wait until a few more of the girls on the street have bobbed their hair before we go and jump on it," Rina continued. "Wait for the designers, the right designers, to get excited."

"What would you do with the look, Helene?" Jed asked.

She twitched her eyebrows provocatively. "I'd milk it for all it's worth."

"But Rina's of Dallas has always been more conservative," he said, prodding her. "You're talking a different marketing approach entirely." He turned to Rina, whose expression was now grim. "Or are the rumors I hear about expansion plans and a move toward the mass market accurate?"

"They're rumors."

Jed shifted his body on the banquette, turning his attention fully to Rina. Helene watched as his prematurely gray head rested casually against his hand and his gold watch sparkled in the candlelight. The suede wall behind him accentuated his strong masculinity.

"Is it such a bad idea?" His voice was gentle, soothing.

Rina tried to remain calm, but Helene could see the man was affecting her. She knew it was his masculinity as much as his question that had gotten to Rina, but Jed couldn't know that.

"It may not be a bad idea for others, Mr. Daniels," Rina managed, "but Rina's of Dallas has its course well planned."

"And you've obviously been very successful with it. But you're in the enviable position of having a desirable business—one desirable to larger firms like my own."

Rina smiled. "It's also desirable to its founder, Mr. Daniels. I like what I have."

"Most entrepreneurs reach a point where they're ready for the harvesting."

The words sounded good to Helene, but Jed Daniels sounded even better. She would never have guessed it could happen so quickly, but after a scant fifteen minutes in the man's presence she knew he was the one.

She studied the contours of his middle-aged face and the leanness of his body. He probably wasn't an André Latrobe in bed, but he'd sure as hell be more than Claude. And he wasn't wearing a wedding band.

Rina had grown uncomfortable in the silence that suddenly hung over them. She scooted toward Helene. "Could I just slip out? I'd like to go to the powder room."

When Rina was gone, Helene found Jed staring at her again. There was desire in his eyes, but there was something more—a trace of whimsy. She looked at him as hard and long as he looked at her.

"Tell me, Mr. Daniels, does your wife mind you running around the country trying to form partnerships with businesswomen?"

Irony touched his lips. "My wife's been dead for several years, Helene. But when Irene was alive she was very tolerant of my business activities."

An involuntary half smile moved over Helene's mouth. "I *am* sorry about your wife," she replied with a languorous Louisiana drawl. "I truly am." Her eyes were gleaming.

He watched her. "Tell me about yourself, Helene. How'd you get hooked up with Rina Chandler?"

"That, Mr. Daniels, is a long story."

"Too long to talk about over, say, lunch tomorrow?"

"Why, Mr. Daniels, that's not an improper proposal you just made, is it? Considering my employer has just left the table, I mean."

"It just might be."

Helene threw back her head and laughed. "Don't tell me all you Californians think us southern girls are just too naive to see what you're up to."

He smiled wryly. "I don't think you're naive at all. It's just that . . . well, I know a little more about you than you're aware. And to be frank, it makes you rather fascinating."

"Something about me? Well now, aren't you being coy. I suppose to find out just what y'all are talkin' about, I'll have to agree to have lunch with you tomorrow."

"Miss Latrobe, I like your subtlety."

October 1

Helene Latrobe walked back and forth across the sitting room of Jed Daniel's suite in a twelve-hundred-dollar red-and-black Nina Ricci silk dress, her drink in hand, her heart pounding nervously in her chest. Christ, first the surreptitious lunch, now the invitation up to his suite for a drink.

She looked toward the bedroom door, wondering when he'd return. She knew she had to keep a clear head and play it very carefully. The next minutes could be the most important of her life.

All his questions at lunch had been about Rina's of Dallas. They had skirted the bounds of propriety, sometimes coming close to, but never completely, putting her on the spot. Helene had been cautious not to disclose much more than Jed likely knew about the company, but she tried to show a spirit of cooperation—to give him hope.

But she had chafed at the direction of their conversation, knowing that Rina's of Dallas was a secondary consideration. What she cared about was him. From the moment she'd laid eyes on Jed Daniels, she realized he was her ticket to paradise.

A moment later the bedroom door opened and Jed reappeared, having removed his suit coat. He looked calm, sophisticated and, as he walked toward her, very much at ease with his wealth. Helene knew with all her heart that she wanted him, and that nothing—not Rina's of Dallas, not even Rina—would get in the way.

"I'm relieved to see you didn't change into your pajamas, Mr. Daniels."

He laughed. "I wouldn't dare—not as long as you insist on calling me Mr. Daniels."

He took her by the arm and led her to the couch where they sat side by side. With his arm resting on the back of the chair, he lightly brushed her cheek with his finger. "You aren't afraid of me, are you, Helene?"

"A wise girl is always afraid of the unknown, Mr. Daniels, and you are a part of the great unknown."

"Call me Jed, please. And, tell me—what do you think I'm up to?"

"I'd say you want me to help you get control of Rina's of Dallas."

"What do you think of that idea?"

"I think it would be in the interest of everybody concerned, including Rina."

"And that's good, don't you agree?"

"I'm a loyal person, Jed." She looked at him, teasing him with her smile.

His finger lightly brushed the silk sleeve of her dress. "Remember last evening when I said I knew something secret about you?"

"Yes. You were to tell me today at lunch, but you didn't."

"It's not so much what I know as what I saw."

"Oh?" Helene had a sense of foreboding.

"Yesterday afternoon I went to Rina's place with her while she changed . . ."

"Yes . . ."

"And while I was looking out the window over the terrace, I happened to see a very lovely sight—something very moving, very arousing."

Helene looked away, wondering what to say, feeling exposed and curiously aroused by Jed Daniels's words. She turned back to him. "Why are you telling me this?"

"I don't know. I suppose I had to see how you'd react."

"What does seeing me naked have to do with Rina's of Dallas?"

"It has to do with us."

"Us?"

"Yes, us."

She waited.

"I feel a rapport, a certain identity with you, Helene. We see things the same way."

"Is that what we're really talking about, then — business?"

"I'm talking about us. Because of who we are, that includes business."

Helene knew the time had come to make her move. "What is it that you really want of me, Jed?"

"Precisely what you said earlier. I want you to help me get Rina's of Dallas and I want you to help me run it."

"That sounds like a business proposal."

"I want you to help me run it from Los Angeles. Rina, or someone else, can do what's necessary here."

She contemplated him, her brain working, knowing she was dealing with both his mind and his cock. She had to be careful — this wasn't just a job they were discussing, though he could hardly know what she was thinking. "I'll talk to Rina," she said after several moments. "I'll see if I can convince her, but I can't promise you more."

He moved closer to her, his breath caressing her cheek. "You bring Rina's of Dallas into the Daniels group, Helene, and your future will be secure."

October 16

Helene stood at the door to Rina's office as a middle-aged man with longish hair and great dark circles under his eyes came walking out. He hardly gave her a glance as she went in the door he'd left open.

"Who was that?" she asked a beaming Rina Chandler.

"Hot damn!" Rina exclaimed. "That, my dear, was Sam Fortney."

"Of Fortney's?"

"The same."

"What was he doing here?"

"It seems our friend Jed Daniels has made an offer to buy out Sam."

Helene's heart stopped. "And . . . ?"

"And it was such a piss-poor offer, Sam came over to see if I was willing to better it."

Helene dropped into the chair across the Rina. "What did you tell him?"

"That I just might be willing to make an offer. But I asked him for a couple of days."

"Are you serious?"

Rina smiled. "As a matter of fact, I am. According to

Sam, Jed Daniels's offer was for not much more than the value of inventory, which is mighty low—even considering the condition Fortney's is in. Hell, the equity in Sam's leases is worth a bunch, never mind goodwill."

"What are you saying, Rina?"

"I'm saying that I've been giving your idea about expanding some thought. If I could do it cheap, in one fell swoop, I might just be willing."

Helene's heart leaped, but her mind began spinning. What had suddenly turned Rina around? The competition with Jed Daniels? And what was he up to? Was he double-crossing her? Jed hadn't said a word about Fortney's, and they had talked twice on the phone since he left Dallas.

"Ol' Sam might just be using you for leverage in his negotiation with Daniels, Rina."

"That's possible, but what if I turn the tables on him and pluck the ripe fruit before he has a chance?"

"That'll take money. How're you going to compete with Jed Daniels?"

"Since my financing comes from my daddy, Daniels has no idea how much capital I can put my hands on. That's the advantage, Helene, of not having to deal with bankers."

Helene sensed her deal with Jed was slipping through her fingers. She'd spent the past few weeks talking up her expansion ideas with Rina, trying to convince her the best way was by bringing in Jed as a partner and using his money. Now everything seemed turned on its head.

"Maybe cutting Daniels out of the Fortney deal will improve your bargaining position with him," Helene volunteered, watching her.

"It'll make him hotter for Rina's of Dallas, that's for sure. Shit, we'd be the major independent in the state." She beamed at Helene.

Helene watched Rina in her glee, feeling helpless. Before she could speak, her secretary stuck her head in the door.

"Excuse me, Helene, there's a long-distance call for you."

"Who is it?"

"I don't know. Someone in Los Angeles."

"I'd better take that." She stepped out and down the hall into her office.

"Hello, Helene. Jed Daniels."

"Well hello, Jed. I was just thinkin' about y'all. How're you doin'?"

"Fine, fine. Thanks. Listen, I'm leaving shortly for Miami, but I've arranged to stop in Dallas. I've only a short layover between flights. Would you mind meeting me at the airport this afternoon?"

A few hours later, Helene sat in the VIP lounge at the airport asking herself if Jed Daniels had intended all along to use her as a spy, then, once her usefulness was over, toss her out like an old wife. She reviewed her conversations with him, trying to remember everything he had told her about his plans, trying to recall if there was something she might use against him if it became necessary.

One thing was clear—she'd never have Jed Daniels unless she managed to deliver Rina's of Dallas. It wasn't enough to be desirable; to snare him she'd have to become an indispensable partner. Then, with luck, she'd convert that relationship into marriage. And what a coup that would be, considering she didn't have anything to her name but her clothes, a few pieces of jewelry, her car, and a couple of thousand in the bank.

Helene knew it'd take every ounce of her skill and energy to carry it off—and she didn't have a friend in the world who'd help. Everything she'd ever gotten had carried a price tag, but someday very soon things'd be different—she'd have money and power, and people'd be beholden to her.

But her immediate problem was Rina and her interest in acquiring Fortney's. Logic and sweet talk had gotten Helene nowhere. It was the ready money of Rina's daddy that was screwing everything up. As long as she had that, Jed's offer was meaningless. The solution, it seemed, was to find a way to break old man Hammond's trust. Turn him against Rina—that was the only way.

"Is that determination I see on your face?"

Helene looked up. "Oh, Jed!" She got to her feet. "I must have been daydreaming."

He took her hands and kissed her cheek. Helene looked

at him and liked what she saw. How refreshing it was to think wealth wasn't necessarily tied to an oversized gut and bad breath. Helene gave him her most charming smile.

"It's good to see you," he said.

"It's good to see you, too."

"I don't have a lot of time, Helene, so I want to bring you up to date on what's happening. You know I've made Sam Fortney an offer to buy his chain?"

Helene nodded, watchful.

"I figured he'd talk to Rina. She'd be the only one who could do much with Sam's operation just now. More so than me, probably." He seemed to look inside of her. "How'd Rina react?"

Helene swallowed hard, knowing the seemingly innocent question, if answered accurately, could make her a traitor. "She's considering it."

"Good."

Helene looked at him with surprise.

"My best chance is if she gets in over her head," he explained.

"It could take years."

"I regard it as insurance. The worst that could happen is that when I finally get Rina's of Dallas, it's a bigger company than it is now."

You may be able to wait, her mind screamed, *but I can't!* "Why are you telling me all this, Jed?"

He studied her. "I know you, Helene. I think we can be mutually helpful."

"Meaning?"

"Meaning I know you left Monroe under less than auspicious circumstances. Meaning I know you're a very clever woman, and you're a fighter. I like that."

Though she was nervous, Helene knew that her future was on the line, and that she couldn't waver. She stared Jed Daniels in the eye. "If we're to have any kind of future," she said coolly, "I'd better deliver Rina's of Dallas to you on a silver platter. Isn't that right, Jed?"

He smiled. "I like your style, Helene."

"I'm going to deliver it—and naturally, I expect to be a part of the new and bigger company."

"I wouldn't be here if that weren't the case." He paused, then said, "Do you have a plan?"

"Rina's got lots of money behind her, that's our biggest problem."

"Yes, I know. Any way around that?"

"I've been thinking about it, and I do believe I've got a solution."

"Can I help?"

"No. This is something I'll have to do on my own. But do be ready to stand up with your money when Rina needs funds and her daddy's not there."

"You apparently know something that I don't."

"Rina didn't get a commitment from her father before she entered negotiations with Sam Fortney. She'd be mighty vulnerable if the old man refused to go along."

"Why wouldn't he?"

Helene smiled coyly. "Let's just say I know something about Rina he doesn't, and if he found out at the wrong moment she'd be . . . up shit's creek, if you'll pardon my French."

"Interesting."

"Rina's marriage to Elmont Chandler gave her credibility with her father that her brother Geoffrey never had. That's why Rina's here with her daddy's money and Geoffrey's in California without it."

"I'm not sure I understand."

"Of course you don't, Jed darlin'. If you did, you might not need me."

Jed grinned. "I think it best I leave matters in your capable hands."

Helene patted his cheek. "You're a wise man."

He glanced at his watch. "I'm afraid I've got to get to the gate. I'll call you in a couple of days."

They both stood. Jed reached into his pocket and pulled out a little package wrapped in silver paper with gold ribbon. "In the meantime, this is a little token for you."

Helene carefully removed the paper from the narrow box. Opening it, she found an eighteen-carat gold-and-diamond Piaget watch. "Jed!" She looked up at his beaming face. "This is no token."

"I'm a wealthy man, Helene. Most everything is a token."

Helene looked into his eyes, exuding every ounce of sex appeal at her disposal. She hadn't remembered feeling so good about a man since she'd first met André Latrobe.

Jed wrapped his arms around her, and Helene sank against him. As he kissed her, Helene's mind turned to the future. Looming ahead was the first hurdle—perhaps the most difficult of all.

A little smile touched Helene's lips as she envisioned the demise of Rina Chandler. In a way it was too bad. But it was, after all, just business.

November 3

Helene stared into the fire, sensing that the evening was going to be the most pivotal of her life. In the dining area behind her, candles cast a mellow glow into the corners not touched by the firelight. The Dom Pérignon was in the ice bucket beside her chair. Asters and chrysanthemums spilled over the Waterford bowl in the middle of the table.

She wore nothing but a filmy caftan, translucent enough to reveal the silhouette of her naked body underneath.

Though the room was warm, she felt a chill run over her skin, and every hair on her body seemed on end. She was nervous and she prayed God she would handle this right.

The doorbell rang and Helene, taking a deep breath, went to the door. Rina Chandler stepped into the candlelit condominium, glancing at the fire and the table set for two. She slowly turned to face Helene.

"Is it safe to assume I'm the only guest?"

"I didn't say there'd be anyone else, did I?"

"When you said there'd be a party to celebrate the acquisition of Fortney's, I just assumed there'd be others." Her eyebrows twitched provocatively.

"Are you disappointed?"

"Hardly."

Throughout dinner, Helene kept the conversation casual and light. After dessert, Rina sipped her champagne, sat back, and smiled. "You know, you'd make somebody a wonderful wife."

"I thought you didn't approve of men, Rina."

"I don't, sweetie, but I'm a realist."

Helene sipped her champagne and gave a half-smile.

"Why did you have this little dinner party—*really?*"

"Because I wanted to do something nice for you. It was a big day, signing your agreement with Sam and all."

Rina nodded. "It was a big step for the company, but a good one, I'm sure of it." She reached over and touched Helene's hand affectionately. "I really have you to thank for it. I didn't see the opportunity, but your talk about expansion opened my eyes. If it weren't for you, I'd probably have pitched Sam out on his ass the first time he came by."

"Rina, I've been thinking. You really ought to sell a half interest in the company to Jed Daniels."

"Sell? Whatever for?"

"Fortney's will be a lot to digest. We could use some high-powered management help and all that capital behind us."

"Helene, I've got all the capital I need. I just pick up the phone and call my father."

"What if he says no?"

"Why should he? I've never let him down."

Helene looked at her, hating the bitch. "Anything's possible, Rina. And you're a fool to count on your father. There's no telling when rumors might get back to him. Your enemies could always use that against you. Now you've got a hell of a package to offer an outside investor. It'd be a perfect time to sell."

Rina was staring at Helene. "If I didn't know better, I'd say Jed Daniels put you up to this."

"I've spoken with him, yes."

"Jesus Christ."

"Your interests have always been in mind."

Rina scoffed. "What kind of a deal have you made with him?"

"I haven't made any deal."

"Then why are you pushin' for me to sell?"

"I'm not pushin', I'm advising. I'd hoped you'd see the light."

"Listen, you little bitch, I don't know what you have in mind, but forget it, just forget it!"

Helene's eyes went hard. "Tomorrow you'll call Jed Daniels and tell him you'll sell a half interest in the company."

"You're out of your fucking mind."

Helene bent her lips into a cold smile. "You'll do it, because if you don't, your daddy'll find out all about the life you lead."

Rina blinked. "He'll never believe you. Not in a million years."

"Maybe not me, but he'll believe pictures. What is it they say, Rina? A picture is worth a thousand words."

"What are you talkin' about?"

"Your photo diary—the one you keep in the bottom drawer of your dresser, under your nighties."

"You bitch!"

"You go on home and look for the shots of that girl with her mouth all over your tits and see if you can find it."

"You goddamned sneaky bitch!"

"Go ahead and call me names if it makes you feel better, Rina. But tomorrow you're going to sell to Jed Daniels."

Rina stared in disbelief before getting to her feet. "I don't know how, but I'll make you pay for this, Helene Latrobe."

"I'll give you till noon tomorrow to tell me you've called Jed. If I don't hear from you by then, I'll send those pictures to your daddy."

Rina glared at her. "I don't give a goddamn if you do. Nobody's ever going to blackmail me. I'd die before I'd give you and that son of a bitch my business." She went to the closet to get her coat.

"Just remember, Rina, noon tomorrow. Otherwise, you lose everything. You're committed to the Fortney deal now and you need your daddy's money. Jed will pay you a fair price, so if you're smart you'll take it and run."

Rina put on the coat and stood on wobbly legs, looking at Helene. "I hope you rot in hell," she hissed.

BEVERLY HILLS

May 8, 1985

6:10 P.M.

Geoffrey's eyes had become glassy, his neck red. "After Rina left Helene's that night, she hit a telephone pole going ninety miles an hour. She was in a coma for three months. When she finally came out of it, she was virtually catatonic. Rina has been institutionalized ever since, although in the last few years she's begun functioning somewhat again."

"Obviously, you blame Helene Daniels."

"Helene wasn't behind the wheel, and she didn't cut the brake cables, but she might as well have."

"So it was your sister's incapacity that enabled Helene to take over the company?"

"In effect, yes."

"Why didn't your father step in? Or did he?"

"No. The irony was that Helene destroyed Rina's relationship with our father without having to. The morning after their fight, Helene waited for the call from Rina, and when it never came she mailed off the pictures, not having heard about the accident. It wasn't until Jed called her the next day that she found out about it. By then it was too late—not that she really cared.

"Actually, it made it easier for Helene with my father out of the picture. He immediately disowned Rina and wouldn't even go to the hospital to see her. I was appointed conservator, and later I negotiated the sale of half of Rina's of Dallas to Jed Daniels."

"Helene didn't participate in the negotiation?"

"Not directly. Being ignorant of what was going on, I turned to company personnel for advice. Naturally, Helene was front and center to advise me. She told me that Rina had already decided to sell to Jed before the accident. It wasn't until a few years ago when Rina finally became lucid again that I discovered that wasn't true."

"What about Helene and Jed? How did they end up marrying?"

"Helene came to L.A. a few months after the deal was put together. Rina—or her estate under my management —retained a fifty percent interest and Jed owned the rest. Since I know nothing about the clothing business, I delegated all management responsibility to Jed, who in turn put Helene in charge. Working together as they were, Helene got her claws into him, and they were married within six months of her arrival in L.A."

"So, our victim got what she wanted from the beginning."

"And a lot more. For a wedding present, Jed gave her his interest in Rina's of Dallas."

"You mean Helene and you ended up as partners?"

"In effect."

Wing studied Geoffrey, realizing he didn't know how important and damning that piece of information was. "But you and she haven't been friendly for years. How did that happen?"

"Once I learned the truth from Rina, I refused to have anything to do with Helene again. I admit I damned near killed her then. I finally ended up threatening legal action, but Jed intervened. He kept us apart, and I put everything in the hands of the estate's accountants and attorneys. I never spoke to Helene after that—not civilly anyway."

"So, Helene still owned Rina's of Dallas at the time of her death?" Wing watched Geoffrey closely.

"No, this spring she negotiated a sale of the entire company. My advisors recommended I agree to the deal, so I did. The company could never mean anything to Rina again, and I wanted to sever all ties with Helene."

"Why did Helene want to sell?"

"She had a movie deal working and she needed capital."

"I thought Jed provided the capital for her movie ventures."

Geoffrey's hand returned to the snuff box. He spun it nervously on the desk. "By that time, Jed and Helene were finished."

"Were you satisfied with the deal Helene had negotiated for the sale of the company?"

"Frankly, at that point I didn't care much. As long as my advisors were satisfied, it was okay with me."

"What did Jed Daniels think of the sale?"

Geoffrey seemed to grow pale. "How would I know?" He looked at his watch and abruptly got to his feet. "It's getting rather late. Can't we take this up another time?"

Wing rose to his feet as well. "Of course. You've been very generous with your time. I appreciate your help."

They headed toward the front of the shop. As they walked past the case with the porcelain, Geoffrey gestured toward it. "Sure I can't interest you in something, Inspector?"

"Thank you, no, Mr. Hammond."

The decorator turned to him with a mischievous grin. "Don't tell me it's a matter of champagne taste and a beer budget?"

"No. The problem is I've been to Hong Kong and, with all due respect, it's your champagne prices, not my champagne taste that gives me pause."

Geoffrey Hammond laughed. "My dear Detective Wing, this is Rodeo Drive in Beverly Hills! What does value have to do with price?"

Wing smiled. "You're right, of course; nothing truly is as it appears."

MALIBU

May 9, 1985

The air was clear as Wing drove up the coast, the horizon over the Pacific a crisp blue line separating the sea from the pink and orange of the sky. When he stopped in front of Leslie Randall's house, he was amazed to find his heart beating in anticipation. The image of her bent over him, her long hair nearly brushing his face, came to mind. He sighed and got out of the car.

On the door was a note:

> Quintin,
> I'm on the beach running a neighbor's dog. Go out onto the deck so that I'll know when you've arrived.
>
> Leslie

Wing folded the note, put it in his shirt pocket, then walked around the house to the deck. Within a few minutes, she neared the house, wearing nothing but a pair of shorts and a tee shirt.

"You found my note."

"Yes."

"Can I get you a beer?"

"Since this visit is only semiofficial, okay."

They watched the sun dropping toward the horizon, drinking their beers in silence.

"Don't you want to ask me some questions about Helene?" Leslie finally volunteered.

"I suppose I should."

"What do you want to know, Quintin?"

"She was your stepmother. Tell me about your life with her."

"I was twelve when my father married Helene. I was twenty-five when she killed him. Much of the time in between was hell."

"I'm listening."

"At first it was the usual jealousy and resentment, I suppose. I was a daddy's girl, and Helene was not the type who shared. She took every opportunity to drive a wedge between us."

"Did she succeed?"

"Yes and no. Daddy and I always remained close, though because of Helene it almost had to be clandestine. As I grew older, I rebelled against everything. Maybe I was trying to punish my father, I don't know. In any case I nearly screwed up my life."

"How so?"

"When I was seventeen I had an affair with a would-be actor. In retrospect, I imagine he was interested in my family's money as much as in my tender body, but I thought I was in love. We ran off to Mexico and got married, but Daddy promptly had it annulled. He paid off Rick, and I never saw him again.

"I went to college to get away from Helene as much as from anything. I was rather wild, to put it mildly. As graduation approached, I met a young lawyer named Steve Randall. We were married in August."

"It wasn't a successful marriage, I take it."

"No. I married Steve for all the wrong reasons. He had the paper qualifications, everybody approved of him, we were physically attracted to one another. After a few years we got bored, and so we divorced. We both knew all along that it wasn't right."

"So what about Helene?"

"Once I left, I arranged to see her as little as possible. The last five years or so she and my father really led separate lives. They were married in name only."

"Prior to that they had a good marriage?"

"No. I don't think you could ever say that what they had was good. It was a bizarre marriage—one of those symbiotic things that makes sense only at some deep level that nobody understands, not even them. To me it was obvious that Helene married him for his money, and I think Daddy realized that, too. But she had some kind of spell over him. It was as though he knew, but couldn't do anything about it."

"What do you mean?"

"Haven't you ever had a feeling you were totally without willpower, when you felt completely helpless to do anything but what you were doing?"

"Yes, I get the picture."

"Well, that's the kind of effect Helene had on my father. There was a perverseness about their relationship—as though she managed to bring out the worst in him, instead of the best."

"Why didn't he divorce her, particularly at the end when they were leading separate lives?"

"I don't know. Maybe it was easier not to. Helene had substantial wealth of her own by then, but she was so bent on a movie empire that she still needed him."

"And yet you think she killed him."

"I know she killed him."

"The authorities in Acapulco regard his death as accidental."

"They say he fell overboard from their sailboat and drowned, but that's because Helene said that's what happened."

"You obviously don't believe it."

"My father was on board alone with Helene at the time, Quintin. They went out together, and she came back alone. Knowing them both as I do—or did—the bitch murdered him."

Wing watched the emotion building in her. Finally, she

got to her feet and went to the railing, standing motionless and staring out at the rose-colored sky.

He looked at her lithe figure silhouetted against the sunset, both equally magnificent. And yet the mood had been broken. Her anger and bitterness over Helene Daniels had come between them.

"I don't mean to be rude, Quintin, but I've got a date this evening and I should go in and get cleaned up."

The words stabbed his heart. He felt intense jealousy. "Do you mind if I ask another question—this one off the record?"

"Sure."

"Since we seem to have a mutual interest in art, would you go with me to Michael's Saturday night? We can enjoy the paintings and maybe cultivate a mutual interest in good food."

She didn't reply immediately; she just stood motionless, reflecting. Wing couldn't see her features in the darkness, couldn't see her well enough to read her reaction. He could tell, though, that she regarded it as a weighty decision.

He waited, his breathing nearly stopped. Then he saw her head moving slowly in assent. "Okay," she whispered, but it was barely loud enough for him to hear.

LOS ANGELES

May 10, 1985

8:10 A.M.

"Jesus Christ, Wing, where in the fuck have you been?"

The detective glanced at Lieutenant Joseph Murdoch, sitting bullnecked in his shirt sleeves at the table, his tie loosened, the top button of his shirt undone. Wing never understood how the man always managed to look as though he had just suffered a tough day, whether it was morning, noon, or night. He slipped off his own suit coat and hung it meticulously on the back of a chair and sat down opposite him.

"Sorry I'm late. Traffic."

The lieutenant pointed an angry finger at the detective. "I had tickets to the Dodgers–Padres game last night and missed the first four innings sitting around here waiting for you."

Wing sighed and turned to the smallish young man with neatly combed hair and a fresh white shirt sitting at the end of the table. "Morning, Tony."

The younger detective smiled weakly. "Quintin."

"Well, let's get down to business," Murdoch groused. "Did you bother to listen to that goddamned answering machine of yours last night, Wing?"

174

"Yes, sir."

"Then you're aware that the subject of this meeting is the Daniels case we're supposedly working on."

"Yes."

"Good." He glanced at Williams, then back at Wing. "Would you be so kind then as to inform the rest of us what you've been doing so that those of us that gotta talk to the press don't sound like we've got our heads up our asses?"

"I guess that's your polite way of asking me what I've turned up."

Murdoch smirked.

Wing reached back and took a gold Cross pen from the inside pocket of his coat. He began writing as he spoke. "I haven't really expanded the suspect list from what Tony had to start with, though I've managed to raise a few more questions and form some opinions about the people we've got."

"That's a start."

Wing ignored the sarcasm. "I think Felice Fallanti is clean. If she did it, she's the world's best actress. I haven't really talked to her in depth about her relationship with Helene Daniels, but it doesn't make sense to me she'd do her in now."

"She's the one married to the movie director who's in the can in Switzerland?"

"Yeah, Adolfo Fallanti. Felice is a cool customer. First-class lady actually, and she's smart. I think too smart to have killed Helene Daniels."

"Whoever did it wasn't dumb. They did a hell of a job covering their trail."

Williams agreed. "We don't have diddly-shit from the lab."

"Well, I'm keeping an open mind," Wing said.

"Yeah. What else have you got?"

"I've also talked to Daphne Stephens, Keith Moore, Geoffrey Hammond, and Leslie Randall."

"And . . . ?"

"Daphne Stephens is a possible, but I don't have solid feelings about her one way or the other. I talked to her and Keith Moore together the other night."

"He's the actor?"

"Yeah. He was protective of her as hell. A little edgy, hostile."

"But he was on an airplane, wasn't he?" Murdoch asked.

"Yes. We got him placed in London for sure the day before," Williams said.

Wing put a check next to Moore on the pad.

Murdoch watched Wing studying the paper, playing with the pen. "You got a feeling about him?"

Wing shrugged. "I'm wondering if we're overlooking something."

"Like what?"

"I don't know." He looked at Tony. "Did you talk to the people who saw him at the airport in L.A.?"

"No."

"It might be worth talking to them—see if anybody actually spoke with Moore, that sort of thing."

"Think it could have been somebody else on the flight, Quintin?"

"It's a thought. When I saw him the other evening he looked different to me than he does on the screen. I think I'd have recognized him on the street without any trouble, but a look-alike might have fooled me."

"He'd need cooperation for an intentional deception," Murdoch said. "Studio double, maybe?"

"It'd be worth finding out about the possibilities."

"What about the other two, Wing?"

"Hammond, the decorator, is nervous as hell. I don't know if he did it, but something's definitely bothering him. I talked to him night before last and thought he'd wet his pants on me."

"What'd he say?"

"He was pretty forthcoming about his relationship with Helene Daniels. Gave me the financial connection that might have put him in the house the night of the murder."

"You mean the documents might have been of interest to him?"

"It looks that way, but I don't think he appreciated the implications. Of course, he had to know it'd come out eventually and might have decided to lay it on me up front. There's definitely something wrong, though. One of the reasons I'm seeing the Fallanti woman today is to talk about Geoffrey Hammond. They're close friends, and she called me last night wanting to talk to me about him."

Murdoch raised his eyebrows. "Could they be in it together?"

"I've considered combinations, but it just doesn't smell like a group thing. Somebody might know something about one of the others they haven't told me, but I don't think there was a conspiracy. I'm hoping I can get them all to help me with each other. Without physical evidence, it may end up being our best bet."

"Hmm. What about the stepdaughter?"

Wing looked at Joe Murdoch, seeing the coldness in his blue eyes. He suddenly felt fear for Leslie. Taking his pen, he wrote her name.

"She has the same motive as the rest of them, and maybe more of a financial interest because of her father's estate ..."

"But ... ?"

"But I have the same feeling about her as I do about Felice."

"You have the same feeling *where?*"

Wing smirked, seeing for the first time in his life how his reputation might actually be hurtful. "I find her attractive, I'll admit—hell, they're all attractive in this case."

Murdoch shook his head in disgust. "You read the lab report on the house?"

"Just bits and pieces from the preliminary."

"Give him a copy, Williams. Maybe you two can brainstorm for a while." He stood. "There's not much there, but I've always believed that when you've got a report without useful information, what's not there can be as informative as what is." He went to the door and left.

Wing took the report Williams handed him. "Anything new I should know before I dig in?"

"A few dead ends. The partial print off the safe is useless. Ballistics tests have turned up nothing. I've looked into the suspects' connection with weapons. No permits have been issued to anyone except Felice Fallanti."

"Felice?"

"Yes, but it was a twenty-two, and it was reported stolen

from her home two years ago during a burglary. Anyway, the murder weapon was a thirty-eight."

Wing scanned the document before him. "Three shots...?"

"Yes, and Sid Hida in the lab says they were probably fired in quick succession and with reasonable accuracy."

"Our killer was a marksman?"

"Maybe."

"Let's check and see if there's any training in any of their backgrounds."

For the next few minutes Wing read the document and studied a diagram of the position of financial documents found on Helene's desk. It was almost as if she had laid everything out to review her financial situation with an accountant, as though she were making a presentation or trying to document an argument.

"Shit, even the documents only had the victim's prints. Whoever the killer was, he came in without touching a thing—or had the foresight to bring gloves."

Williams said nothing.

Wing stabbed at the report on the table. "Hey, Tony, it says here Sid dusted two glasses in the bar. 'Cocktail glasses containing approximately eight to ten ounces of liquid.'" Wing looked at the diagram of the house as Williams opened his own copy of the lab report.

"Yeah, but only the victim's prints were on them."

"Well, all that means is that she was the only one that touched them. People don't drink from two glasses at the same time, do they?"

"Yeah, I see what you're getting at. To be honest, I never noticed them."

"Fortunately, the lab boys did, but it doesn't say what kind of liquid was in the glasses. I wonder if anybody checked."

"I don't know. I can call Sid, if you like."

"Yeah, do that. The kind of drink she served might tell us something about the guest—possibly even who it was, if the drink was distinctive."

"Yeah, but how do we know the drinks weren't there for several days, from some other occasion?"

"We don't, unless somebody can verify the bar was clean prior to that night."

"The maid, for example?"

"Bingo."

"I'll call Sid now."

Wing leaned back, trying to remember what everybody had been drinking at lunch that day at the Hotel Bel-Air. Geoffrey Hammond had pretty well been into his cups. A recollection of martini glasses came to mind, but he couldn't be sure. With Felice and Daphne he drew a complete blank. Shit. Why didn't he pay attention? If Felice hadn't been playing with his prick, he might have been more alert.

Leslie had a beer with him on her deck—of course, that didn't mean that was all she ever drank. Daphne Stephens and Keith Moore were drinking wine the evening he visited their place, though that wasn't conclusive either. Everyone's drinking habits would have to be verified.

"Sid's going to check, but he's pretty sure no analysis was done," Williams said when he hung up.

"Shit."

"He said he had three men out there and is going to talk to each of them and call me back."

"Good. Why don't you go back out to the house? I want an inventory of the kinds of glasses that are in the bar. Oh, and Tony, tell me whether she kept vermouth in stock."

"Why?"

"Just a hunch."

Williams made another note.

BEVERLY HILLS

May 10, 1985

1:05 P.M.

Wing arrived at Nate 'n Al's on Beverly Drive five minutes late and was surprised to find Felice Fallanti already there and just being seated at a corner table. She looked up as he made his way to the table.

"Quintin!"

"I thought you abhorred punctuality," he said, grinning.

She smiled up at him, her adornments—two-carat canary diamond stud earrings, chunky gold bracelets, and rings—glimmering, alluring, provocative.

"You wore the tie! How sweet." She was looking him over, contemplating him like a piece of sculpture. Her fingers caressed the back of his hand. Then she lapsed into a contemplative mood. Neither of them spoke. They both were thinking.

"Geoffrey's upset," she volunteered at last, pulling her hand back onto her lap.

"What about?"

"You. The investigation."

"He has nothing to worry about . . . if he's innocent."

"I know that. You know that. But Geoffrey doesn't believe it."

"I don't see why."

Felice gave him an impatient look. "Please don't play policeman, Quintin. This is serious. I'm worried about Geoffrey."

"What do you want me to do? Call off the investigation?"

"Can't you say something to reassure him that you're not out to hang him?"

"Is that what he thinks?"

"He's worried."

"I'm not, Felice."

The waitress came, and Wing ordered the matzo brie at Felice's insistence. She had corned beef and a salad.

"What did you say to Geoffrey that upset him so?"

"I didn't say anything. I just asked him a few questions and he talked. He told me about Rina and how he had come to be Helene's partner in the clothing business."

"What a nightmare that was!"

"Yes."

"Maybe reliving all that upset him. Maybe that's all that's bothering him."

"No, Felice, I think there's more. He's holding something back. Some key piece of information. I can't put my finger on it, but there's something." He watched her eyes, trying to look beyond the glamour, the voluptuous femininity.

"Was there anything else that happened between Geoffrey and Helene?" he asked. "Anything that might make him want to kill her?"

"Wasn't what she did to Rina enough?"

"That was a long time ago. Why would he wait until now?"

"Quintin, you know I won't rat on a friend. But I will tell you in all honesty I think Geoffrey's innocent."

He smiled. "You don't want anybody to have done it."

"Not one of my friends. Of course not. Why don't you just blame it on a serial killer and let bygones be bygones?"

"I wish I could."

"Do you?"

Wing wondered what Felice was really up to and if going to bed with him had only been a part of it. "Can you tell me anything about Geoffrey's business dealings, especially his partnership with Helene?"

"Geoffrey is my best friend, but we never talk about business, Quintin. That's the truth."

"Who do I talk to, then?"

"Donald, I suppose. Donald Lawrence was Geoffrey's lover and business partner in the shop. They were together for years."

"What happened?"

"They had a falling out. Late last year."

"Why?"

"I consider that a confidence. I won't tell you."

"Where do I find Lawrence?"

"I believe he's a consultant at Sotheby's now."

"Geoffrey's a martini drinker, isn't he?"

Her eyebrows rose. "What a strange non sequitur. To answer your question, though, Geoffrey is an inveterate martini drinker. Why?"

"I consider that a confidence."

Her face filled with amusement. "Touché."

"What's *your* drink, Felice?"

"Quintin, this conversation is definitely taking on the character of an interrogation. Are we going to let this murder come between us?"

"It may already have, Felice."

They fell into silence. Felice was studying him.

"Things aren't the same between us, Quintin, are they?" He was silent. "It's someone else, isn't it?"

"Yes."

"Is she connected to the case?" Silence. "My God—it's Leslie!"

"I hadn't intended this."

"Don't worry, Quintin, I'm not going to get maudlin. That's too predictable. I've got a better idea. Let's drive down the coast to Laguna and I'll tell you the whole story about me and Helene Daniels. How does that sound?"

He grinned at her. "You know my weaknesses, don't you, Felice?"

BEL AIR
1984

November 17

Jed Daniels climbed the sweeping spiral staircase, drink in hand, his stocking feet sinking into the pale celadon wool carpeting. It was new and had followed the peachy melon that Helene had decided she hated after only three weeks. Surely, no other man in Southern California had lived through three different carpets in the space of just a month. Thank God the downstairs was hardwood—though there had been the threats to change all the orientals as well.

Jed's mind turned—as it had off and on all day—to the sour news on earnings that had come from accounting the previous afternoon. Whenever there was a setback, he was certain he had expanded beyond his ability to control things. When business was good, he had an insatiable desire for more. Life, it seemed, consisted of either eating or shitting.

He paused to listen to the thumping of his heart from the climb up the stairs, then opened the door to Helene's suite. She was in her mirrored bath, stark naked, her hair perfect from a late afternoon visit to the hairdresser. She was applying skin cream to her face as she glanced up at him in the mirror.

Jed sat in Helene's white silk lounge chair that had a matching ottoman. He sipped his Scotch and watched her, vaguely amused by her indifference. Jed casually regarded her body. She was thirty-nine and still exquisite. Her ass and breasts were firm, her thighs thin and toned, her waist trim. Only the tiniest protrusion at her tummy betrayed age. With her sister the queen of fitness and beauty in L.A., Helene wasn't about to let herself slip.

She was examining her face in the mirror and touching the wisps of her carefully blond hair that was loosely swept over and back on the side. Helene stretched her neck taut, running her fingertips along the skin on either side of her throat. Jed drew on his Scotch. "What are you wearing tonight?"

"I bought a dress. A Bill Blass." She began applying concealing cream under her eyes with a makeup sponge.

"Felice Fallanti warrants a new dress?"

"You can be damned sure the bitch will be in something scintillating. I just haven't figured out what."

"Bitch? I thought you considered Felice a friend."

"She is. I happen to be talking about clothes at the moment."

"Then it's war."

"Jed, don't be naive. It's always war."

"When do I get to see your suit of armor?"

"Don't be snide." When she had finished applying foundation she went to the closet and brought out a red silk crepe sheath with a high neck and long sleeves. "What do you think?"

"I'd say two thousand dollars would have been an adequate statement. What did I pay for it, four?"

"*I* paid four thousand. All the money in this house is not yours, Jed."

"What else did you buy for tonight's contest?"

She glanced at him impatiently. "I thought I'd wear the diamond earrings and necklace from Fred's you gave me."

He smiled, knowing no compliment was intended. "Are you sure that's enough ammunition?"

"I wish you'd stop being so cynical. You do the same thing. Just differently."

He knew she was right.

"Felice will spring something on me," she continued. "You can be sure of that."

"Maybe she doesn't care, Helene."

"Felice is married to Adolfo Fallanti. She cares."

"I wonder if Adolfo is pleased with all the attention."

Helene gave herself a little smile in the mirror that Jed understood better than she would have guessed. She was applying eye shadow, first a pearl gray for highlight, then a smudge of smokey gray for contrast.

Jed knew that he fit in somewhere in Helene's plans for the Fallantis; he just wasn't sure quite where. The dinner party definitely had a purpose beyond the shoulder rubbing Helene had been engaged in for the last six months. She had been fairly discreet about her newfound obsession with the film business, and he knew it was a sure sign she was serious. Dead serious.

"I think Adolfo likes me," she announced matter-of-factly.

Her bluntness was somewhat unexpected, but Jed wasn't completely surprised. "Wonderful. I'm pleased for you, Helene."

Hearing the sarcasm, she looked up at him in the mirror, a touch of irritation on her face, but she didn't respond. Instead, she began applying her mascara. "Can I count on your support?"

"What kind of support?"

"If some kind of opportunity arises to do a film with Adolfo."

"You say that like you're expecting something. What about Felice?"

She looked at him over the mascara brush. "I don't believe she approves of me, as a competitor."

"Competitor for Adolfo, or for his talent?"

"Jed, it's important that I know. How much money can I count on if an opportunity arises?"

"That depends on how much I like what I hear."

Jed waited, wondering what she had planned and how willing she was to kiss his ass in order to accomplish it.

When Helene greeted her rival, her heart sank.

Felice had cut her hair since she had last seen her. It was short and swept up in the Beverly Hills version of the new punk style. The raven color of it in the firelight, the large, dark Italian eyes, and high, patrician cheekbones gave an impression both electric and elegant. Felice's beauty touched even Helene. She was weaving a skirt of silver-and-black horizontal lamé stripes and an embroidered black cashmere sweater that Helene's trained eye told her was a Gloria Sachs. Felice had pulled out all the stops.

"You look gorgeous, Felice," she said, brushing the other's cheek with her own, smiling for an instant before turning to Adolfo, who was eyeing the clinging contours of her sheath.

He stepped over and kissed her cheek, his thick hand embracing her skin through the crepe of her sleeve. His sharp, pungent cologne was as unsubtle as he.

"Adolfo, how are you?"

"Me, I am fine, dear Helena," he said in a husky whisper. "But you . . . *bellisima!*" There was a faint tremor of emotion in his voice. The heavy dark-rimmed glasses and curly salt-and-pepper hair exuded an artistic countenance.

Helene touched his jaw affectionately, smiling into his coal black eyes, sensing more than seeing the curl of his lip under his narrow, hawkish nose. Though he was comparatively short and a touch stocky, Adolfo Fallanti was dynamically appealing.

"What would you like to drink?" Jed asked them as the maid approached. "Felice?"

"Maybe a Black Russian this evening."

"Adolfo?"

"Campari, no ice."

"All right. Helene, darling, what will you have?"

"Vodka tonic, Jed. You know that's all I ever drink."

"I'll have a Scotch, Teresa. Do you have all that?"

"Yes, sir."

As the maid withdrew, Felice gave a little laugh. "Jed, you'll never guess what happened to me at the IRS this morning." She laughed again.

But Helene was looking at Adolfo, whose eyes were

still on her. She decided instantly that Felice may have won the battle, but she was going to lose the war.

"But you are wrong this time, Felicita!" Adolfo said, his eyes flashing. "I know it!"

"Adolfo, you have wonderful artistic judgment but not much common sense when it comes to the marketplace."

"That's stupid. *Sciocco!*" he retorted, stabbing his fork at her across the table. He gave a sideward glance at each of his hosts, then glared at his wife. "What do *you* know? Art is business and business is art. They go together like two . . . two . . . fishes in a pond!"

"Adolfo," Felice, said, her voice hardening with impatience, *"The Lovers of Trevi* is a classic film and it doesn't need remaking from a commercial standpoint. I'm sure you would do it beautifully, but it won't sell!"

Helene had been listening to husband and wife arguing for the past several minutes, taking secret pleasure in their tiff. Her heart beat more sweetly as Adolfo's temper flared.

"Won't sell, won't sell?" He thrust his chair back abruptly and got up, walking in a circle behind it. "Beauty sells—beautiful pictures, beautiful images, beautiful emotions. That's what sells!"

"Adolfo, there's no point in abusing Jed and Helene's hospitality with our professional differences."

"The Lovers of Trevi is in my soul. All the business principles in the world will not kill it."

"Perhaps your soul is a suitable hiding place for it, Adolfo."

"Ha! Now you are the funny one." He sat down again. "Well, my dear, there is a solution. You are not the only producer in the world, just as I am not the only director."

"True, Adolfo."

"You think there are not others who trust my vision?" Adolfo asked, his excitement building again.

"Why don't you ask a few?" Felice shot back.

"I will! You think I won't?"

They eyed each other like two alley cats, each waiting for the other to strike. Finally Adolfo whipped off his glasses, this time leaning toward his hostess instead of his wife. "Helena," he said, taking her hand. "You have listened to this. You know *The Lovers of Trevi*. You know my work. What do you think? Felice says it would flop; I say it would be a success."

Helene didn't bother to look at Felice. Her eyes were on the temperamental genius holding her hand. "Adolfo, I couldn't agree with you more. I think it would make a marvelous movie."

"There, you see!" he said to Felice. "Perhaps it is you who is wrong."

"Perhaps Helene is confusing the artisan with his work." There was steel in her words.

Helene slowly turned to Felice, giving her a level look. "Felice, I'm a businesswoman, too. I never let emotion color my business judgment."

"Oh. An instant expert."

"Instant?"

"I knew you went to the movies. I hadn't yet heard you made them, too."

Helene could see Felice had bared her dagger. "I know you carry the title producer of Adolfo's films humbly, Felice, but I wasn't aware that it made you a filmmaker."

"Anyone who knows the industry, dear, can tell you that business judgment is half the success of a film."

"Then by your standard I ought to do well."

Felice smiled. "Maybe you ought to ask Jed to give you some money so you can throw the dice."

"You seem to have done pretty well with Adolfo's talent and your father's money. Maybe I'd have the same luck."

"Ladies," Jed said, interrupting, "maybe we ought to have some dessert—"

"No, Jed," Felice cut in. "We're having a serious discussion. Adolfo here has a strong conviction about his project, which Helene seems to share. Maybe I'm the one who's out of line. I mean, who am I to stand between two such kindred spirits?"

Jed fidgeted uncomfortably. He looked at Adolfo.

"The last time you invested in one of my films, you did well, Jed."

"Yes, but that was only a thirty percent interest. Do you have any other backers?"

"It's only a concept. I...we haven't done budgets or—"

"You don't even know if you can get the rights to the film," Felice cut in.

"Eh," Adolfo said, gesturing with both hands. "That's no more than a trip to Rome. Panelli has the rights; he's my friend."

Felice and Helene's eyes met.

"It sounds like someone ought to go to Rome," Helene said to her, "and see if it can be done."

"If you're offering your services to Adolfo, Helene, I doubt seriously if he'd turn you down." She looked at her husband.

"Felicita..."

"Don't give me your cow eyes. You've got a live one. If I were you, I'd reel her in before she comes to her senses."

Adolfo looked at Helene. His eyes were filled with supplication and promise.

"But I'm warning you, Adolfo," Felice said over the silent seduction. "Not a cent of my money is going into the project. Helene, you might as well know that he is wonderful at spending other people's money."

The director ignored his wife and took Helene's hand, kissing it ceremoniously. "Helene, we go to Rome at *my* expense."

Felice turned to Jed apologetically. His expression was stoic. He reached over and patted her hand. "Can I interest you in a chocolate hazelnut torte, Felice?"

LAGUNA BEACH

May 10, 1985

Quintin Wing stood at the bar looking out at the open terrace and the Pacific beyond. Felice sat at a table near the railing, her head turned upward toward the afternoon sun, unseen eyes behind her dark glasses watching the gulls soar and swoop in the wind.

"Phone around I could use?" Wing asked the bartender.

The man pointed to the rest room sign over a doorway across the lounge. "In there."

He found the phone next to the men's room, inserted some coins, and dialed. "This is Wing. Williams in?" he asked the desk operator. "Tony? Quintin. Anything new?"

"I went back out to the house. The place has been cleaned up, no glasses on the counter."

"That's what I figured."

"Talked to the Daniels' maid. She doesn't remember seeing the two glasses on the bar prior to the day of the murder and said if they had been there, she'd probably have cleaned them up."

"So there's a good chance those drinks were for Helene and her killer."

"Looks that way."

"What else?"

"There were a couple of different kinds of vermouth, and they all were opened. I checked the glassware like you asked—they had every kind of drink glass imaginable in that bar, mostly Waterford crystal, all matching."

"Martini glasses, too?"

"Yeah."

"Did Sid get back to you?"

"Yes, and we might have something there. One of the technical guys took samples of the contents of the glasses, put them in his kit, and then forgot to check them out back at the lab. It was just luck that he took them, because normally a sample wouldn't have been taken under the circumstances. The guy was just curious. He's coming in tomorrow morning to find the samples and run the tests."

"Thank God for small favors. How about Keith Moore? Anything on him?"

"Yeah. I went to the airport. Just got back."

"And?"

"Nobody talked to him. But one of the passenger agents saw him getting off the plane. She said it sure looked like Keith Moore to her."

"What about the crew?"

"They're to hell and gone, but I'm trying to track them down and arrange a meeting the next trip through L.A. But the passenger agent told me she talked to the flight attendant in the first-class cabin about Moore because she's a fan of his and was curious. Apparently, there was little interaction, and he was asleep most of the flight."

"I would imagine Moore sat alone."

"I didn't think to ask. Want me to get the first-class passenger list and try to run them down?"

"Not yet, I think the crew's your best source of information. Why don't you concentrate on the studio next? See if Moore has a stand-in and how close the resemblance is, that sort of thing."

"Okay. What are you up to?"

"I'm at the beach and ready to head for Rome."

"What?"

"Tell you when I get in."

Wing returned to the nearly deserted terrace.

"So where were we, Quintin?"

"You had just given Adolfo and Helene your blessing to leave for Rome."

"It wasn't exactly my blessing. Actually, it was a miscalculation on my part. I didn't realize how serious both of them were. I thought it would blow over and be forgotten, but Helene had a foot in the door, and nobody was going to keep her out. The next day she was on the phone to Adolfo, making plans. Two weeks later they got on a plane and were gone."

"That must have put a strain on your relationship with your husband—when he left for Europe with another woman, I mean."

"Actually, it didn't. Not then. I don't think Adolfo had anything in mind except to slay a fat hog—that, and maybe give me a lesson in humility. His Italian pride was always bruised a bit at having a wife who controlled the purse strings. He was glad to assert his independence in that regard. Plus, I think he really did want to make that film.

"Helene, on the other hand, just wanted her name in lights. I realized that at the time, but what I didn't count on was how important it was that her name be right up there with Adolfo's. She envied me my husband and our professional relationship. She didn't just want fame, she wanted it at my expense."

"Why would that be?"

"I don't know, exactly, unless it was somehow sweeter that way."

"Obviously, letting them go off together was a mistake."

"It cost Adolfo his freedom and perhaps our marriage—though that remains to be seen." Felice took a drag on her cigarette, watching the detective with unseen eyes.

"Do you know what happened between them in Rome?"

She grinned. "Of course. Adolfo confessed everything. His last hope was the truth. After Rome, I didn't see him again until I visited him in the Swiss prison. And then the poor dear wasn't exactly in a power position."

ROME, ITALY
1984

December 14

The Alban Hills district lay to the southeast of the capital, its villas imperious and fortified against the crowded sprawl of Rome. Helene Daniels stood at the great French window in the Fallantis' master suite, waiting for Adolfo to take her to lunch. Then that evening there was the party at the home of Antonio Zucconi, the director and Adolfo's good friend.

The past week or so had been a whirlwind of activity, but activity carefully orchestrated by Adolfo. He had made it a long and excruciatingly precise seduction, which she had let herself enjoy, though his unexpected reserve had thrown her off balance. The man was more subtle than she had thought.

Helene glanced at the rumpled bedding on Felice and Adolfo's great canopied bed—the one she had occupied alone for the past ten nights. She wondered when he would finally get around to joining her.

On their flight to Rome, he had taken her hand affectionately several times during the course of their conversation, and she was sure he would invite her to his bed, but he hadn't. To the contrary, since their arrival he had been the model of decorum—polite, solicitous, gentlemanly. It made Helene want him all the more, and she knew he knew it, too.

As she walked impatiently about the room, Helene thought of Felice's admonition that Adolfo was good at spending other people's money. It had begun to trouble her. Since Jed's call the previous day, she had started doubting Adolfo's judgment. That—more than just money—was what concerned her.

Jed had been coldly matter-of-fact on the phone, and that made her suspicious as well. What could he be up to? Had he and Felice banded together? She shivered at the thought, remembering his words.

"Helene, everyone I've talked to thinks three hundred thousand for the story rights to an old film like that is ridiculous. From what I've been able to learn, a hundred thousand would be absolute top dollar."

That night Adolfo insisted that it was the best they could do, until she told him she wouldn't pay that much. Then he decided they might do better, and promised he would talk to Panelli again the next morning, which was where he was now.

Helene hated Jed for making her doubt herself, but she had given Adolfo a hundred-thousand-dollar limit for the rights. Neither Felice nor Adolfo realized it yet, but before he got any money out of her he would have to commit a lot more than his body for a few weeks. The price she would exact would change all their lives. She would show Felice that she, too, had balls. And Helene would end up with everything she needed—including Adolfo Fallanti.

As she pondered her situation, there was a soft knock at the door, and Helene turned. "Yes?"

The door slowly opened and Signora Buoni, the housekeeper, a slender, middle-aged woman with a somber face and deeply suspicious eyes, appeared. *"Mi scusi, signora.* The signore called on the telephone to say to you he is late and please to be patient. If you wish some fruit or refreshment before lunch, I am to bring it to you." The words were pronounced as though duty bore heavily.

Helene looked at the woman, knowing instinctively not to trust her. It was obvious she didn't approve of her employer being in the house without Felice present—and to occupy the master suite had probably been doubly shocking. But Adolfo had insisted she take the suite, and Helene agreed, assuming it was only a matter of time until they shared it.

"Thank you. I'm not hungry."

"I will do your room if you would wish to wait for the signore in the salon, signora."

"I'm comfortable here, thank you. Tell Signore Fallanti I'm here and ask him to come up when he arrives."

"*Si, signora.* As you wish." The woman inclined her head slightly and withdrew.

Staring at the heavy wooden door, Helene decided that the housekeeper would be the first thing she would replace —even before the furniture. She returned to the window to wait for Adolfo Fallanti, liking the vaporous atmosphere and the mysterious labyrinth of the city that he would, in the coming months and years, unravel for her. It was a very different place than Los Angeles, yet it appealed to her. In L.A., money was the end, but here, Helene sensed, it was the means.

Twenty minutes later, Adolfo came to her room. "Helena, forgive me for being late, but I have good news."

"What did Panelli say?"

His controlled expression turned into a broad grin. "He cut the price in half, Helena! I made him do it. *The Lovers of Trevi* is ours for a hundred and fifty thousand!"

"A hundred and fifty is not a hundred, Adolfo."

"Yes, but I have thought about it. There is another solution. I have this friend, the Baronessa Nica di Valerga, who has wanted to invest in a film of mine for many years. Perhaps we can get her to put in with us the fifty thousand we need if we give her a ten percent interest."

Helene heard a treachery in his words. "Perhaps your friend will put up the entire hundred and fifty, Adolfo, and then you won't need me."

"Helena. You are my partner, not the baronessa. I have

no use for her. It is just that you and I together could use her money if we want our *Lovers of Trevi*, no?"

Helene eyed Adolfo.

He took her chin between his thumb and fingers. "I will be honest. The baronessa has a daughter who has been in several films here in Italy, but without great attention. As an actress she is . . . adequate. In exchange for a part for this daughter, and perhaps five percent, I think we can have the fifty thousand dollars. I don't know it for sure, but we can ask."

"We?"

"Yes, tonight. The party I told you about at the house of Antonio Zucconi—Nica will be there. I will talk to her, and you will meet her. We are a team, my little pet."

"Is that what you really want, Adolfo?"

"Yes. It is what I want with all my heart."

Antonio Zucconi was a Renaissance man in the modern sense of the word—artist, cinematographer, society figure, politician, businessman, and aristocrat. Though untitled, Zucconi was accepted, and to some degree revered, by broad segments of Italy's nobility. Some affectionately called him the crown prince of the nation's culture, and his palatial villa in the Alban Hills was always temporary home to some count, princess, duke, or marchesa, not to mention celebrities and luminaries from around the world.

Zucconi, a tall and rather Aryan-looking man, save his olive skin, was in his mid-fifties, wealthy, and happily married to the daughter of one of Milan's greatest industrial families. Some of their five grown children always seemed to be in residence at the villa, not to mention members of both husband and wife's extended families, which occasionally included fourth and fifth cousins. All of Italy above a certain economic stratum belonged.

"So, Signora Daniels," Zucconi said, taking Helene by the arm, "Adolfo tells me you are becoming a brilliant producer in Hollywood and that you will make a film together."

Helene was surprised to feel herself blush. "I've primarily been an investor till now, but my judgment seems to have been pretty good, so I'm doing more with this one."

"A remake of *Trevi,* isn't it?" he asked over the hum of conversation in the great vaulted drawing room.

"Yes, Adolfo has this wonderful vision, and I'm very excited about it."

"Adolfo is very good. He understands the American audiences like many of us don't in Italy."

"Tell me, Signore Zucconi, what do you think of the idea of redoing *Trevi?*"

"This is a decision for you and Adolfo, no?"

"I'm interested in your opinion."

The boyish innocence turned calculating. "More important is what Nica Valerga thinks."

"You've heard."

"We Romans survive by gossip, signora."

"You won't tell me what you think?"

"I do not know the American market, so I have no opinion worth stating. Adolfo Fallanti, on the other hand, does."

"Tell me about Nica Valerga."

Zucconi smiled. "You have that wonderful American quality of going to the bottom line, Signora Daniels."

"I am Helena."

"Wonderful . . . Helena. Call me Antonio, or Tony, if you prefer. So you want to know about the baronessa . . ."

"Yes."

"Nica is a lovely person. Clever and very down to earth, as you say, for a noblewoman. Like many of our gentry, the land reforms in the forties pushed her family into the real world—the real economic world. Nica chose the arts as her field of interest."

"What about the baronessa's daughter—the actress?"

"Ilaria?"

"Yes. Is she a friend of Adolfo's?"

"Helena, I am beginning to understand the reasons for your success."

"Success in business is fifty percent information, Antonio."

"And the rest?"

"Knowing what to do with it."

Zucconi reached over and patted Helene's hand. "I must compliment Adolfo once again on his choice of women."

Helene studied him. "The prior occasion being Felice?"

"I understand you and Signora Fallanti are friends."

"We are. But I have come to realize that Adolfo and I see more eye to eye than they do. You may as well know that. Adolfo and I have more than just a business relationship."

"I assumed, but . . ."

"He's a gentleman, but there's no need for him to carry a burden among his friends." She smiled. "I trust I'm not being presumptuous in assuming our friendship?"

Zucconi bowed his head graciously. "Helena, I am honored."

"Now, about Ilaria . . . I assume her relationship with Adolfo ended when he married Felice, but I would be very interested to know the Roman gossip about them—without asking you to betray any confidences, of course."

"It's common knowledge that she and Adolfo had an affair. Nothing earthshaking there. The tragedy, however, was that it was Ilaria who introduced him to coke."

"Cocaine?"

"You were aware of Adolfo's problems, were you not?"

Helene's mind began spinning, but she quickly seized control. "Well . . . yes, but I thought that was all over."

"Felice was a demon about it—very much against drugs. It was a condition of their marriage that he stop. But I would have thought as her friend you were aware of that."

"Oh yes, of course. I just didn't know about Ilaria."

"Well, then, I have been a good Roman host, have I not? I have sealed our friendship with a gift of information." He looked into her vaguely vacant face. "I hope you use it well."

December 15

Adolfo Fallanti poured ample portions of Rémy Martin into two brandy snifters and carried them to where Helene lay waiting on the couch. He was in his shirt sleeves, his tie loosened at his neck as he stood over her.

"Helena, you were magnificent with Nica tonight. You played her to perfection."

"Thank you. But I couldn't have done it without you." She smiled up at him. "I think we played off of each other rather well, don't you?"

"Like swallows in flight." He beamed. "You know what it means, my little dove—*Trevi* is ours."

"It's yours, Adolfo. I'm just the prop behind your genius."

He sat down on the edge of the couch next to her, handing her one of the snifters, his eyes glistening.

Helene could see that his attitude toward her had shifted from calculating to desirous now that he had gotten his film. She gently touched her glass against his. "To *The Lovers of Trevi*. And to Felice," she added wryly, "for making this possible."

"No, not to her," he said. "To you, Helena, the woman

who believed in me." He leaned over, his mouth hovering inches from hers as he touched her cheek with his fingers.

Helene sensed her dreams, her empire, her future were at her fingertips. She opened her mouth, accepting his tongue into its recesses, savoring the pungent taste of him.

"Helena," he whispered into her lips, "tonight we make love."

He kissed her again, letting his broad chest press down more heavily against her breasts. When he pulled away, Helene watched him as he toyed with the edges of her gown that plunged to her waist, gently caressing the swell of her breasts. She could see the pleasure of the seduction had turned to hunger.

"I want you, Helena."

She stroked his face lightly with her fingers, not giving her assent just yet.

"And I want you, Adolfo, but I want it to be special, memorable."

He touched her hair. "But it will be our first. That is, by definition, memorable. Or am I wrong?"

"I know it will be special, but I want it to be different, too."

He stroked her. "What would be different?"

"I want to be on top of the world. I want to own it. I want to own you when you come."

He chuckled softly. "It sounds to me like you are talking about drugs."

Helene's eyebrow lifted.

"There's a history with me and cocaine, you know."

"Can we do it, Adolfo?" she asked, ignoring his comment.

"You want to snort coke and make love? What makes you think I have any?"

"Do you?"

"Between Felice and me coke is a big problem."

"I'm not Felice, darling."

"It can be very wonderful, it it's done right."

"Do you know how?"

"What do you think? Would you like some tonight, my little dove?"

"You have some?"

"Yes. It's easy, very easy to get, but I have hidden a large stash from when I promised Felice not to use it again. I didn't have the heart to get rid of it."

"What about that promise, Adolfo?"

He contemplated her mouth. "It was only as good as our partnership. She violated our trust first, not me."

Helene's insides began to burn with desire. "Tell me what it's like," she purred.

"No, little one, I will show you." He kissed her lips. "Wait for me." He rose and walked slowly into the dining room.

Helene lay still for a moment, enjoying the glow of triumph. Finding another lever Adolfo would respond to was a stroke of luck. And she could see the wedge she had managed to force between him and Felice would soon go deeper.

In the next room she could hear the sound of a chair being dragged across the floor. Curious, Helene got up and crept in stocking feet to the doorway. Across the dining room she saw Adolfo standing on a chair in front of a large antique china cabinet. He was removing the lid from an old apothecary jar sitting on top of it. Seeing him remove a small plastic sack, she quickly retreated, heady with the power she now felt at her fingertips.

December 19

Helene sat back in the passenger seat of the borrowed Ferrari, watching the late night lights of Rome whisk by as Adolfo hurled expletives at offensive drivers. She felt mellow from a day at the beach. When they finally entered the courtyard of the villa, she felt ready for bed. Adolfo would sleep with her as he had the past four nights, but there would be no more sex. No human body was capable of more than what they already had had. As they approached the master suite, they both saw a light shining under the closed double doors.

"Who do you suppose has been in there?" he mumbled more with curiosity than alarm. "Signora Buoni is never here past four." He reached for the handle and slowly pushed the door open.

"Well, the prodigal son and daughter return!" It was Felice, sitting up in bed, a magazine open across her lap.

"Felicita!"

"Surprise, dears."

Helene stared in disbelief.

Adolfo drew himself upright, puffing his chest. "What are you doing here?"

"This is my home, Adolfo. I wasn't aware I needed an invitation."

"No . . . but . . ."

Felice watched him sputter for a moment, then looked at Helene. "I hope you don't mind, dear, but I had the house-keeper move your things to the guest room. Under the circumstances that somehow seemed more appropriate."

Helene glared at her, speechless.

Felice looked at her watch. "My, it is late. You two been to a party? She smiled at Helene, taking in her disheveled countenance with one long sweeping look. "It's hell going to a strange place without your hairdresser, isn't it, dear? You look as though you walked into a butcher shop. Remind me in the morning and I'll give you the name of the best hairdresser in Rome."

"Felice, I demand to know what you are doing here. You sit there talking to me like I am some sort of school-boy."

"Adolfo, I am in *my* bed in *my* house and that requires no explanation." She glanced at Helene. "I won't embarrass your *guest* by asking what *you've* been doing here. Let's leave that discussion till morning, shall we?"

"Felice—"

"Please, Adolfo, there's no need to go through the motions of defending your honor. You're in the presence of two women who know you. There are things that do need to be said, but that's best done in private."

"Helena and I have made a deal for *Trevi*. We're going to make the film together."

"Congratulations."

"And we're going to stay in Rome to organize the production."

"I see. When are you scheduled to begin shooting?"

"I haven't worked out the schedule yet. The financial details must be completed first. We're still in the preliminary stages."

"I must say, I'm surprised. I didn't think you'd put a deal together—this quickly anyway. Perhaps I should have called before coming. It would have saved me swinging down here to talk to you."

"What do you mean?"

"I'm on my way to Switzerland to meet with Bernard Gutzman."

"Gutzman? What for?"

"He's got a wonderful script for *Julius Caesar* based on Shakespeare—an epic production that I'm seriously considering investing in."

Adolfo's eyes rounded.

"Bernie called last week to see if we'd be interested in—"

"We?"

"Yes. He asked whether you might be available to direct. I said you were in Rome looking into another project and—"

"You didn't tell him no?"

"No, I said I'd have to check and see how committed you were . . ."

Helene felt her stomach drop. The whole thing was obviously a ploy—one of Felice's tricks. "We're committed, Felice. We've bought the rights to *Trevi.*"

Adolfo looked at her. "This is true, Helena, but the timing is not certain. I'm sure we could put up a small amount of money and option the rights instead. After all, it is a remake, and timing is not essential."

"What are you saying? You're backing out?"

"No, no, of course I'm not backing out . . ."

"Felice comes in with a half-baked idea and all of a sudden you're willing to drop what we've worked on for weeks?"

"No, I didn't say that. I just think it's something we should hear." He looked back and forth between the women. "Maybe something for all of us. How about Helena, Felice? Is there room for her as well?"

Felice looked at Helene coldly. "I don't know. Bernie doesn't like working with amateurs."

Adolfo took off his glasses and rubbed his head miserably. *"Gesu Cristo."*

"Don't worry about me, Adolfo," Helene said, her voice nearly quivering with anger. "I made my statement when I proved I believe in your talent and judgment. If that's not good enough, then so be it." She spun on her heel and went back down the hall, trying a couple of doors until she finally found the guest room.

Inside she went to the window and stared into the black of night. She swore bitterly. The bitch couldn't accept defeat gracefully — she had to try and bribe him away.

There was a knock at the door and Helene turned to see Adolfo, his face contrite, his palms turned upward in supplication.

"What do you want?"

"Helena, a word. I must explain."

"There's nothing to explain, Adolfo."

He walked to where she stood and held her by the shoulders. "I had to say those things in front of Felice. It is you I want to work with, not her."

"Then why didn't you tell her so?"

"It is not easy. Don't forget, my little dove, there are complications. You are married to Jed, whom we are both dependent on for money at the moment . . ."

"*I* have money, Adolfo. Before I left I made arrangements to put Rina's of Dallas on the market. I'll use Jed's money to the extent I can, but it's only temporary, until we're established." She turned to the window. "That's what I was thinking anyway — until tonight."

"And it can be that way, too. At worst I take several months out to do Gutzman's film. No artist — director or actor — could turn him down. His films are always successful. You know this as well as I."

"Then do it, Adolfo."

"I promise you and I will make *Trevi*, no matter what. Tomorrow I will go to Panelli. I will ask for an option instead. If he agrees, we will do the film sometime within the year. If he says no, then I will tell Felice I cannot leave Rome and we will do *Trevi* now."

Helene was skeptical as she faced him. "Really?"

"I swear it on all that is sacred."

"Then talk to Panelli, Adolfo."

He kissed her softly on the lips. "And don't forget us, my little dove. Films are only part of what we share."

Helene smiled weakly and watched him steal silently from the room. She stared at the closed door, knowing Adolfo Fallanti was one of the biggest liars she had ever met. How stupid did he think she was? She and *The Lovers of Trevi* were nothing more than insurance—just in case the Gutzman deal didn't work out. And there was no risk in his promise to do *Trevi* now if Panelli wouldn't option the rights. Why shouldn't he give an option? The price was absolute top dollar and nobody else wanted to make the film.

No, Helene knew she'd lost...unless she could find some way to turn Felice against Adolfo.

December 20

Felice Fallanti climbed the steps to the villa, her body wrapped in a Fendi mink for protection against the evening cold, her arms full of packages.

Signora Buoni opened the door. Her expression was glum. "Signora, that woman is still in the house."

"I expected as much. She's not the kind to give up easily."

The housekeeper closed the door and took the packages from Felice.

"And Signore Fallanti?"

"He has been gone from the house all the day."

"Where is she?"

"In her room."

"Go and tell her I'm in the salon if she'd like to join me for a cocktail."

"Si, signora."

Felice tossed her coat onto a chair in the entry and went into the sitting room, where she sat near the fire, staring at the flames. Helene Daniels was not given to subtlety. It was time for some frank talk.

In ten minutes Helene appeared at the doorway. She walked toward Felice slowly, her expression bland.

"Sit down, Helene. I think it's time to talk."

Helene sat without a word.

"Let's skip the bullshit," Felice said dryly. "What's the bottom line?"

"Adolfo wants me."

Felice raised her eyebrows. "He does?" She stared at Helene evenly. "Are we speaking professionally or personally?"

"Both."

"Oh, a sweep. Aren't you clever."

"If you have something to say, Felice, say it. Otherwise, I'm going back upstairs."

"Since we're such good friends, I thought you might like to tell me what's been happening here in Rome—the unsanitized version."

"Obviously, Adolfo and I have been having an affair."

"How genteel. Tell me, how do you find him?"

Helene smiled icily. "I thought I was invited down for a drink. Or must I endure your wifely pique first?"

"No, you shouldn't have to hear that refrain again. You've doubtless heard it before." She got up and went to the liquor cabinet in the corner. "Actually, I thought we ought to discuss how we can make your disengagement as civilized as possible."

"Have it backwards, don't you, dear?"

"Strange as it may seem, Helene, I know Adolfo better than you. He's a good deal more clever than you realize. Italian men value their whores—though not as much as their wives—and say what they must to keep them happy."

"Your tolerance astounds me, Felice. Or is it desperation?"

Felice gave Helene a little smile. "What'll you have, dear? Vodka tonic?"

"Actually, I don't feel like a drink. Adolfo has turned me on to the pleasures of coke, and this conversation has left me . . . wanting. You wouldn't mind, would you?"

Felice's mouth fell. "What are you talking about?"

"I'd prefer cocaine."

Felice began to shake. "You're lying!"

She watched Helene walk across the salon toward the dining room. Incredulously, she waited at the door as Helene climbed up on a chair and took an apothecary jar from the top of the china cabinet. When Helene had gotten down she turned to Felice.

"Same hiding place, or has he changed it?"

Felice was speechless, but she didn't move. She waited as Helene fished out a handful of tiny pouches, letting them slip through her fingers into the jar. Then, taking one, she walked toward Felice, smiling triumphantly.

"Amazing what this stuff does."

Just then they heard the sound of the front door opening. Both turned toward the entry hall as Adolfo appeared, the smile on his face fading as he began to sense the drama he had walked in on.

"Well . . ." he said, looking at each of them in turn, hoping for an explanation.

"Felice and I were just talking, Adolfo. It seems she doesn't approve of our relationship."

He looked at his wife, whose face was nearly drained of color. He saw the violence in her eyes. "Felicita?"

"Is there cocaine in that jar?" she asked with a quivering voice.

"Felicita . . ."

"Is there?"

"It is old, from before. I didn't have the heart to throw it out. I haven't used it. I swear . . ."

"Except with your whores?"

He looked at Helene, desperate.

"Except with your whores?" Felice repeated, her voice shrill.

"Only a couple of times, Felicita, and only because of the film. I swear it."

Felice walked to the doorway, past Adolfo. She stopped and turned around, looking first at him, then at Helene. "You had to destroy him to get him, didn't you, Helene darling."

"Felice!" Adolfo shouted after her. But it was too late. She was gone.

* * *

Helene heard the taxi door slam and then the sound of the vehicle driving away. Several moments later Adolfo came back in, his face twisted in anguish.

"Why did you do this to me, Helena? Why couldn't you have waited? Now Felice is going to Switzerland without me. How can I possibly be involved in the film with her against me?"

"Is that all it is, Adolfo, the Gutzman film?"

He looked at her with surprise. "Of course."

"It's not Felice?"

"No, I told you last night. It is an opportunity no artist would pass up."

"Then perhaps I should buy into the project."

"You?"

"Me. Why not?"

Adolfo began walking in a circle, his glasses off, his hand on his forehead. He stopped and looked at her. "But you don't know Gutzman."

"My money is just as green as Felice's."

"It's not that simple."

Helene drew a long breath, feeling things slipping from her. "Are you telling me no?"

"Helena, our project is *Trevi*. It is a good one." He sat in the chair opposite her. "Today I talked to Panelli. He's agreed to the option. For fifty thousand—"

"You're wasting your breath, Adolfo. I won't pay it."

"But Helena, there is no risk. We will make the film. You have my word on it."

"Adolfo, you're either with me or you aren't. I won't put a leash around your neck like your wife has, but I've got to know you're on my side."

He stood and made another circle around the room, shaking his head. Then he stopped. "First I must go to Switzerland. If you will not wait for me, Helena, then it is you who is not trusting."

She glared at him coldly.

"I'm sorry, but this is how it must be." Adolfo's look was apologetic. He hesitated, then strode from the room.

Helene watched him go, then fell back against her chair, her mind reeling. In just hours, Felice had snatched her dreams, her plans from her. And Adolfo, the bastard, had let her do it.

He had been so cavalier—using her, taking from her, but deserting her when the chips were down. Helene knew she couldn't let him get away with it. If she had to go down with the ship, he would, too. There was no way she'd let him waltz off to Switzerland unscathed. She'd make him pay. One way or another, she'd make him pay.

SANTA MONICA

May 11, 1985

4:55 P.M.

The world was on its head—Old Glory up the street was upside down, the palm tree outside Wing's window soared toward the ground, even the sweat from his body was running up his neck and into his hair. After a few more deep breaths, he strained again, curling his body upward, reaching for the antigravity boots hanging from the top of the doorframe. This time his fingertips barely made it to the middle of his shins before his burning muscles collapsed and he hung, strung out like a fish on a line.

The telephone rang.

"Shit."

Wing extended his arm toward the phone that sat on the dresser next to the door. His fingers didn't quite reach the receiver, so he flexed his aching stomach muscles to pull himself closer. Finally, breathlessly, he managed to grasp the receiver as the rest of the instrument went crashing to the floor.

"Wing?"

"Who's this?" he gasped.

"Williams. What's wrong?"

"Shit, Tony..."

"Quintin, are you all right?"

"Yeah . . . just glad . . . you're not a wrong number."

"What the hell are you doing?"

"Getting laid. What does it . . . sound like?"

"Wing . . ."

"I'm in my gravity boots. Shit."

Williams laughed. "I figured on a Saturday you'd just be hanging around."

"Very funny. Is this a social call . . . or what?"

"No, I thought you'd like to know what I dug up on your pal, Geoffrey Hammond."

"Yeah, what?"

"I tracked down his former boyfriend, Donald Lawrence."

"And?"

"The guy was pretty bitter toward Hammond. He wouldn't say much at first, but he finally unloaded. Seems they broke up because Geoffrey got a new lover."

"Oh?"

"Yeah. Lawrence said it was late last year or early this. Somebody in the film business, but he didn't know who."

"Films?"

"That's what he said. I tried to find out about his business dealings with Helene Daniels, like you asked, but Lawrence insisted that once the sale of the Dallas company was arranged, the relationship between Geoffrey and Helene was over. He was sure Hammond's problems had to do with this lover of his, not our victim."

"Hmm. I wonder if somehow there might be a connection."

"What do you mean?"

"Between Hammond's affair and Helene Daniels."

"How?"

"I don't know, but Geoffrey's somehow tied up in the murder—I'm fairly sure of that. He may even have done it. Any word on what was in those drink glasses, by the way?"

"No. Sid's off today, and I don't know whether his guy came in or not. I forgot it's Saturday. Maybe he wasn't coming in until Monday."

"Anything else, Tony?"

"Yeah. I did some checking on weapons training. Two of your people have had some."

"Who?"

"Keith Moore was in the service and had training in small arms, including pistol. The other was Leslie Randall."

"Leslie?"

"Yeah. Took a self-defense course a couple of years ago here in L.A. It included pistol marksmanship."

"Hmm. What about the others?"

"Nothing I've been able to turn up."

"Look at Geoffrey Hammond especially closely, will you, Tony? I think we should focus a little on him."

"Okay. What about Moore?"

"Find anything on his double?"

"The studio office was closed today. I thought first thing Monday morning."

"Good. I'm going to see what I can find out about Geoffrey Hammond's affair. There's got to be a connection."

"Could it be that Italian director, Felice Fallanti's husband?"

"Not unless Hammond was in a Swiss prison recently. Of course, Lawrence might have been off on the timing. I suppose we have to keep an open mind. Speaking of which, my head is about to burst. I've got to get off the phone."

"Okay, Quintin. Hang in there."

"Very funny, Williams." Wing dropped the receiver, aiming for the cradle on the floor below him, but missed.

SANTA MONICA

May 11, 1985

8:15 P.M.

The Diebenkorn over Leslie's shoulder looked for all the world like it belonged there. The mustards and beigy pigments were in her hair, the gray green of her clinging jersey dress blended perfectly, even the Christofle silver in her hand was a natural part of the collage of canvas, flesh, and furnishings. Wing tried not to stare.

"If I'd known you were a regular, I'd have suggested someplace else," he said, hoping she didn't really mind.

"I love Michael's, Quintin. To be honest, I was so impressed that you could get in here on a Saturday night that I had to come with you." Her smile was heartrending. "What's your secret? Protection?"

He laughed. "No, I can't even take credit personally. My mother is responsible for two of the canvases on the walls. One was formerly owned by a doctor friend of hers, the other a dealer had committed to her before Michael McCarty fell in love with it. So, we tend to get tables."

"You'll never believe who turned *me* on to this place."

"Who?"

"Felice Fallanti."

"Really?"

"Felice knew about my interest in art and thought it would be fun."

"I hadn't realized you were that close."

"We weren't. It was one of those spontaneous things. I was at the house in Bel Air one time when Felice and Adolfo had come over to talk about a project with Daddy. She and I talked for a while, and a couple of weeks later she invited me out. I think she was aware of how badly Helene and I got along and took pity. She's a good-hearted person."

"Yes, she seems rather generous." Wing was noticing the gloss on Leslie's full lower lip, thinking how sensuous it looked and how much he would like to taste it. He leaned back in his Breuer chair, savoring the vision of her.

"How's your investigation going?" she asked after a while.

"Slowly."

"Is that because you're thorough or because it's a tough case?"

"Maybe a little of both." He contemplated her, not wanting to break the spell of the evening, but knowing she was potentially a rich source of information. "There's one area where I'm a little stumped, though."

She touched the rim of her coffee cup with her finger. "What's that?"

"I know you and Helene were not at all close, but are you aware of any connection between her and Geoffrey Hammond—apart from Rina's of Dallas?"

"Not after they sold it, no."

"How about a third party—someone who might have linked them in some way?"

"What do you mean?"

"Geoffrey had a lover about six months ago, give or take, who was in the film business. I thought it might somehow involve Helene, too. Any ideas?"

"I'm afraid neither of them were exactly part of my crowd. Have you asked Felice?"

"She's rather protective of Geoffrey."

"Do you think he did it, Quintin?"

"It's my job to think everybody did it."

"That's rather comforting."

"Present company excepted."

"I'll bet you say that to all the girls."

A few minutes later Wing had paid the check and they were walking along Third Street toward Wing's car.

"Why do you think films are somehow involved in Helene's murder?"

"She was rather keen on being an industry star, and little things keep popping up—like Geoffrey's mysterious lover."

"And like Felice and Adolfo, Keith and Daphne?"

"There seems to be a pattern of sorts."

"Helene's career was rather short-lived. After the fiasco in Rome, she made another stab, but that flopped, too."

"What was that?"

"Bernard Gutzman's epic on Julius Caesar. When Felice got tied up with Adolfo's arrest and trial, Helene tried to slip in the back door. She needed my father's backing because it would have taken everything she'd gotten out of the sale of her stores and then some to make it. When he cut her off, it did her in. That's why she killed him, Quintin."

He let her words settle. "You really miss him, don't you?"

"Yes. Terribly."

They came to Wing's black '57 MG Roadster. He opened the door for her, took her arm, and helped her in. By the time Wing had gone around and gotten into the driver's seat, Leslie had her purse open. He watched with curiosity as she opened her wallet, slipped a photograph from the plastic holder, and handed it to him. "This is the last picture of us," she said simply.

Wing tilted the photograph toward the window and street light nearby. In it he saw a smiling young woman in shorts, the familiar shapely legs, and next to her a tall, fair man in his fifties, also in shorts. They were standing on what appeared to be a dock in front of a sailboat, his arm around her waist, a vague smile on his lips.

"Last fall in Balboa," she said.

Wing handed it back to her and put the keys in the ignition, starting the engine. He watched as she put the photograph away, noting even in the darkness the film of moisture on her eyes. Then, when she looked over at him, Wing touched his hand to her face, leaned over, and softly kissed her on the lips.

WESTWOOD

May 13, 1985

9:55 A.M.

Quintin Wing put money in the pay phone on the corner across the street from Daphne Stephens's Wilshire Boulevard spa. He dialed and waited.

"This is Wing. Williams in?"

"No, sir. But he called in on another line asking for you a few minutes ago. He's talking to Lieutenant Murdoch now."

"Listen, tell Murdoch I need to talk to Tony. Can you cross-connect me?"

"Sure. Hang on."

"Quintin?"

"Tony, where are you?"

"At the studio. Boy, do I have news for you."

"Yeah, what?"

"There's a stunt man, bit actor who works here named Paul Clark, who they say looks enough like Keith Moore to be his brother. He does a lot of stand-in work for him."

"Did you talk to him?"

"No, that's the point. The guy's disappeared. Didn't come into work last week, and nobody's been able to locate him."

"Jesus."

"I've got an address, and I'm headed out to Glendale to see if I can get a line on him."

"Good. Did you tell Murdoch?"

"Yeah. He's got a couple of guys going out to the airport this morning."

"Good work, Tony. I'm going to see Daphne Stephens in a few minutes. See you this afternoon." Wing hung up just in time for a break in the heavy traffic. With his tie flying, he ran across the street.

Inside, he was told Daphne was working out with an aerobic dance group, but leaning against a wall watching was Keith Moore.

Wing turned his attention to the dancers.

"I figured you'd turn up here," the actor said, going over to Wing.

"Actually, I was hoping to find *you* here. Tell me about Paul Clark, Mr. Moore."

"Why?" Keith asked warily.

Wing shrugged. "I'm curious. I understand his resemblance to you is uncanny."

Moore studied the detective. "He's my double, that's all."

"Have you heard? Clark has disappeared. Hasn't been seen since sometime last week."

"Paul Clark and I are not friends, and we're not working together on anything at the moment. I have no idea what he's doing."

"Any chance he was in London about the same time you were?"

Moore's expression hardened. "What are you getting at?"

"I understand you had quite a time on the flight back from London—playing cards, doing scenes from your movies for the other passengers, that sort of thing."

"Wing, you're nuts. I slept most of the trip."

"Oh. Maybe I'm confusing your flight with Paul's."

Moore stared at him for a moment, then gave a little laugh. "Ah, I'm beginning to understand. This is an allegation."

"No. A question."

"With the proper lighting Paul Clark looks like me, Wing, but he doesn't play me. Ask anybody. Shit, ask the stewardess on the flight—I must have talked to her for fifteen minutes. Hell, all you have to do is talk to customs in London or here. I think I even signed an autograph. Yeah! A lady in first class—it was during a meal. Paul Clark doesn't do my signature. Find the lady; ask her. She was a Brit, I believe."

"Thanks for the suggestions."

They watched the dancers in silence, Wing beginning to feel fairly certain Joe Murdoch was going to be disappointed.

Wing glanced at Daphne, who was kicking her legs up to her outstretched hand. "Mrs. Stephens is quite a woman, isn't she?"

"A hell of a woman, Wing. And I wish you'd lay off her."

The detective started to respond, but Moore cut him off.

"Yeah, I know. Duty. But Daphne's as innocent as I am."

"We spoke briefly about your run-in with Helene Daniels that first day we met, but not in detail. Would you mind discussing it now?"

"If that's what you want."

"How'd it happen—your confrontation with Helene?"

"Supposedly, it was over Bernie Gutzman's film—she wanted to screw me out of the lead. But the truth is, Helene was jealous of Daphne."

"Because of her relationship with you?"

"Because of who Daphne was and how she'd gotten there. You see, Jerry Stephens, Daphne's ex, might have rescued her from life as a waitress in Bakersfield, but he didn't make her, like Jed made Helene. When Daphne and Jerry divorced, they owned three marginal little gyms up in the San Fernando Valley, a tract house with an enormous mortgage, and the clothes on their backs. Out of the settlement she got one of the clubs and turned it into the empire she has now. Helene never forgave her for doing it on her own."

"And ending up with one of Hollywood's most eligible stars?"

Moore shrugged.

"So what happened with you and her?"

A smile slipped across the actor's face. "It was at the grand opening for Daphne's new resort spa in Palm Springs last February..."

PALM SPRINGS
EARLY 1985

February 16

Felice Fallanti's handmade white silk pumps clicked on the marble steps leading up to the door. She heard a car pulling under the portico behind her and the light toot of a horn. She spun around, the full, white silk taffeta skirt of her Carolina Herrera swishing in the vaporous air of the building's ecosystem, the high-necked, long-sleeved black sequined net top glittering in the floods.

"God, Felice, you're beautiful!" It was Geoffrey, hanging out of the window of a white Rolls Royce. The black-faced chauffeur was in a white uniform, Geoffrey in a black tuxedo. The car had hardly come to a stop when the decorator was out of it and bounding up the steps toward her. They embraced.

Then he held her at arm's length. "I won't ask you how *you* are. How did Adolfo take it? My God, eighteen months, wasn't it?"

"I'd rather talk about me, Geoffrey."

He gathered her to him again. "When did you get back?"

"Last week."

"My poor little Felice."

"That's what I get for marrying a gigolo."

"It will be over before you know it. Don't fret."

"Fret! Christ, I wish they'd given him ten years." Felice looked at the Rolls. "Isn't that a little ostentatious, dear?"

"It's a black-and-white party—my party as much as Daphne's, you know. I was the one who suggested it."

"That's right. I'd forgotten. This place is your *pièce de résistance,* isn't it?"

"It'll keep me in bread for a year or two—that's what counts."

She took his lapel between her fingers. "And what's this? Herringbone?"

"Yes. Bijan."

Her eyes rounded. "At this rate, you'll be lucky if bread is all you eat for the next two years. What's gotten into you?"

He brushed the question aside. "It was a gift." He took her arm. "Shall we go in?"

As the door swung open and they stepped inside, Felice gave a little involuntary gasp. "Geoffrey, it's fabulous!"

Astonishingly, he had taken art deco and created a masterful blend of the practical and the luxurious. Dusty peach walls contrasted with smokey gray carpeting and shiny white columns. For accent there were Erté etchings and sculpture.

"You've really outdone yourself."

He beamed amidst the swirl of black uniformed help moving through the lobby toward the exercise room, which had been turned into a ballroom for the occasion.

Daphne Stephens emerged from the studied tempest in a clinging white sequined Bob Mackie, her skin richly tanned.

"Aren't you the picture of health," Geoffrey enthused.

"You look great," Felice added, extending her arms. They embraced.

"Thanks. And you're elegant, as always, Felice. I'm so glad you came."

"It wasn't easy, considering *she's* going to be here."

"She?" Geoffrey said.

"Yes, I didn't want to tell you," Daphne explained, "because I was afraid you wouldn't show, but I invited Helene."

"Oh, God. Well, I suppose I can always drive around the desert and look at the moonbeams on the cactus."

"You're not going anywhere." Daphne took his arm.

He turned to Felice. "And *you* knew she'd be here?"

"Yes, Geoffrey."

"Bitch."

Felice took his other arm, and they headed toward the party.

"Then why did you come?"

"I'm supposed to cower? No, Geoffrey, the only way to handle Helene is to look her in the eye. Adolfo insists she set him up, but couldn't prove it. I have my doubts as well as my suspicions, but I'd sure as hell like to hear what she has to say."

He turned to Daphne. "Why in God's name did you invite her?"

"Business. Besides, we're having fun with it. There's a pool to see whether she'll be in black or white."

"God, it'll be black. What else?"

"Don't be so sure. My sister's perception of herself is not the same as everyone else's."

"I couldn't guess what she'd be in," Felice said, "so I came two-toned."

They were at the entrance to the ballroom and Keith came over to them. "Felice!" He leaned over and kissed her, then shook hands with the decorator. "What do you think of the place now that it's occupied, Geoffrey?"

"Looks pretty good. At least the caterers didn't slop up my delicate balance of color."

"Which way's the smart money going?" Felice asked. "Black or white?"

"Who knows."

"Ugh," Geoffrey groaned. "I think I'll go out and look at the pool. I may have to be here, but I don't have to see her."

They watched him go.

Keith touched Felice's arm. "Sorry about Adolfo."

"So am I, I think."

A tray of champagne came by, and Felice took a glass.

"You think it's true she's cut herself into Gutzman's film?" he asked.

"He needs investors. I haven't talked to Bernie since I had to bow out, but I'd say Jed is the key. He's got the money and knows the business, without wanting to call the shots. He's a perfect investor."

"Helene's been talking like they're her dollars not Jed's."

"I don't know if she'd have enough even if she used every cent she has. My guess is Jed's making her put up a bunch and he's covering the difference."

Keith and Daphne exchanged glances. "I suppose that means she has to be reckoned with," he said glumly.

"I haven't seen Jed since I've been back from Switzerland, but from what I've heard she's really got the reins. It would be interesting to hear what *he* says—if Helene will let anybody talk to him."

Keith frowned. "Hell."

"That's where she belongs," Felice agreed. She lifted her glass. "To a speedy trip."

Keith was standing near the tall arched windows, looking out over the pool and garden, when he heard several gasps and a hush fall over the room. He turned and there, across the polished floor at the entrance, stood Helene and Jed Daniels—he in a black tuxedo, looking tall and dignified.

She was wearing a shocking pink strapless Mary McFadden and, judging by the expression on her face, she had managed to get the exact reaction she had intended. For an instant, no one moved, and Keith sensed he had better get over to them. He made his way across the room as the din of conversation gradually picked up again.

"Well, Keith," she said, beaming, "I was beginning to wonder if everybody had shrunk into the woodwork. How are you?" She touched his arm and he gave her an obligatory kiss on the cheek. As he shook hands with Jed, Daphne approached.

"Well," Helene said with a tight smile, "long time no see."

Daphne gave a slight nod. "Hello, Jed."

He leaned over and kissed her cheek. She looked at her sister hesitantly. "I'm glad you came."

"Are you, Daphne? Now that I'm here?" She looked imperiously at the many faces around the room still turned her way. "Did the invitation say black and white? I hadn't really noticed."

"It doesn't matter," Daphne replied.

Keith could tell she was angry. "Jed looks thirsty, Daphne. Why don't you take him to the bar? I'll show Helene around the spa."

Helene smiled at him as Daphne and Jed turned away. "No need for the chef's tour, Keith, but I would like to talk to you."

"And I'd like to talk to you, too, Helene."

"Could we have a bottle of champagne?"

Keith signaled a waiter, who stepped immediately to his side. He ordered a bottle and glasses to be brought to the lounge off the lobby. Helene took his arm and they went back into the foyer, across the polished marble floor, and into an intimate little salon.

"Well," she said, sitting on an overstuffed deco sofa, "was it your idea or Daphne's to invite me?"

"We both thought it would be a good idea."

Helene raised her eyebrows. "She obviously is seeking reconciliation. What did *you* have in mind, Keith?"

There was a knock at the door, and the waiter entered with the champagne. They watched him for a moment opening the bottle. Helene glanced around the room. "Who did the decorating, Geoffrey Hammond?"

"Yes. Don't you like it?"

"I like Geoffrey's work better than I like him. Let's put it that way."

The waiter poured the champagne, placed the bottle in an ice bucket, and left the room. Keith handed Helene a flute.

"To our mutual success," she said in toast.

They touched glasses and sipped the wine.

"So, you were about to tell me your intentions as regards this little tête-à-tête."

Keith looked at her, feeling almost as though he were at court. But despite her regal air there was a suggestiveness about her. "I thought we might talk about Bernie Gutzman's film."

"Julius Caesar?"

"Yes."

"Bernie's and *my* film, darling."

"You've made your deal?"

She smiled coyly. "We're working out final details, one of which involves agreement on the leads. Since this is our first film together, I couldn't exactly ask for artistic control. But it appears we're coming to a happy compromise."

As Keith contemplated her, Helene reached over and placed her hand lightly on his thigh.

"I understand you're interested in playing Brutus."

"My agent's been talking to the Gutzman people."

"You know how many actors want that role, darling? God, and they're mostly like you, the Mark Antony types. Why is it that all you pretty boys feel the need to be bad once in a while?"

"Serious actors look at roles for their dramatic potential, not their image."

Helene gave him an inviting look. "So you're serious about playing Brutus."

He waited.

Helene looked around again, running her hand over the sofa cushion. "Enough to *be* Brutus?"

"Be Brutus?"

"Well, Daphne *is* a little queen of sorts—her empire and all. You've been a faithful lieutenant, if that's the word, and I just wonder if that isn't inconsistent with your future —as an actor."

"Helene, what are you getting at?"

"Let me be direct. You want to play Brutus, and it's within my power to grant your wish. Unfortunately, my favors are not gratis—not when there's something I want as well."

"And what might that be?"

"You. I want us to get to know one another better. I want you to spend the next two weeks here with me in Palm Springs—at my place."

"Me? Helene, you're crazy."

"Am I?"

"You can't be serious."

"Dead serious. You want to play Brutus, you've got to be Brutus. Isn't that what good acting's all about?"

Keith stood. "My God, you *are* nuts."

She also stood, her expression hardening. "That's hardly calculated to win my favor."

He looked at her incredulously. "What about Jed—never mind your sister?"

"Daphne means nothing to me, she hasn't for years. And as for Jed . . . we're married in name only. Business partners are what we really are. He has his life and I have mine."

"That may be fine for you, Helene, but I love Daphne."

"Yes, and we all love Caesar—when he's Caesar. Think of your career, Keith. I'm offering you the opportunity of a lifetime. If Newman and Redford hadn't gotten beyond the pretty-boy stuff, they'd have withered on the vine, and you will also, if you don't come to your senses."

"Helene, I can't believe you."

"I'm going to be a power in the industry—a major power. This discussion hasn't been a casting couch interview. I'm offering you my friendship, a career opportunity if there ever was one."

Hearing her, Keith was left speechless. He just stared into her vicious, beautiful face, shaking his head.

"Maybe you need time to think about it, to weigh what you have against what you'll get."

"No, Helene. I don't need time. I know exactly what I want—and it's not you." He smiled at her sadly. "Thanks for the offer, though. I *am* flattered."

Helene gave him a bitter smile. "That's it, then?"

"I'm afraid so."

"All right, Keith. I accept that."

He was surprised at the gracious turn.

"Maybe we should toast our parting of the ways," she said.

"If you like."

Helene bent over and took her champagne flute. Keith took his. "To what could have been, Keith," she said sweetly, "if you hadn't been such a horse's ass!" With that, Helene threw her champagne in his face.

Keith Moore stood staring incredulously, his face and the front of his tuxedo dripping. At that moment, he knew hatred like he had never known it before.

Daphne looked out from the ballroom onto the pool area where Felice Fallanti, Jed Daniels, and Geoffrey Hammond stood talking. The tables around them were covered in black silk with white tapers flickering atop them. In addition to the candles, there were black ceramic vases containing white orchids, freesias, and *Phalaenopsis.* Daphne felt awfully proud, but she worried about Helene. Her very presence was pernicious, she could feel it.

Outside Felice was doing most of the talking. Jed had a sober expression on his face and shook his head from time to time. Daphne had little doubt about the topic of conversation.

She wondered about Jed, though—why a man as decent as he would stay with Helene. Something told her it couldn't last for much longer, that things were building to a breaking point. Beneath Helene's cool veneer there was desperation. It seemed the higher she climbed, the more frenetic she became. What could she be saying to Keith?

"How's it going, doll?" Felice asked, coming back into the room.

"I hope it was worth having her here. It's spoiled the evening for me already. I saw you talking to Jed."

"Yes, we were comparing notes. In some ways the poor man strikes me as awfully naive."

"It's probably easier for him that way."

"Helene will eat him alive if he isn't careful, but I'm not telling *you* anything." Felice looked around. "Jed said she's off somewhere talking to Keith."

"Yes."

"About *Julius Caesar,* I take it."

"Keith wanted to enlist her support."

"God, I think all men are naive—when it comes to women, anyway. What do you suppose she's after?"

"God only knows."

"I'll lay odds it's him."

Daphne gave Felice an uncomfortable look.

"Adolfo thought he had a filly he could ride, and look where *he* is."

Daphne looked across the room and saw Keith making his way through the black-and-white throng.

"I think we'd better talk, Daphne."

"You bitch!" Daphne Stephens slammed the door behind her and stood glaring at Helene, her hands on her hips.

"Please, spare me your outraged indignation. I've got better things to do with my time."

"I'm not going to spare you anything."

"Listen, if you're upset over Keith, don't bother. His stupidity has already been proven. You're welcome to him."

"I appreciate your sisterly generosity—considering he's already mine!"

"You may not like what I did—but you know what? It was honest. I don't sneak around. I don't have to anymore."

"Helene, I don't understand you. I swear I don't. How in God's name you could have turned out this way is beyond me. Where is your heart?"

Helene laughed. "Daphne, you should have been an actress. Your holier-than-thou routine is marvelous—an admirable performance."

Daphne looked at her. At some deep, intuitive level she sensed how frightening and dangerous the monster before her was. "You know, I would have thought even you— even hardhearted Helene—would have passed up this one. I know you don't love me. I don't think you're capable of loving anyone. But I would have thought after what you've done in the past, you would have at least wanted to stay clear."

"I don't know what you're talking about."

"I'm talking about when that boy, Ray Wicks, raped me. I don't know exactly how, but I know deep in my heart that you were responsible."

Helene stood frozen, staring at her sister.

"I knew it at the time, but I couldn't believe it. I thought surely it had to be my fault—not yours, not his, but mine. It was like a horrible truth I couldn't and wouldn't accept.

It was easier, better, to blame myself, and maybe him, than my own sister."

Helene sipped her champagne.

Tears began flowing down Daphne's cheeks. "Damn it, Helene, I was hoping that once, just once, you'd do what was right."

"If this is a plea for a part in my film for your ever-faithful lap dog, Daphne, save your breath."

"No, goddamn it!" Daphne screamed. "It's a plea for decency! Can't you see that?"

They looked into each other's eyes for a long time. "That's all in the past, Daphne," Helene finally said, her lack of denial convincing Daphne she had been right about what her sister had done long ago. "You know, Daphne, I've had my triumphs, but they haven't come cheaply either. I've paid dearly for everything I've gotten in my life. But it's been worth it, because I do things my way, and I'm going to keep on doing things my way—no matter who gets hurt!"

"Even if it kills you?"

"If that's what it comes to." She shrugged.

"Good luck, Helene."

"No, dear. *You're* the one who needs the luck."

At home that night, Helene watched as Jed packed a suitcase. "Where are you going?"

"Acapulco."

"Acapulco? Whatever for?"

"I want to get away to think."

Helene sensed something momentous. There was something different in a man's voice and demeanor when he had slipped from a woman's grasp. "Am I permitted to ask about what?"

"I'm going to reassess our relationship, Helene."

"I take it at some point you'll deign to inform me what this reassessment involves."

"I've already come to several decisions. You may as well know those now."

She contemplated him, feeling uneasy. "Yes . . .?"

"I'm pulling out of the Gutzman deal. What you do is your business. I refuse to be involved."

"Refuse? You've already made a commitment."

"It's been conditional all along. After what I've learned

tonight, I wouldn't give you the money to open a Chinese laundry."

Helene's mind scrambled for ploys, levers, entreaties. She realized she had left herself without any, having relied entirely on inertia in her relationship with Jed. "Am I to have the opportunity to hear the evidence against me, or am I already convicted?"

"You were aware, weren't you, that when Adolfo left Rome he was headed for Switzerland to meet with Bernie Gutzman? Not to mention the fact that Felice had already entered into negotiations with him."

"Yes, of course."

"I won't bother to ask what happened that last evening. As far as I'm concerned, it's enough that you meddled. More serious crimes aren't even necessary."

Helene could see that he was determined, but there was no point in joining battle at the moment. Better she do what she could to prepare for a future engagement. "If that's the way you feel, I suppose I ought to do some reassessing of my own."

"Yes, that might be wise."

"How long will you be gone?"

"I don't know. A week. Perhaps more."

"Shall I expect the worst?"

"Expect what you wish, but as far as I'm concerned, enough has finally become enough. I've taken your behavior for granted, Helene, as much as you've taken me for granted. It's been a mistake on both our parts." He closed the lid to his suitcase and zipped it shut. Then he looked at her.

Helene could feel how dead the space was between them. There was nothing really to appeal to. She eyed him blankly.

"What's most telling is that I don't really feel anything. Not even anger."

She didn't respond. She stood tall, her breasts arched under the silk of her gown. Her entire career was about to disappear out the door with Jed Daniels, and she didn't know what to do about it—how to respond. But Helene did know it was just a temporary setback. She would find a solution. She always had.

LOS ANGELES

May 13, 1985

2:15 P.M.

Quintin Wing listened to Lieutenant Murdoch relating the results of the day's investigation of Keith Moore's flight from London the night of the murder.

"Looks like the bastard was on the plane," he said glumly. "I thought sure we had something with that double."

The door to the squad room opened, and Tony Williams entered, looking less fresh than usual. "Christ."

"What happened?"

The young detective dropped into a chair next to Wing. "I've been holding Joan Clark's hand for the past couple of hours."

"Joan Clark?"

"The wife of the stunt man. She got hysterical when she found out we were looking for him, too. She's sure he ran off with another woman."

"Did you find out anything that'd help us?" Murdoch asked.

"Yeah. It looks like Clark was with her at a friend's birthday party that night. She gave me the guy's name, and I tracked him down at a car dealership in Glendale. He confirmed the wife's story. 'Course it's possible they're both covering for him."

"Naw," the lieutenant said, tossing down his pencil, "we've pretty well placed Moore on the plane. We found a passenger from first class who talked to Moore during the flight—even got his autograph. She's visiting from England—staying with relatives in Pasadena."

"Did she still have the autograph?"

"No, she mailed it back to her granddaughter in Birmingham. But she was sure the man she talked to was Moore. Wing suggested we check with immigration to compare the signature on the customs declaration."

"Actually it was Moore who suggested it. I don't know whether he's cocky because he planned this thing so damned well or because he's innocent. But I'm inclined to go with the latter."

"You're the number one boy on this one, Wing," Murdoch said after a while. "Where are we?"

"I still think Geoffrey Hammond is the key, but I can't figure out why."

"Maybe we ought to dig into him a little more, try and trace his movements around the time of the murder, that sort of thing."

"It wouldn't hurt, but the motive is still bothering me. He hated her enough—they all did. The timing is critical, though. Why was she killed when she was? Why would Geoffrey do it then?"

"Any ideas?"

"At first I thought because of the documents on her desk a financial connection was key. Then it looked like Geoffrey's mysterious lover was somehow important—if he could be connected to Helene Daniels. Now I'm beginning to think this film deal they all were involved in is the critical factor."

"Including Hammond?" Murdoch asked.

"I don't know."

"Are you going to find out?"

"That was part of my plan."

Murdoch smirked. "Are you going to divulge the rest of your plan, or do we have to wait for the TV movie of your life?"

"Obviously, I've got to talk to Hammond again. I'd like something to scare him with." He sat upright. "By the way, any word from the lab on those drinks?"

"Yeah," Murdoch said, flipping open the file in front of him. "Preliminary analysis shows both glasses to contain alcoholic beverages. One was concentrated, the other diluted. The diluted one had traces of carbonated gas, corn syrup, citric acid, sodium benzoate, and quinine."

"Quinine? That's probably tonic water. A vodka tonic?"

"Could be."

"That was probably Helene Daniels's. She drank vodka tonics. What about the other?"

"Eighty-six proof alcohol."

"That's all?"

"That's all Sid said."

"Shit. That doesn't tell us anything. Ask Sid whether it was vodka or gin, and vermouth—whether that could average out to eighty-six proof. Surely, they could tell if there was vermouth in the glass." Wing shook his head. "For Christ's sake, they ought to be able to smell the stuff and tell us what brand it was."

"What I got was just preliminary, Wing. Sid's boys should be able to pinpoint it down to which barrel in which distillery before they're through."

"Good, because I want something to hit Hammond between the eyes with." Wing got up.

"Where you going?"

"To call Felice Fallanti and see if I can talk to her some more about *Julius Caesar,* et al. Geoffrey Hammond's in the cast somewhere, and I'm going to find him."

BEL AIR

May 13, 1985

4:20 P.M.

"Afternoon, Mr. Wing." The houseboy, Jimmy, stepped back, gesturing for the detective to enter. "Mrs. Fallanti is upstairs. She said when you come to send you right on up." He grinned a toothy smile, and Quintin Wing headed for the staircase.

He found the door to her suite open, but there was no sign of Felice. He knocked lightly on the door.

"Is that you, Quintin?" came her disembodied voice.

"Yes."

"Come on back. I'm in the bathroom."

Grinning, he walked through the bedroom, glancing at the bed that had been the scene of such a delicious encounter. He stuck his head in the door and found Felice in the sunken malachite tub, covered to her chin with a mound of bubbles.

"I do hope you don't mind asking your questions while I bathe. I like doing more than one thing at a time, whenever possible. Amazing how it expands one's day." She smiled.

"Are you sure you want me in here?"

"Of course. We *are* acquainted, aren't we? Or have you already forgotten?"

"No, of course not."

She lifted a slender arm from the mountain of bubbles. "There's a stool," she said, pointing. "Appropriate, don't you think, if you're going to be milking me for information?"

He gave her a little smile.

"So, how's Leslie?"

"Fine."

"I've been thinking about it. You two would make a lovely couple. And your babies would be delicious—exotic and beautiful."

Wing smiled with embarrassment. "I think that's a little premature."

"Nonsense."

"We went to Michael's for dinner the other evening. Leslie said she'd first gone there with you. She spoke very highly of you, Felice."

"I'm fond of her. I really am. Actually, Leslie reminds me a lot of myself when I was young. There are major differences, of course, but they're generational as much as anything. But you didn't come to hear about the good old days." She looked him over.

"Tell me about Geoffrey Hammond, Felice."

She grimaced. "Lord, you'll have me a Judas yet. Quintin, the man's innocent."

"Then help me prove it."

"How?"

"Help me connect Geoffrey to the Gutzman deal."

"There is no connection. Believe me."

"Geoffrey's hiding something. I'm absolutely sure of it, Felice."

She sat immobile for a time, then slowly rose Botticelli-like from the water. Wing, surprised, stared at her glistening flesh and the soap bubbles—some sliding down her body, some clinging.

"Quintin, will you hand me my towel please?"

Wing grabbed a monogrammed bath sheet and handed it to her. She stepped from the tub, wrapping herself from chin to toe. She looked up at the detective. "I'm as certain of Geoffrey's innocence as you are of Leslie's, but you're right. He *has* been withholding something." She closed her eyes. "God forgive me," she mumbled.

ACAPULCO, MEXICO EARLY 1985

February 21

Helene Daniels hated Mexico as much as Jed loved it, maybe *because* he loved it. Acapulco in particular was depressing. It always looked tired to her, like tarnished gold.

Their house belonged to a forgotten generation, and it annoyed Helene that Jed should prefer Acapulco over places like Cancún or Cabo San Lucas, where important people who mattered went. Looking out the window of her limousine at the brightly lit boulevard ringing the bay, the sun long having set beyond the old town at the west end of the city, she decided that this was going to be her last trip here.

As they swept along the endless row of high-rise hotels, punctuated by shops selling junk or overpriced imported goods, Helene pondered the state Jed was likely to be in when she arrived. Doubtlessly, he had been sailing much of the time—he did when he brooded.

She remembered the long week she had spent there several years after their marriage. She had sat on the veranda overlooking the sea, while Jed went sailing, thinking about a financial crisis he was involved in at the time. Finally, one afternoon the monotonous runs stopped, and he came back up to the house and announced they were returning to Los Angeles.

At Jed's insistence Helen had learned to sail, but after that excruciating week she resisted going to Acapulco whenever she could. Since then, he had more often than not gone alone.

As the limousine circled the Diana Fountain, Helene considered her strategy. It was the smart move—to confront him here at his retreat before he had regrouped. Once he had made up his mind, Jed was a difficult man to deter.

Once they had left the bay and were in the dark twisting streets on the hill above the yacht club, Helen readied herself. The notion of surprising him, catching him off guard, pleased Helene because it gave her a controlling hand. She would start by trying to charm him. If that failed she would try to reason with him. Finally, if necessary, she would threaten him.

The limousine stopped in front of the house, and Helene waited for the driver to help her out. Then, standing at the foot of the cobbled walk, she looked through the growth of tropical shrubs toward the door. The house looked dark. Helen wondered if Jed might have gone out for dinner.

Helene made her way to the door in the darkness, the moon providing just enough light for her to find her way. Behind her the chauffeur padded along, carrying her bags.

"Leave them here," she said when they had come to the porch. She handed the man two twenty-dollar bills and waited as he retreated down the walk. She started to ring the bell but stopped herself. Instead, she put her hand on the door handle and, finding it open, entered.

The sitting room, an airy chamber with high ceilings and large, shuttered windows opening onto the sea, was dark, but there was a faint light coming from the adjoining dining room. There was the soft murmur of voices, then laughter. Jed's laugh was distinctive, higher than his voice, a little forced. Helene wondered who he could be entertaining.

She quietly stepped to the arched doorway overlooking the dining room three steps below. Facing her at the candlelit table was Jed. Another man sat opposite him, his back to Helene. As she moved into the aura of the candles, her husband saw her and his eyes rounded in surprise.

The other man, seeing Jed's shocked expression, spun around. It was Geoffrey Hammond.

The decorator jumped to his feet, the bathrobe he was wearing swinging open to reveal his naked body. He quickly pulled the edges of the garment closed.

"Helene," Jed said in a low, halting voice, "what are you doing here?"

She smiled sardonically. "Maybe I should be asking *you* that question."

Geoffrey backed away as she slowly descended the steps, taking in the scene—the bottle of wine on the table, the candles, and Jed, like Geoffrey, in a bathrobe.

"Why didn't you call?"

She stopped at the chair the decorator had vacated and rested her hand on its high back, eyeing Geoffrey, who was touching the table to steady himself. "I was curious what *boys* do when left to their own devices." She raked her eyes up and down her rival. "I guess now I know, don't I?"

Geoffrey was still white, but the surprise on his face gradually hardened into anger. Helene could feel his hatred. She turned to Jed.

"So, Jed darling, it's not enough that you threaten to ruin me financially, you have to humiliate me by shacking up with a raving faggot."

"What is it you want, Helene?" Jed's voice had taken on an edge.

"I came down here hoping to work things out with you . . ." She glanced at Geoffrey. ". . . but *this* seems to have changed things."

"Oh? What's different?"

"How do you think I feel? Discovering that my husband is not a man?"

"He's more of a man than you are a woman," Geoffrey snapped.

Helene turned to face him. "Is that right?" Her eyes bore into him. "How would *you* know anything about men? *Real* men. And it's for goddamn sure you don't know anything about women!"

"I know the difference between a whore and a lady."

"Geoffrey," Jed cut in, "just drop it."

"No, Jed, you aren't the only one who's suffered at the hands of this bitch."

"I don't give a goddamn what you think," Helene shrieked.

"Maybe so, but you're going to hear it whether you like it or not."

"Oh, go to hell!"

"That's your destination, not mine. I may be gay, but I've never been a whore. You fuck everybody you come into contact with, figuratively and literally—your own sister, Rina, Felice and Adolfo, Keith, me, even your own husband and stepdaughter."

Jed shifted in his chair. "Geoffrey..."

"No, somebody needs to tell her, Jed." He turned again to Helene. "You know how many lives you've ruined or nearly ruined? You think Leslie would have jumped into that marriage as a kid if she hadn't had such a screwed up stepmother tormenting her, destroying what she had with her father?"

"Well, if this little soap opera is over, I'll thank you to get the hell out of my house!"

"This is *my* house, not yours, Helene," Jed said evenly.

"That's something else that needs to be discussed," she replied icily, "but this is not the time. I've got a terrible headache. I'm going to bed, but I'd like to speak with you in the morning, Jed." She turned, pausing to look at Geoffrey. "I trust you'll be gone by then."

Helene went to the steps and slowly ascended.

"My bags are on the porch," she said, without looking back. "Would one of you so-called gentlemen be good enough to bring them up?"

February 22

Jed Daniels was standing in his sloop, hoisting the mainsail, as Helene slowly made her way out on the dock. She said nothing, waiting until he finally turned around and saw her.

"Making a habit these days of sneaking up on people, aren't you?"

"You knew I wanted to talk to you this morning. Why did you leave?"

"I wanted to go sailing."

"At least you didn't bring *him* with you. For Christ's sake why couldn't you at least have had the decency to be involved with a woman?"

"Frankly, your embarrassment came pretty low on my list of considerations."

"Obviously, you didn't think of me at all."

"For once you're right. I didn't think of you at all."

She watched him rig the jib. When he had finished, he reached over for the tie lines, ignoring her hovering presence.

"Jed, we're going to talk about this."

"I'm going sailing," he replied without looking up.

Helene stepped into the boat without hesitating. "God-damn it. We're going to talk about it *now.*"

Jed moved past her, releasing the other tie line and push-ing off from the dock as the sail luffed above them. He sat at the stern and began taking slack from the sheets. Helene dropped onto a cushion, ducking under the boom as it moved across the boat in the light breeze. The sail caught just enough wind to move slowly into the channel.

Jed was looking into the bay, ignoring her. Helene watched him nervously fingering the tiller. "Have you de-cided to destroy my career in films? Is that what it's come down to?"

"I haven't decided anything. I don't care about your career."

"You made a commitment to me, and now you're trying to pull the rug out from under my feet."

"I never committed to help you with your dirty tricks."

"Oh, for God's sake, Jed. This is business. I haven't done anything you or any other businessman doesn't do as a matter of course."

"It's still my right to choose whom I associate with and where I invest my money."

"And leave me out to dry?"

"Maybe that's part of the risk you take."

She looked at his cold, unyielding face. "I didn't marry you for business reasons. I thought you were my husband, not an adversary. But I'm beginning to see I was wrong. At first you doled out your largesse under the guise of gener-osity. But I see now that wasn't your real objective—you were just trying to control me with your money, make me dependent and beholden to you."

"Well, I'm sorry my money has been such a problem."

"It's been a weapon, and you know it. You never really gave a shit about me. It was owning me that you cared about, that's all that's ever mattered. And do you know why? Because you're not capable of winning anyone's love."

"Helene, you'd sold your soul to the devil long before I ever came into the picture. You just don't like the short end of the stick now that it's in your hand."

They had moved out into the bay, and Jed began tacking

into the wind in the direction of Roqueta Island. Helene ducked as the boom swept across the boat.

"I can take an occasional setback, that's not the problem. You want to know what the real problem is? You can't stand the fact that I'm successful. Every day I grow bigger and stronger, and it galls you. You can't bear the thought of a wife who can stand on her own two feet. *That's* the real problem."

Jed scoffed. "You're worth more today than most people could earn in two or three lifetimes and you're accusing *me* of using *you?* You've got it backwards, Helene darling. If anyone has been used, it's me."

"Oh sure! You've been generous all right—giving just enough slack to keep me on the line. But every time I'm on the verge of really doing something that counts, you reel me back in. No, Jed, I haven't used you, you've manipulated me. And every time I've become a threat to your goddamn male ego, you've repressed me, kept me down."

He laughed. "Jesus Christ. How many people on this earth would like to suffer the kind of repression you've had to endure?"

Helene's blood began to boil. "Do you deny it? Do you deny that you're killing the Gutzman deal just to cut me down to size?"

"I didn't kill the Gutzman deal. I just refused to put my money in it."

"It's the same thing!"

"Get your money somewhere else."

"Yeah, sure!" She glared.

Jed tacked again and Helene ducked, wanting with all her heart to kick him in his goddamned pompous face.

"Maybe the time has come to terminate our financial relationship," he said calmly.

"Maybe it has." The warm sea breeze was nothing compared to the fever inside her. "Maybe it's time to terminate our relationship—period. I'll be damned if I'll have people thinking I'm sharing with that goddamned faggot."

"There's nothing between you and me but my money. There hasn't been for years."

"You and I know that, but now it's time for the world to know it."

"You want a divorce, then?"

"Yes. But I won't settle for what was in that premarital agreement. It was an unequal contract. You forced it on me and you can't make it stick."

"Sounds like you've already been to see your divorce attorney."

"Let's say I'm prepared to fight you to the bitter end."

"Well, threaten if you like. I know that agreement will hold up. It's a damn shame you'll get that much though, considering what you deserve."

She gave him a hateful smile. "I'll beat you one way or another—even if I have to drag your other 'woman' into it."

"No court cares about that, and you know it."

"I'm not concerned with courts. I'm going to ruin your reputation if you don't give me what I want."

The ice on Jed's face broke and he began to seethe, his neck turning red. "You're just a good-for-nothing slut."

"If this is going to get nasty, you'll find out you've never really known me at all."

"What's left?"

"Your darling daughter. Have you forgotten Leslie? What do you suppose she'd think of her big strong daddy involved with faggots?"

"Helene, you wouldn't."

"Oh, wouldn't I?"

His eyes narrowed. "For two cents I'd kill you, right here and now."

She laughed. "Aren't we brave, though?"

They had passed the mouth of the bay and were in open seas. In the heat of the argument Jed had let the wind get abeam and the boat began to tip. He threw his body against the rising gunwale, frantically loosening the sheets to slack off. The tiller slipped from his grasp. Jed lunged for it and slid, the swinging boom catching him on the side of the head.

Helene clung to the boat. A wave washed over the side, drenching her. She was frozen, immobile. Then she saw Jed clinging to the far gunwale. He was dazed, his body half in the boat, half out of it.

He was just inches from her feet, helpless and teetering.

Helene suddenly realized her physical advantage. His death flashed before her, and she calmly lifted her foot and gave him a shove. Two or three pushes and she managed to roll him over the side.

As he slipped from sight, Jed frantically reached up with his hand and grasped the gunwale. An instant later his face reappeared over the side of the boat. There was fear in his eyes as he peered at her, the rushing water tugging at him.

"For God's sake, Helene," he gasped. "There are sharks..."

Then, as she watched, he lost his grasp and slipped away.

"Helene!"

She stared at him waving frantically as the boat silently moved off. Then Helene calmly slid over to the stern of the craft and took the tiller, still watching him bobbing in the waves. "No, Jed darling," she whispered. "I'm sorry, but you're worth more to me dead than alive. I'll let the sharks have you."

BEVERLY HILLS

May 14, 1985

1:40 P.M.

Wing and Williams found Geoffrey Hammond behind the desk of his private office. He looked back and forth between the police officers. "I feel outnumbered."

"You don't have to talk to us if you don't wish to."

"Oh shit, better here than under your bright lights." He sighed. "Let's get on with it."

"I understand you were in Acapulco when Jed Daniels died, Mr. Hammond. Why didn't you tell me during our earlier conversations?" Wing asked.

"There's nothing that says I had to volunteer it, is there?"

"It doesn't exactly make you look good."

"That's why I didn't tell you—it's a damned-if-you-do, damned-if-you-don't situation."

"Well, I know now, so why don't you tell me what you were doing in Acapulco."

"Jed and I were having an affair."

"How long had your relationship been going on?"

"A few months. It was a casual thing, certainly nothing that would drive me to murder."

247

"But you had an encounter with Helene Daniels over it, didn't you?"

"She walked in on us, yes. Obviously she wasn't pleased, but it was really Jed's problem, not mine. I spent a miserable night after she arrived and left early the next morning. I went to the Princess Hotel for a couple of days, then came home." He cleared his throat. "I wasn't even aware Jed had died until I got back."

"You don't know what transpired between them after her arrival?"

"No. I was gone before either of them were up."

"You heard nothing? No arguments, fights?"

"No."

"But Helene was clearly upset about your relationship with her husband."

"She didn't like the idea of being upstaged, regardless of the circumstances. She didn't give a damn about Jed. It was his assertion of independence she couldn't stomach."

"You say you and Jed Daniels had only a brief relationship. Did he have any other gay affairs that you are aware of? Did Helene know?"

"Jed was essentially bisexual. To my knowledge there was no one else at the time."

"Was Helene surprised to find you together?"

"Yes. She didn't know about us—or about Jed's sexual preferences."

"You and Helene didn't discuss the matter again?"

"I never laid eyes on her after that night."

The phone rang; Geoffrey ignored it, but his clerk didn't.

"Excuse me, Mr. Hammond," Richard said from the doorway, "but William Burrows is on the phone. I told him you were busy, but he insisted it was urgent."

Geoffrey twitched nervously, then glowered at his employee. "Take a number. I'm not to be disturbed."

The clerk withdrew, and Geoffrey rocked back in his chair, observing the detectives.

"Does this Acapulco business put me in the soup?" he asked.

"I have a feeling you aren't coming clean," Wing replied. "Call it a sixth sense."

"Excuse me, Mr. Hammond." It was Richard again. "He absolutely insists he must speak with you."

Geoffrey grimaced. "Sorry," he said to the detectives before picking up the phone. "Yes? . . . Look, this is not a good time to talk . . . Oh." He glanced at Wing. "Well, the piece you wanted hasn't arrived. I suggest you go ahead and make that contact you were talking about."

He hung up, turning his attention once more to his visitors. "Seems as though when people give you a little business they think they own you."

"We're obviously taking up a lot of your valuable time." The police officers rose.

"Mr. Hammond," Williams said coolly, "I think it might be best if you didn't make any out-of-town trips without checking with us first."

The decorator got to his feet, searching Wing's face.

"Our options are somewhat limited," the detective said. "With Mr. and Mrs. Daniels both dead, you're about the only one we can discuss this with—unless perhaps there's someone else Helene Daniels might have talked to about what happened in Mexico?"

"I don't know who."

Just then, Wing remembered Leslie's insistence that Helene had killed Jed.

MALIBU

May 14, 1985

2:55 P.M.

As he drove, Wing's mind drifted back and forth between Leslie and Geoffrey Hammond. He had a vaguely uncomfortable feeling there was a piece of the puzzle he was missing. He knew his subconscious mind was trying to communicate with him, but he didn't know what it wanted to say.

On the ride back downtown to drop Williams off, he and Tony had compared impressions of Geoffrey Hammond, but Tony hadn't been around the decorator enough to have gleaned the same insights. Nevertheless, he agreed that something was wrong with the man—something more than having been caught with Helene Daniels's husband.

Wing was a quarter of a mile from Leslie Randall's place when, on an impulse, he swung into a gas station to use the phone. He dialed Robbery–Homicide, then waited for Williams to come onto the line.

"Quintin, I'm glad you called. The lab sent up a detailed report on those drinks."

"Yeah . . ."

"One was a vodka tonic, like you thought. The other was straight Scotch."

"Straight Scotch? No water, no melted ice cubes?"

"That's right. A blended Scotch whisky. Sid says if they went out to the house, they could tell which bottle it came out of."

"Scotch?"

"Yeah, you were hoping for a martini, weren't you?"

"Expecting a martini, let's put it that way. Shit."

"Back to the drawing boards?"

"No, not necessarily." He thought for a moment. "Well, the reason I called was to see what you thought about the idea of putting a tail on Hammond."

"What for?"

"I don't know, exactly. I just have the feeling he ought to be watched."

"Want me to talk to Murdoch about it?"

"I was having trouble justifying it in my own mind and wanted your reaction."

"What the hell, he may not mind a short surveillance. I think the captain's putting pressure on him. This could have gone to Divisional Homicide, you know..."

Wing was staring idly at the traffic, half concentrating on Williams, half concentrating on his own rambling thoughts when his mind focused on a red Porsche on the far side of the street stopped at a traffic light. He immediately recognized Leslie Randall by her tawny hair. She turned her head just enough to reveal the familiar, lovely profile, but couldn't see him from where she was.

"Listen Tony, I've got to go. Talk to Murdoch about the tail, will you?" He hung up just as the light changed and traffic began to move. Leslie's window was up so there was no point in shouting at her. Wing jumped into his unmarked car.

She was well up the street and out of sight by the time Wing got across the flow of traffic and headed down the Coast Highway in pursuit. He maneuvered his way through the flow of cars, hoping he was gaining ground, but unsure because the Porsche was still not in sight.

Wing was just beginning to wonder whether he'd lost her when he caught a glimpse of the Porsche ahead, weaving through the traffic. Wherever Leslie was headed, she was in a hurry.

The detective managed to stay about fifty yards behind her, though it wasn't easy. But by the time they got to Venice, they were in heavy traffic, and it became stop and go. Wing got stuck behind another car, and Leslie went through the light at Rose Avenue on caution. Swinging around the car in front of him, he went through the red light, receiving a blast from the horn of an angry motorist. Around 18th or 19th, Leslie turned toward the beach and, judging by the way she slowed, began looking for a place to park. The detective paused at the head of the street until he saw her pull into a spot.

Leslie jumped from the Porsche and began half walking, half running up the sidewalk. Wing couldn't find a place to park and finally stopped in front of a fire hydrant. He got out of the car and ran after her.

At the foot of the street Leslie crossed the freeway and went directly to the boardwalk. It was obvious she was not just out for a casual stroll.

Wing dropped back a discreet distance, but Leslie was still moving very quickly. He wished it were a weekend, because it would have been easier to hide in the crowds. Still, Leslie didn't appear at all concerned about the possibility of being followed. She seemed too much in a hurry to be worried about anything.

Then, suddenly, there was a shout over the sound of the wind in the palms and the traffic on the freeway. Farther up the walk, a man was waving his arm, and Leslie took off for him in a dead run.

Wing watched in disbelief as the woman of his dreams —the tawny-haired beauty with the fabulous body—threw herself into the arms of the man, a stranger. He stared at the couple embracing, feeling his guts seeping from him and spilling onto the sidewalk.

Wing couldn't see the man's face, but he saw Leslie's. She was smiling, joyful. After a long time they separated, but the man still held Leslie's arms. He was shaking his head, and she was beaming up at him.

The detective felt betrayed, stung by her affection for another. He eyed the man's back and slightly rounded shoulders, his gray blond hair, realizing he was older, probably double Leslie's age.

From time to time Leslie pressed her head against the man's shoulder. Wing decided it had been some time since she had seen the guy—a former lover? But watching them, he read something in their behavior that didn't compute. While he struggled with the confusion in his mind, the couple went to an empty bench.

Wing drifted to one nearby but on the opposite side of the walk. It was occupied by an older couple who looked at him with annoyance for intruding. Ignoring them, he glanced up and saw that Leslie's back was not to him and for the first time he had a clear look at the man's face.

Wing froze. Recognition struck. He remembered the photograph he had looked at under the street light sitting in his MG with Leslie. The man with Leslie was none other than Jed Daniels!

A dead man—the pivotal person in Helene Daniels's life—wasn't dead at all. The detective's mind was spinning as he tried to sort out the implications. Helene, Leslie, Geoffrey—Geoffrey! He *knew* that Daniels was alive. And now here was Leslie, sitting talking to the man the world thought was dead. But her excitement at seeing him—the mad rush to Venice Beach—had to mean she'd just found out that her father was alive. God Almighty.

Whatever was being discussed, it wasn't just a light-hearted family chat, judging by Daniels's expression. The man's face looked pained, somber. He shook his head and touched Leslie frequently—at one point she put her head on his shoulder and he held her. It looked to Wing as though she might be crying.

After another five or ten minutes, Leslie Randall and her father stood. She headed back down the walk toward Wing, who pivoted on the bench, away from her line of sight. Jed Daniels walked off in the other direction.

When Leslie had passed him, Wing rose and went the other way, in pursuit of her father—the man who supposedly had died in Acapulco Bay.

VENICE

May 14, 1985

4:35 P.M.

Quintin Wing stood in a phone booth staring at an old rundown building across the street, the telephone receiver against his ear.

"Murdoch, this is Wing. Listen, I'm in a pay phone across the street from the Palm Dunes Motel on Venice Boulevard out by the beach. Jed Daniels is in room twelve. I tailed him here."

"Jed Daniels? He's dead."

"That's what I thought, too. But he's here, big as life."

"Goddamn."

There was silence.

"How'd you find him?"

"A chance thing. I'll tell you about it later. Right now I'd like for you to get some people out here to watch him."

"What about you?"

"I'm going back to Beverly Hills to talk to Hammond again. This gives me something to hit him over the head with. Tell Williams to meet me there, will you?"

"Okay. But why don't we pick up Daniels while we're at it?"

"I'd like to find out what he's up to, first. It's something, that's for sure. I talked to the clerk at the motel. Daniels is registered under the name William Burrows. It didn't hit me at first, but then I remembered that while Tony and I were at the Beverly Hills shop, Hammond got a call from somebody named Burrows."

"You think Daniels'll sit tight?"

"The clerk said he mostly stays in his room, paid a week in advance, and has been there two days. I'm sure he didn't know I tailed him."

"Okay, I'll get somebody out there. Shouldn't be more than twenty or thirty minutes at the most."

BEVERLY HILLS

May 14, 1985

5:15 P.M.

Tony Williams was already in Hammond's shop when Wing arrived. "Where's Hammond?"

Williams grimaced. "The clerk here says he took off just after we left this afternoon."

Wing stepped over to the man. "Any idea where he went?"

"No. He didn't say anything except make sure I closed up properly."

The detectives looked at each other.

"Sounds like he isn't coming back today."

Richard sighed. "I just hope it's not another trip."

"Another trip?"

"After Acapulco he was only back for a couple of days, and then he took off for Rio." He looked up at Wing. "Don't you think that's a little much? I'm not paid to run this place, but it seems like I'm here alone most of the time."

"When did Mr. Hammond get back from Brazil?"

"I don't know. A couple of weeks ago, I suppose." He looked at his watch. "Can I go now? I don't get paid for overtime."

"Yeah, in a minute." Wing turned to Williams. "Anybody try him at home?"

"Richard here tried when I arrived. No answer. He said he also tried earlier when he had a question for a customer. No answer then either."

Wing looked at the clerk again. "Do you know anybody named William Burrows?"

"Yes. Well, I don't know him. He's a friend or customer of Mr. Hammond's. He's been calling here the last few days."

"Has he come by the shop?"

"No."

"You've never seen him?"

"No."

"I'm going to call headquarters, Tony."

"Anything on Burrows?" he asked when Murdoch came on the line.

"Yeah. He skipped."

"Skipped?"

"When the team got there he was already gone."

"Shit, I wonder what happened. I'm sure he didn't see me."

"No. Apparently, he paid the clerk to tip him if there were any calls or people looking for him. I guess he got the word right after you left. Clerk said he left in a cab. We're tracking down the dispatch."

"Hammond's disappeared, too. I think we'd better put out an APB on both of them."

"Right. I've already got one out on Daniels. I'll add Hammond. Looks like these are our boys, Quintin."

"Yeah."

Wing hung up, then glanced at the shop clerk. "One more call."

"Hello?"

Hearing Leslie Randall's voice, Wing's heart leaped. "Hi, it's Quintin."

"Hi."

He heard nothing in her voice that betrayed the weighty events of the day. "Any plans for dinner?"

"No."

"Can I take you out for a bite?"

"Sure."

"I'm just wrapping up a few things, so it might have to be a late meal, if you don't mind."

"No, I can wait."

"I'll give you a call when I'm on my way."

"Fine."

Wing hung up, feeling a great sense of relief. Williams was looking at him, shaking his head. "Jesus, Quintin. I don't take the time to call my wife, and you're making dates?"

"Shit, Tony. You don't want me hurting my mom's feelings, do you?"

"Your mom?"

LOS ANGELES

May 14, 1985

As they were driving back downtown, Wing and Williams got the news over the car radio that Hammond had been tracked down.

They found the decorator at a table in the interrogation room, his head in his hands. He looked up when the door opened.

"Thank God, a familiar face."

Wing furrowed his brow. "Not so friendly as in the past, Geoffrey. You haven't been playing straight with me."

Geoffrey closed his eyes. "God, why don't you just shoot me and get it over with?"

"Do you suppose if I asked you for the whole truth I'd get it this time?"

"God, will you believe *anything* I say?"

"That depends. Start by telling me where Jed Daniels is."

"I wish I knew."

"This is another inauspicious beginning."

"It's the truth. I lied when I told you I never saw Jed after the night Helene arrived because I was trying to protect him—that's the only reason."

259

"It'd be a shame," Williams interjected, "if Daniels took off and left you holding the bag, after you've been so loyal to him."

"If that's calculated to induce something, it won't do any good." His eyes flashed. "I'm telling you the truth."

"All right, Geoffrey. Why don't we take it from the top. Tell us exactly what happened since that night Helene arrived in Acapulco, and please, no little white lies."

"Okay. Acapulco." Geoffrey shuddered, then looked squarely at Wing. "What I told you this afternoon was true. I left the morning after Helene arrived before either one of them came down. But, contrary to what I said earlier, it wasn't the last time I saw Jed."

"We're listening."

"I took a cab to the Princess, had a couple of martinis in the bar, and went up to my room. Like I told you, I hadn't slept well the night before. I fell asleep soon after I lay down. A couple of hours later, the phone rang and woke me up. It was Jed on a house phone down in the lobby saying he needed money to pay a cab.

"I went down and found him half soaked, his hair a mess. I paid the driver, and we went upstairs."

"What happened?"

"They had gone sailing. Jed was hit in the head by the boom and, while he lay stunned, Helene had pushed him overboard. She just sailed away, leaving him to drown. Jed's a good swimmer, and he managed to swim and float for an hour, but sharks taunted him, and he could see he wasn't making much progress. He'd just about given up when some American tourists in a pleasure boat happened by and pulled him from the water.

"He didn't tell them what happened, trying to decide whether he ought to go to the police. But he started thinking about it and figured Helene would deny his story. The most he could have hoped for was her disappointment. The more he thought about it, the more he realized that revenge would be sweeter if he waited and showed up later, at some particularly dramatic moment."

"Like when she was about to spend his money?"

"Yes, that sort of thing."

"All right, so then what happened?"

"Jed told the people who picked him up that he had been out alone, the boat sank, and so forth. He acted terribly humiliated, thanked them profusely, and after they had put him ashore, they went on their way. Then he came to my hotel."

"And enlisted your support in perpetuating the hoax."

"Yes, I suppose you could put it that way."

"So what did you do?"

"At first Jed wanted to lay low for a few days, rest and enjoy the anonymity of death. I hid him in my room without any trouble, and we discussed—planned, I guess—his revenge on Helene. Before long we had a pretty elaborate scheme worked out, designed to magnify the impact on her—to hurt her the most."

"Like kill her?" Williams asked.

Geoffrey looked at the detective. "No, we never even considered it. We wanted to shock and humiliate her."

"Okay," Wing said, "go ahead with your story."

"We realized it would be difficult to stay in Acapulco and too risky to come back here to L.A., so we ended up deciding to go to South America for a couple of months."

"How did you manage without a passport for Daniels?" Williams asked.

"First we went to Mexico City. We needed money, so I had several thousand transferred from my bank, and then we arranged to buy a forged passport under the name William Burrows.

"There was a wait for the passport, so I came back to L.A.—to make arrangements for my shop. Jed wanted me to talk to Leslie and tell her what was up, so she would know he was all right, but she was away somewhere grieving, and I couldn't find her. When I had things in order here, I returned to Mexico City."

"And?" Wing prompted.

"Jed had picked up his passport, but we were out of money again. I brought a little more with me, but I'm not a rich man. Fortunately, Jed had one of those hidden accounts in the Cayman Islands, so we flew there on our way to Rio. Once we got there, we rented a villa in a lovely part of town and settled in." Geoffrey had a wistful expression on his face.

"We spent two wonderful months in Rio and realized we didn't really want to come back. But Jed wasn't going to leave Helene with his money, so we knew we'd have to return for a while. Besides, I wanted to sell everything here, and Jed was still worried about Leslie. He didn't want to take the chance of calling her, so he agonized and ended up leaving things as they were.

"Late in April we decided it was time to come back and drop the bombshell on Helene. The prospect was really a glorious one, because we both hated her guts."

"So you both came back?"

"No, not exactly. Just before we were scheduled to leave, Jed got ill. We didn't know what it was, but he looked terrible. He assured me he'd be all right—just needed a day or two of rest—and told me to go on without him. I was worried, but I decided he'd tell me if there was something serious. So I came on back."

"And he stayed on in Rio?"

"Yes."

"Did Jed come later, then?"

"That's just it. I waited, expecting to hear from him, but no call from the airport, no call from Rio."

"Did you call him?"

"Not at first. I was back for three or four days when I got up one morning and read that Helene had been murdered. God, what a shock—considering. You don't know how much I was anticipating seeing her face when Jed walked in—that was the biggest disappointment about the whole mess. God."

"What about Jed?"

"Of course, I called Rio immediately. It was a little difficult communicating with the household staff, but after three or four calls, I finally got the impression Jed had left the house a couple of days earlier. Needless to say, I was worried sick. I finally sent a cable to Jed in care of the owner of the villa, under the theory that he could get it to him if anybody could."

"What was in the cable?"

"I told him about Helene being murdered."

"Any response?"

"No, that's what's strange. We never made contact. As a matter of fact, I've never seen Jed since I left Rio."

Williams scoffed. "You took a call from William Burrows while we were visiting you this afternoon."

"Oh, I've talked to Jed. He's called me several times in the last few days."

"The last few days?"

"Yes, the first time I heard from him was two days ago."

"Did he explain where he's been?"

"Not exactly; our conversations have been very brief."

"What'd Daniels say when he called?" Wing asked.

"He was upset about Helene's death."

"Upset?"

"Well, the bitch did rob him of his big surprise, didn't she?"

Williams slowly walked around behind the decorator. "Maybe he decided on a different sort of surprise."

Geoffrey turned around. "What are you trying to say? That Jed killed Helene?"

Williams gave a quirky little smile. "The thought has occurred to me."

"No, I'm sure he didn't. He was worried about me and Leslie; that's mainly what he talked about. Of course, I told him you were breathing down my neck—all our necks."

"He didn't say where he'd been and what he was doing?" Wing asked.

"Well, he said he'd been sick and then, when he got my message about Helene, he started worrying. He realized that it might not be an auspicious time to make a reappearance, so he decided to lay low for a while."

Wing leaned forward, watching Geoffrey's eyes. "You said he got your message. You mean the telegram?"

"Well, I suppose that's what he meant."

"When, exactly, did you send it?"

"Let's see. When was Helene shot?"

"Late the night of Friday, May third, or very early Saturday morning."

"That's right, a Friday night. I started calling Rio the next day when I heard. But I don't think I sent the cable until the day after that, on Sunday."

"Can you give us the name of the landlord and the address you sent it to?"

"Sure. I have it here in my address book." Geoffrey reached into his jacket and took out his address book. He pointed to a page and Wing jotted down the information.

"So Daniels didn't tell you exactly where he'd been and when."

"No. Like I said, he was very brief. He was concerned about Leslie and me."

"What did he say when he called this afternoon while we were in the office?"

"Well, not much. I guess you heard, I was trying to cut him off because you were there."

"What'd he say?"

The decorator sighed. "He said you guys were getting too close and he couldn't risk sticking around any longer."

"What else?"

"He said he'd see me in Rio."

"I thought you didn't know where he's headed?"

"I don't know how he's getting there or where he went after the call."

Wing stood. "Tony, tell Murdoch it's probably Rio."

Geoffrey groaned as he watched Williams leave the room. "I'll never forgive myself."

Wing leaned over the table as the door closed across the room. "There was something else you said on the phone, Geoffrey."

"You mean my comment about something hadn't arrived? That was just talk to make you think I was speaking to a customer."

"No, not that. You said something to Jed about making contact with somebody. What was that all about?"

"Leslie. I was trying to tell him he'd better get off his ass and see her if he was going to."

"Hadn't he seen her yet?"

"No, he was afraid to until things had cleared up regarding the murder. But then he called me from the airport before your cohorts came to arrest me and told me he had seen her this afternoon."

"What else?"

"Nothing much else. It was a forty-five-second conversation. What could the man say? He was upset, I know that. I did tell him he ought to stay and help clear things up, but he just hung up on me."

They both looked up as Tony Williams came back into the room.

"They're on it. Murdoch had four guys out at the airport. He's sending a couple more."

"I'll never forgive myself," Geoffrey mumbled.

Williams inclined his head toward the decorator. "Murdoch said to do whatever you wanted here."

Geoffrey's eyes were closed. "God, what I wouldn't give for a martini." In the ensuing silence he opened his eyes and looked at the two detectives. "I'm afraid to ask."

"What?"

"Am I going to spend the evening at Spago or San Quentin?"

"Geoffrey, since you've been so straight with us, I'm inclined to say Spago—if you can get a table."

The decorator's eyes rounded. "Really?"

Wing nodded.

"Bless you, Inspector Wing." He smiled happily. "May you have many children."

Williams laughed. "Odds are he already does."

Wing smirked. "One more question, Geoffrey."

"Yes?"

"What's Jed Daniels's drink?"

"His what?"

"His drink. When he's having a cocktail, what does he like to drink."

"Scotch."

"Soda or water?"

"Neither, he likes to drink it straight, no ice cubes, no nothing. A habit he picked up in the service, I think."

Wing and Williams looked at each other.

"Why ever would you ask a question like that?"

"We thought we'd send him a bottle in Rio."

"You think he made it?"

"There's the door and freedom, my friend. Maybe he'll call and let you know."

MALIBU

May 14, 1985

Wing knocked softly and waited, his gut tight, his brain sour with dread, though he was anxious to see her. In a moment the door swung open and Leslie stood before him in crisp narrow jeans and a white cotton vee-neck sweater. Her sleeves were pushed up to the elbow. He was still savoring the vision when she stepped onto the deck and slipped her arms around his neck. She kissed him long and tenderly on the lips.

"I'm glad you're here," she whispered.

He just looked at her, unable to speak.

"I hope you don't mind eating here instead of going out."

He shook his head. "No."

Leslie took his hand and led him inside to the kitchen. "Pour yourself some wine, if you like. Glasses are in the cupboard."

"Would you like some?"

"If you are."

Wing poured while Leslie took the steaks to the barbecue out on the deck. When she came back into the kitchen he handed her a glass. "To your art," he said, touching his glass to hers. "May I soon have the privilege of seeing it."

They sat at a little drop-leaf table in the corner of the living room, a single candle flickering between them, Andreas Vollenweider playing on the stereo, and the sound of the pounding surf coming in the partially open slider.

"Quintin, there's no point in hiding it. My father called me from the airport. You probably know already, don't you?"

The surprise at her remark only lasted a moment. A feeling of regret stabbed at him. Wing knew they would have to face it eventually and, by bringing it up, Leslie had given him license to pursue the subject. "Did he admit to you that he killed your stepmother?"

Leslie bowed her head. "Yes."

"I figured he told you this afternoon at the beach."

She looked up with surprise.

"By chance I spotted you on the way to meet him and followed you."

"You followed me?"

"I was on my way to see you when I saw you driving down the Coast Highway, Leslie. My intent wasn't to spy on you . . . it just worked out that way."

"I guess I can't fault you for that." She searched his face. "I'm just so relieved to know he's alive."

He pulled her hand to his lips and kissed her fingers.

"Daddy made it out of the country, didn't he?"

"Yes, we think so."

"Thank goodness."

He watched her, a half-smile on his face.

"If you were there this afternoon, why didn't you arrest him?"

"I didn't have any cause. The fact that he was alive and not dead made him a possible suspect, but we didn't get the whole story until we talked to Geoffrey Hammond later this afternoon. By then it was too late."

"Then you know about Geoffrey, too?"

"You mean the fact that they were in Acapulco and Rio together?"

She nodded.

"Yes, Geoffrey told us everything. When did you find out?"

Leslie shivered involuntarily. "Daddy told me," she said, dropping her eyes.

"It was a rough day for you, wasn't it?"

"I'm so relieved, though."

"I am, too. I've hated this case from the minute I laid eyes on you. I'm sorry about your dad, but I'm glad it's over."

"What about my father?"

"As long as he's careful and stays in Brazil, he's probably safe."

"Thank God," Leslie said with sigh. "Want some dessert?"

"No thanks. It was a great meal, but I couldn't eat anything else."

"Want to go out on the deck and get some air? There's a big moon coming up over the hills."

They went out into the night, Leslie sinking immediately against him, the cool salt air caressing them both. They watched the moonlight on the surf. Wing held her close.

"Life is strange, isn't it?" she said. "This was the last way on earth I ever thought it would happen."

Leslie looked up at him and he kissed her, drawing her long, voluptuous body against him. They kissed deeply, their bodies melding together.

"Quintin," she said, her lips against his neck, his arms encircling her protectively, "would you like to see my paintings?"

The curtain billowed slightly in the breeze that washed over their naked bodies. Wing looked at her skin, bathed in moonlight.

Strands of her hair crisscrossed her face, silver threads in the moonlight. He knew he loved her.

Leslie moaned slightly and moved in her sleep, easing her body near his.

Wing savored her closeness. Though he was tired, he couldn't let go, he couldn't abandon her.

Feeling moved by the spell, he lightly touched her

breast, amazed that she was really there and that he had actually made love with her. What was it about her that affected him so?

Leslie didn't move. Wing stared. There was something unfathomable about the woman. He didn't understand it. Perhaps no one could, not even Leslie Randall.

WESTWOOD

June 5, 1985

2:30 P.M.

Kathryn Wing looked at her son over the pile of exam papers on her desk. "You know, dear, you never cease to amaze me."

"Why's that?"

"Do you remember when you were in high school and seduced that little Filipino maid we had?"

"What about her?"

"I thought that would be the height of your capacity for surprise — as regards women, I mean."

"What are you trying to say? That you're shocked Leslie and I are living together?"

"No, dear, of course not. My students are even younger than you, don't forget. Young people now do all sorts of things with each other, including living together without the benefit of matrimony. Lord, my younger colleagues on the faculty do as well."

"What have I done that shocks your sensibilities, then?"

"That's overstating the case, Quintin. I was alluding to the fact that your young lady is the daughter of the man you exposed as the murderer of her stepmother."

270

"It was an unusual family, I'll admit. But I hope you won't hold that against Leslie."

"Of course I won't. I'm pleased that the two of you are coming to dinner this evening."

"Leslie's been anxious to meet you. I just wanted you to know I'd moved in with her before we came over."

"I must admit I'd begun to worry when you never answered your phone." She contemplated him. "Are you going to give up your condo, or is that too personal a question?"

Wing smiled. "Mother, you'll be the first to know."

"So, how are you enjoying your retirement? Or is *that* too personal a question?"

They both laughed.

"I'm enjoying it. And I'm especially glad my last case is behind me."

"It must have been trying...considering Leslie's involvement. When did you discover that her father was the culprit?"

"Not until the eleventh hour."

"And he's in South America now?"

"Yes. In Brazil."

"Could you get a conviction?"

"Admittedly, the case has a number of holes from a legal standpoint, though I doubt he'll ever be brought to trial."

"What sort of holes?"

"We don't have a weapon or much in the way of physical evidence. There's the drink—the straight Scotch—we found at the scene of the murder. Apart from his flight and confession to Leslie, that drink is, to my mind, the most damning piece of evidence, though I realize it wouldn't be overwhelming in court."

"It sounds as though everybody is satisfied Mr. Daniels did it, though."

"Lieutenant Murdoch is a little frustrated at the loose ends, but he's glad we've identified the killer anyway."

"What loose ends?"

"Murdoch wanted Daniels placed in L.A. the night of the murder, but we haven't been able to do it."

"*We,* Quintin?"

"They."

Kathryn grinned at her son.

"There's no record at customs of his coming into the country, and nothing that the airlines have been able to give us. The best bet is that he entered via Mexico or something of that sort. It makes sense."

"What about verifying when he left Brazil?"

"Murdoch is working on that. As a matter of fact, the captain went to an FBI training school with a high official in the Rio police. He called down there to ask for a little help in tidying up the file. From what I understand they won't do much for us officially, but Murdoch said the captain thinks as a favor they might unofficially verify some things for the department."

There was a knock at the door. Kathryn looked at her watch. "An anxious student," she said. "He's early."

"Well, I'll run along," Wing said, getting to his feet. He went to the door. "See you tonight, Mother."

"Yes, dear. I'm very anxious to meet Leslie."

MALIBU

June 5, 1985

4:50 P.M.

Wing touched her chin with his index finger, then ran it slowly down her neck, across her chest, up the mound of her naked breast, and over the erect nipple. Leslie trembled.

"God, Quintin. Every time I think I couldn't possibly do it again, you touch me and I want you some more."

He leaned over and lightly kissed her lower lip, nibbling at it with his teeth. She slipped her fingers into the hair at the back of his head and pulled his mouth hard against hers.

"Do you know how many times we've made love in the past three weeks?" she mumbled into his lips.

"I lost count the third day."

She pushed him back a little. "Are you serious? Were you really counting?"

He grinned coyly.

"Probably trying to break your own world's record," she teased.

Wing kissed her again.

The phone rang.

"Dammit," Leslie said.

"Want me to get it?"

273

"I can't move. You'd better."

Wing got up from the bed and padded out of the bedroom.

"If it's for me," she called after him, "tell them I'm booked up for at least a month—if I live that long."

Wing was smiling as he picked up the phone.

"Quintin, how's the man of leisure?"

It was Murdoch.

"Shit, a sound for sore ears."

The lieutenant laughed. "Bet that's not all that's sore."

"What'd you do, bug this place?"

"No, just looking for independent confirmation."

"Murdoch, you really should put in for transfer to vice. Your natural talents lie that way. What do you want?"

"Just a courtesy call, Quintin. I'm keeping you informed on the Daniels case, since you worked on it."

Wing glanced into the open door leading to the bedroom. He could see Leslie's nude body on the bed. "Yeah . . . ?"

"The captain's buddy in Rio came through for us."

"Oh?"

"Hell of a surprise."

"What?"

"They traced Jed Daniels's movements after Hammond left the country."

"And?"

"Daniels suffered a mild heart attack the evening Hammond left and checked himself into a hospital. He was there from May first until the morning of May eighth— four days after Helene Daniels was shot."

Wing's heart stopped. He blinked, trying to comprehend. "Are you sure?"

"The captain's friend is third in command of the Rio force. They discussed it at length. That name and address you got on the landlord was the key apparently. The guy is sending documentation from the hospital as a favor. I don't know why it wouldn't be the truth."

"Shit."

"I'm sort of shorthanded around here. Aren't looking for work by any chance, are you?"

"No, Murdoch, not under any circumstances."

"Oh well. No harm in asking, is there?"

Wing paused. "Joe, the truth. Is this on the up and up?"

"Yeah, Quintin. It is."

Wing hung up the phone went back into the bedroom. Leslie looked up at him through heavily hooded eyes. "Who was that?"

"Murdoch . . . from the department."

"What did he want?"

Wing sighed. "For me to reenlist."

"What did you tell him?"

"That I wasn't interested." He looked down at her.

Leslie reached over and took him in her hand. "Is there anything *I* might interest you in?"

He looked at her pretty face and sank down onto the bed beside her.

BRENTWOOD

June 5, 1985

7:20 P.M.

Wing stared out at his mother's garden. Twilight had fallen and a peculiar light lay over the yard, illuminating it with the same warm amber as stage lights. Behind him, back somewhere in the house, he could hear their voices — Leslie's and his mother's.

Leslie was getting the grand tour — a look at the childhood domain of Kathryn Wing's son. He could tell by the laughter that they were getting on famously. It pleased him that they both cared enough about him to try so hard.

Murdoch's message had come as one of the biggest surprises of his life — not just his professional life — but his entire life. He had so badly wanted the case solved. He wanted to forget. And now here it was again, pursuing him, as though he were the hunted rather than the hunter.

The women's cheerful banter was drawing closer, and he knew they were about finished with their tour. He turned from the door as they returned to the living room.

"Quintin," Leslie said, "it's wonderful how your mom has kept your room just as it was when you were a kid."

"Don't tell me you showed her my chemistry lab in the closet, Mother."

"I showed her everything, Quintin."

276

"Even the stack of *Playboy*s on the top shelf," Leslie said, and smiled at Kathryn. "What an understanding mother you had, Quintin—*buying* you a subscription."

"She was afraid I'd never develop an interest in girls."

Leslie looked at Kathryn as they slowly walked toward Wing.

"You don't have to tell me how naive I was, dear. I learned that rather dramatically one afternoon a long time ago."

Leslie turned to Wing. "Oh?"

"I shan't embarrass the poor boy by telling on him." Kathryn laughed. "Maybe on your next visit."

Leslie was giving him a mischievous little smile that made him want her again.

Seeing they might want to be alone, Kathryn turned and headed for the kitchen. "Quintin, why don't you get the drinks while I check on dinner. I'll have my usual Tom Collins."

Wing and Leslie looked at each other. He reached over and lightly touched her nose. "Sit down and relax. I'll get you a drink."

Leslie dropped into an overstuffed chair, and Wing went to the far side of the room, stepping behind the wet bar. He opened the cabinet below the sink and glanced over the myriad of bottles. "I'm afraid Mother keeps a rather modest bar. Trevor, her doctor friend, drinks Scotch and she drinks Tom Collinses. Does either suit you?"

"I'll have a Scotch."

Wing slowly turned to face her. "Water or soda?"

"Neither, just straight up."

He looked at her across the room. "Ice?"

"No, I have it like my dad always does. I don't drink Scotch very often, but when I do it's like he taught me."

Wing swallowed hard. He expected it, but it was the sort of thing that had to be played out. There was no surprise but it hurt anyway, like that blow to the groin the day they met.

"One Scotch, straight up," he mumbled, and began mixing the drinks.

When he had finished he took the Tom Collins to his

mother in the kitchen, then rejoined Leslie in the living room. "Would you like to go out into the garden?"

Leslie got up. "Sure."

He handed her the Scotch and went to the slider, pulling it open. They stepped out into the balmy air, strolling across the patio.

"It's a lovely evening, isn't it?"

His heart was pounding. "Yes, beautiful."

"Oh, look!" she said. "The evening star."

Wing looked up where she was pointing to the west. "Venus."

Leslie took his arm, pressing her breast against it. "Your mother's wonderful. I love her."

"She's quite a lady."

They stopped at the edge of the garden and looked at the carefully pruned shrubs and statuary in the half-light. Leslie glanced down at her drink.

"You know, she's a far cry from the woman I grew up with, but much as I hated Helene, I've got to admit that if it weren't for her we'd never have met."

"That's true."

"Maybe we owe her a debt of gratitude."

He didn't respond.

Leslie looked at his somber face. "Quintin, there's something wrong. I can tell. What is it?"

He took a deep breath. "That call this afternoon. Murdoch didn't phone just to recruit me back to the force."

She studied his eyes, a touch of trepidation on her face. "What did he say?"

"That they'd learned from the Brazilian police that your dad was in a Rio hospital the night Helene was killed."

Leslie's mouth dropped. Then, after a moment, she lowered her eyes. "What does that mean?"

"There's something else you don't know."

"What?"

"We found two drinks in Helene's bar after the murder. They had never been served. One was for her—a vodka tonic. The other, we think, was for her killer."

Leslie stared at him. Neither spoke for a long time. She finally volunteered, "Scotch. No soda, no water, no ice."

He nodded.

There was dead silence around them. The air was calm. The evening seemed to be dying as they stood there. Leslie's eyes began to brim.

"Please kiss me," she whispered.

He leaned down and softly touched his lips to hers.

Leslie looked across the table at Wing. Her heart hadn't slowed a beat since their conversation in the garden. Her lover, the man who had discovered the awful truth, somehow looked at peace, serene. She glanced at his mother, hoping the woman wouldn't notice her trembling fingers.

Leslie forced herself to eat, but her stomach was a knot. Just sitting there, not knowing what he'd do, what he was thinking, was torture.

"Leslie," Kathryn said, "I don't mean to bring up unpleasant subjects, but you undoubtedly know that Quintin has told me all about your father."

Leslie's heart stopped.

"It must be terribly hard for you," the woman continued, "but I thought it important that you know that what your father has done is not an issue for me. I just don't want you to worry or feel uncomfortable in any way."

Leslie nodded weakly. She didn't have the strength to speak.

"There's no conviction, Mother," Wing interjected, "not even an indictment."

"I appreciate that, dear. I, of all people, recognize the importance of the technicalities of the law. I was thinking of your young lady's feelings."

Leslie was watching Wing, agonizing over the horrible uncertainty.

Kathryn reached over to pat Leslie's hand reassuringly. She turned to her son. "You said this afternoon the case was a weak one."

He nodded. "If the murder weapon is at the bottom of San Pedro Bay and they don't force a confession, there's no way there'll ever be a conviction."

"Or an arrest," Kathryn added.

For the first time his eyes swung to Leslie. "That's another issue entirely."

She felt the blood draining from her veins and her life right along with it.

Kathryn Wing got up to clear the table just as the doorbell rang. "Good heavens. Who could that be? I'm not expecting anyone."

Wing looked at his watch. "Punctual to a fault," he mumbled.

His mother looked at him with surprise. "Are you expecting someone?"

"Yes. Lieutenant Murdoch."

Leslie's eyes closed involuntarily.

"Murdoch?" Kathryn said. "Whatever did you invite—"

"Please, Mother, I'll explain later. Would you mind getting the door?"

The woman left the room, and Leslie and Wing looked across the table at one another. Tears were trailing down her cheeks. She looked at him beseechingly. "Quintin?"

"I'm sorry," he said in a husky voice. "I couldn't go through life pretending."

She bit her lip, trying not to sob. "What's going to happen?"

"It's not my case anymore. That's up to Murdoch." Wing slowly got to his feet. "Come on. I'll go with you into the living room." He went around the table to take her arm.

As they made their way to where the police were waiting, Wing glanced toward his mother's gallery. Inside was the Jasper Johns she had promised him one day for a wedding present. He sighed, thinking how close he had come.